A POSITION TO BE FILLED

Pandora was taken aback by her own brazenness when she practically forced herself into the drawing room of the Duke of Heron. Beggers, however, could not be choosers, and Pandora was forced to virtually beg Heron for a position of governess.

But Pandora felt her bravado draining away in the presence of this flawlessly elegant, totally commanding lord. She felt weaker still when he asked in a cutting voice, "And where did you hear that I was in need of a governess?"

"Why, from something Lady Margerson said," Pandora replied, already edging toward the door.

"I'm afraid you misunderstood," said Heron, his eyes traveling over Pandora's person with an amused, speculative gaze. "You see, her ladyship's quest—self-instigated, I assure you—is to discover for me the perfect wife." Then Heron smiled, a smile that stopped Pandora in her tracks. "But please, Miss Carlyon, don't go just yet. . . ."

A Highly
Respectable Marriage

A
Highly Respectable
Marriage

by
Sheila Walsh

A SIGNET BOOK

SIGNET
Published by the Penguin Group
Penguin Books USA Inc., 375 Hudson Street,
New York, New York 10014, U.S.A.
Penguin Books Ltd, 27 Wrights Lane,
London W8 5TZ, England
Penguin Books Australia Ltd, Ringwood,
Victoria, Australia
Penguin Books Canada Ltd, 2801 John Street,
Markham, Ontario, Canada L3R 1B4
Penguin Books (N.Z.) Ltd, 182–190 Wairau Road,
Auckland 10, New Zealand

Penguin Books Ltd, Registered Offices:
Harmondsworth, Middlesex, England

Published by Signet, an imprint of New American Library,
a division of Penguin Books USA Inc.

First Printing, October, 1982
11   10   9   8   7   6   5   4   3

 REGISTERED TRADEMARK—MARCA REGISTRADA

Printed in the United States of America

1

"Well, of course you shall have a letter of recommendation, my love, if you really feel that it will answer. . . ."

Lady Margerson's gentle voice held its habitual note of vagueness.

"Only, I cannot help thinking that it is not precisely what your poor dear mama would have wished. . . ."

One plump hand clutched ineffectually at a shawl of fine Norwich silk while the other sought absently for the comfit dish which was always placed conveniently close to the sofa.

Pandora Carlyon, leaning forward to steer the dish unobtrusively toward those indecisively hovering fingers, thought Lady Margerson the most indolent person she had ever known. Had she not been so certain that a kindly heart beat within that immense bosom, such slothfulness must have shocked her deeply.

But no one could be offended by Lady Margerson—there was something ineffably endearing about her vagueness, which Pandora suspected of being little more than a convenient pose adopted that she might not be obliged to make the least push to involve herself in anything of a disagreeable or energetic nature.

Her task accomplished, Pandora sat back, pushing into place an escaping strand of the fair hair which so obstinately refused to take curl or even remain neatly braided for any length of time.

"But Mama is no longer with us, dear ma'am, or Papa either, for that matter," she argued with determined cheerfulness, her hands clasped about her knees in a manner as youthful as it was earnest. "Although Courtney is

1

now head of the family, we are agreed that he must finish his term at Oxford, in spite of having his head filled with notions of buying a pair of colours and following in Papa's footsteps at the first opportunity . . ."—here a tiny frown creased her brow—"though how *that* is to be managed I cannot at present think, for there is William to be considered too. . . ."

Lady Margerson was almost shaken from her indolence by an involuntary spurt of indignation. She had grown quite fond of Pandora in the short time they had been acquainted; she could even admire the indomitable spirit which had enabled the young girl to pick up the pieces of her shattered life and strive to hold her family together in circumstances which would have crushed the daughters of most of her friends.

And insofar as her ladyship could bring herself to own to an obligation, she felt it incumbent upon herself to lend at least her moral support to this daughter of her late godchild. (Though what had possessed Arabella to marry a widowed Colonel of artillery and go traipsing around battlefields in his wake with her children in train must forever remain a mystery. It had come as no surprise to her ladyship when a Fever had finally carried her off.)

But now here was Pandora with her disconcertingly candid grey eyes and little else to distinguish her narrow sensitive face except for the slight dusting of freckles over the bridge of a straight, "no-nonsense" sort of a nose (and they could hardly be accounted a bonus!). Not a dissembling bone in her body! Quite unlike her beautiful mother, but bent upon behaving every bit as foolishly, worry over her brothers' needs without a thought for herself. And as for the elder boy's wishing to enter the army . . . After all the scandal-broth that had surrounded Colonel Carlyon's unfortunate demise not six months since, such a step seemed foolish beyond belief!

"One would suppose your family to have had its fill of the army," she said with unaccustomed crispness, and immediately wished the words unsaid as she saw the colour come and go in the expressive young face.

But the answer came clear and steady. "Oh, as to that,

ma'am, I believe that events have only made Courtney the more keen to prove himself."

"That is very well if he had only himself to consider." Lady Margerson, now unwittingly launched upon a line of reasoning, felt obliged to follow it through. "But your brother is, as you have said, the head of your little family now—and if you are really minded to quit Mrs. Hamilton's protection, which I am bound to say I think decidedly foolish in you, for although she don't move in first circles, she can still claim a fairly distinguished acquaintance—and she *is*, after all, your sister—"

"My half-sister." Pandora was quick to make correction. "We had not met above twice—and that many years ago—until we came back to England after Papa's death. It was Papa's lawyer, Mr. Lewis, who arranged that we should stay with the Hamiltons. I daresay it seemed the ideal answer to him, and besides, there was no other course immediately open to us—Courtney was in rooms at Oxford and thus unable to help, and Mr. Lewis thought it quite improper that I should take rooms for William and myself . . ."

"So I should hope, my love!"

Pandora smiled at the horror evident in Lady Margerson's voice.

"Well, I can't see why, except that of course the funds might not have run to it. However, Octavia it had to be. But we have nothing in common, you know. She is all of ten years my senior and is forever prosing on about how we should thank heaven that she and Frederick received us so generously into their home. Only, I believe Mr. Lewis came to some arrangement with Frederick that our annuity is paid to him while we remain, and though I cannot think it amounts to a great deal, Frederick is appallingly clutch-fisted! And Octavia makes shameless use of one and has the unerring knack of making one feel beholden to her for the merest necessities in a way that is fast becoming insupportable!"

"Oh, dear!" sighed her ladyship, shrinking a little from the light of battle in her young companion's eye. "Well, if that is true . . ."

"Besides which," Pandora concluded with the triumphant air of a magician producing his *pièce de résistance*, "she is constantly picking on poor William. He tries so very hard not to vex her, but it is not easy for a boy of ten to adjust to her notions of propriety when he has been used to a vastly different way of life."

Lady Margerson found herself recalling all too vividly the one and only occasion upon which Pandora had brought her younger brother on a morning call. He had *tried very hard* not to fidget with her collection of Sèvres figurines, until her nerves were set to jangling. She had little opinion of Octavia Hamilton—a hard, encroaching female if she ever saw one, and as different from Pandora as could be imagined—but just for an instant she owned to a pang of fellow feeling for Pandora's half-sister.

"I cannot see how leaving Mrs. Hamilton's roof will solve your difficulty in that respect," she reasoned faintly. "You can hardly hope to take William with you, should you succeed in securing a position, of whatever kind."

She had touched upon the one obvious flaw in Pandora's reasoning. The young girl rose agitatedly and walked away a little, then came back to stand looking down anxiously at Lady Margerson.

"Yes, well . . . I'll allow that I have not as yet quite worked out how that may be overcome," she acknowledged. And then, with renewed firmness: "But I mean to do so. The answer of course is for Will to go to school, and that in turn depends upon the amount of our annuity. I am not precisely certain at the moment how much we may count upon. Mr. Lewis spoke to Courtney about it, of course, but that was small use, since Courtney hasn't a grain of interest in money matters. He was quite irritatingly vague when I asked him to explain, and until now I have hesitated to interfere. But I'm sure it only requires a little resolution, and if we are pinched, I have several pieces of jewellery of Mama's which I can sell, so you see we are not quite destitute."

Lady Margerson looked at her with something approaching exasperation. Could she think of nothing but her wretched brothers? Standing there in her simple high-waisted mourning dress which emphasised the thinness of her figure, she looked little more than a long beanpole of a child—and an undernourished child at that—but there was an obstinate set to Pandora's chin which belied her apparent frailty, and Lady Margerson found herself wondering, not for the first time, at the stamina which had enabled her to follow the drum all those years.

"But your own prospects, my love?" she wailed. "Only consider—if you do as you suggest, it will quite ruin your own chances of making a respectable marriage!"

"Oh, that!" Pandora laughed. "My dear ma'am, I cannot allow that to be a consideration, for who would have me? With no portion to speak of, and no possible claims to beauty by way of compensation, I must be the least eligible of creatures!"

This was so close to the truth that Lady Margerson could find no immediately convincing argument to refute it. Really, it was quite tiresome to be obliged to stir oneself, but there seemed no other way. It crossed her mind briefly that she might take Pandora for a companion herself; to be sure, she was a very capable girl and could well prove invaluable, but the spectre of William loomed ominously, and she put the thought from her. Still, there might well be others less sensitive to the presence of a restless young boy.

"Very well, child. I will furnish you with this letter, but do not, I beg of you, act precipitately. I have any number of friends and might yet come up with a more fitting solution to your little problem." She brightened momentarily. "There is Heron, of course, though that may be flying a trifle high. . . ."

"Heron?" Pandora queried.

"The Duke of Heron, my love. You *must* have heard of him! Oh, well, perhaps not . . . but I'll warrant Mrs. Hamilton has, for he is quite the most-talked-of man in London at the present. . . ." Just for a moment Lady Margerson's gentle features took on a look of almost malicious amusement. "Such a hobble to find himself in . . . saddled with two young children—and French children at that! You may imagine how *that* has set all the gabble-grinders by the ears!"

Since Pandora could not imagine anything of the kind, she sighed and wished the old lady were not so prone to wandering from the point.

"There can be no denying, of course, that he adored their mother or that his relationship with her was not somewhat unusual. Mariette de Choille, you see, was the daughter of a widowed French émigrée who escaped from the Revolution at the same time as Heron's maternal grandmother, the Comtesse de Valière. In fact, it was Heron who went with his father to Paris to spirit them away. He was but a boy at the time, and we all thought it prodigiously romantic, I remember!"

Pandora smiled and tried to look interested.

"And then Madame de Choille passed away and Mariette was brought up by the Comtesse. At seventeen she was a beauty." The old lady sighed. "Heron was so in love with her—I swear he would have married her then, but alas, she proved sadly willful and flighty, spurned his offer, and flirted shamelessly with every disreputable rake who looked her way . . . and many did! Finally she quarrelled irrevocably with the Comtesse and Heron, and ran away. Then next we knew she was living with a French royal duke . . . and now, poor wicked girl, she is dead!"

If only Lady Margerson could have been persuaded to write the letter earlier, Pandora fretted, it might be possible to make one's excuses and leave. But the letter was essential to her plans, and if she didn't hold her ladyship to it now . . .

"No one is clear as to why Heron has accepted responsibility for Mariette's children, but to infer that they are his side-slips as some are doing is a great piece of nonsense! I was quizzing him about it at Sybil Gresham's levee only last evening . . . well, I have known him almost from the cradle, you know, and may take liberties not accorded to everyone . . ."

With her ladyship's peroration now dwindling inevitably into vague chitchat about her cronies, Pandora turned her attention to the various options open to her.

She had formed the habit of removing Frederick Hamilton's *Morning Post* from the breakfast room when she was sure he had finished with it, so that she might scan the columns of advertisements. Only this morning there had been one requiring the services of a genteel young woman for the post of companion, and two for governesses, but all were well out of London and all stipulated the need for references.

". . . and finally he said to me, 'Well, then, Lady M., you had best find me someone!' I daresay he was only funning, but the more I consider it, the more I see how splendidly it would answer, solving his difficulties as well as yours."

Pandora's wandering thoughts came back to the present in time to hear the old lady say: "Yes, indeed . . . I believe I really must arrange for you to meet Heron!" She wondered briefly if she had missed anything of importance, but dared not ask for fear of setting Lady Margerson off again.

On the way back to Brook Street with the letter safely tucked in her reticule, however, little threads of her ladyship's meandering conversation strung themselves together in her mind, and hope began to stir. If she had remembered it aright, there was a friend—a duke who had become guardian to two French children and might be in need of someone to care for them. . . . Excitement quickened her step, and the little abigail who accompanied her was several times obliged to run in order to keep up with her.

Upon reaching Brook Street, Pandora stepped out to cross the road, still lost in thought, and at the very same moment a horseman rounded the corner at a brisk canter.

For one terrifying instant she stood transfixed by the gleaming muscles that rippled across the shoulders of the powerful black hunter as it bore down upon her, nostrils snorting with its wild unease.

The abigail screamed, the rider uttered a furious expletive, and just when it seemed that nothing could save Pandora, the horse, superbly controlled, swerved and was reined in a tight circle.

Shoulder capes flapping, the rider loomed above her, contemptuous anger in the heavy-lidded eyes that raked her comprehensively from head to toe, killing the apology that hovered on her lips before it could find utterance. For a moment it seemed that he would demolish her with a tirade of abuse, but as she glared back at him defiantly, he appeared to think better of it. With an abrupt dismissive gesture he wheeled the restive horse full circle once more and left her staring after his retreating back as the hoofbeats gradually faded away into silence.

"Well, really!" she exclaimed.

"Oh, miss!" breathed the abigail on a stifled sob. "You might've been killed!"

"Nonsense, Cassie!" said Pandora bracingly, ignoring the traitorous trembling in her knees. "Some people," she declared with a sweeping disregard for her own culpability, "are not fit to be on the road!"

It was in this same pugnacious mood that she entered the Hamiltons' house and at once became aware of an atmosphere that was becoming all too familiar. There was no sign of William, who was usually to be found lurking somewhere close at hand watching for her return. Schooling her feelings and her temper, she remarked upon his absence to Binns as she stripped off her gloves and prepared to mount the stair.

"I regret to say, miss, that young Master William has been banished to his room—following upon an unfortunate incident concerning the use of his catapult."

"Oh, Binns! He didn't break another window?"

"No, miss." The butler's manner was the very model of correctness, but anyone looking closely might have detected a faint gleam behind the eyes which betrayed where his sympathies lay. "This time, I fear, the damage was of a more . . . personal nature and involved Miss Eliza. An accident, I feel sure," he hastened to add. "It could not be otherwise. And Miss Eliza, I am relieved to say, sustained no lasting harm beyond a slight cut— though it did bleed quite alarmingly at first, which naturally sent Madam into one of her acute spasms, so that what with one thing and another, Dr. Marston had to be sent for."

"Oh, that wretched boy!" exclaimed Pandora, her foot already on the stair. "How *could* he, after promising me most faithfully that he wouldn't so much as touch that dreadful weapon again within the bounds of Mrs. Hamilton's house!"

"No more he did, miss." The butler was quick to William's defence. "The incident took place in the park, Miss Prosset having taken both children there some little while earlier for an airing. It was, I believe, some kind of bird perched upon a low branch which precipitated Master William's enthusiasm—"

"Thank you, Binns, you need say no more!" Their eyes met in rueful recognition of William's undoubted temptation. Then Pandora shrugged and mounted the stairs, preparing herself for the inevitable.

"Is that you, Pandora? I know it *is* you, so do not be thinking to creep past the door!"

Octavia's voice rang out almost before she had reached the landing, its strident tones confirming Pandora's worst fears. She drew a deep breath and pushed open the drawing-room door to find the curtains half-drawn, casting deep shadows over the gold-striped chintzes. She was just able to make out her beautiful half-sister prone upon a sofa placed at right angles to the fire, a vinaigrette clutched in one hand, a crumpled square of cambric and lace in the other. On the floor beside her a child of some seven summers knelt playing with a doll, dark ringlets falling across a pretty, slightly petulant profile which, though as yet undefined by the years, already showed a distinct resemblance to her mama's.

Pandora decided that a frontal attack was her only hope. "I had no intention of creeping past; in fact, I wished most particularly to see you. Binns has told me something of what happened. It was a most unfortunate accident, but William must of course be punished for his carelessness—"

"His carelessness? Is that how you term it?" Octavia's mouth was working in a most unbecoming way, her shrill voice quivering on the air. "I am amazed that you can take the matter so calmly! But then, you are not a mother and can have no conception of how it feels to have your child viciously struck down, to know that she might have been fatally wounded, the delicate bloom of her youth snapped at a stroke!"

"She looks remarkably healthy to me," Pandora cut in, unable to endure such a farrago of nonsense one moment more. She walked across to Eliza and bent down to put a hand under the child's chin. Eliza looked up and in so doing revealed a small piece of sticking plaster adorning one cheekbone and another, even smaller piece covering part of her earlobe.

"My!" She smiled encouragingly. "How bravely you are bearing your battle scars!"

Eliza was torn between this affecting and somewhat heroic view of herself, and her running grudge against William. In the end she compromised. "I bled and bled," she lisped. "And Mama says that now William will *have* to go away!"

Pandora's glance flew to Octavia, who sat up, swinging her legs gracefully to the floor, her pose of distraught mother, its purpose served, discarded. She patted her impeccably coiffured hair and looked at Pandora, hard-eyed.

"I am sure that I have been patience itself where William is concerned, but there is a limit to even my goodness . . . and Miss Prosset declares she can no more! The boy consistently disrupts lessons by asking unanswerable questions so that it becomes impossible for her to proceed."

Pandora's opinion of Miss Prosset led her to declare most unwisely that the governess's inability to answer William's questions might well stem from her own inadequacy rather than any great degree of difficulty in the questions themselves.

"There is nothing wrong with Miss Prosset! She is a perfectly adequate governess and I do not intend to lose her on William's account! Frederick will have to make enquiries first thing tomorrow about finding some suitable alternative. I doubt any school will be found willing to

10

take him this late into the year, but we shall have to see. Until such time as a solution may be found, however, he will have to study alone. I can no longer allow him to share Eliza's lessons."

"William ought to go to Charterhouse," said Pandora quickly. "It is where Papa went, and although Courtney never followed in his footsteps—for Mama could not bear to be parted from him, you see, and there was a very able tutor in Lisbon who prepared him for Oxford—the circumstances are now quite different. I am sure that Papa would have wanted at least one of his sons to follow him. . . ."

Octavia stared. "My dear girl, you must have windmills in your head! Even if there were sufficient funds, which there are not, do you suppose that Charterhouse would take him?"

"I don't see why not. William is very bright, you know. . . ."

"William, or had you forgotten, is the son of a man who ordered his batteries to open fire on their own comrades!" Octavia said harshly. "That he was also an ex-pupil of Charterhouse is, I would hazard, the very last thing they would wish to be reminded of!"

Pandora felt anger rising to choke her. "It wasn't like that!" The words were forced out. "Lord Wellington himself completely exonerated Papa . . . you know he did! There was a tragic blunder in communications . . . and it happens sometimes when the weather is appalling and everything is in disorder. Papa wasn't even present when the order was given, and the captain in charge of the battery was little more than a schoolboy with no experience—"

"But Father accepted responsibility." The hard voice was unrelenting.

"Of course he did! They were his men—under his command! What would you have had him do?" Pandora dashed a hand across her eyes. "Oh, what is the use . . . you will never understand! You never really knew Papa! He would have given his life for any one of those men—indeed, he did exactly that, very soon after!"

"So you have told me, *ad nauseam*. All I can say is

11

that it was very convenient for him to be dead and well out of it, but thanks to that Ibbot woman, who seems determined to make his name a byword, it is we who continue to bear the stigma." Octavia lifted an impatient hand as Pandora, horrified by such selfish insensitivity, would have said more. Her beautiful face was unrelenting. "No, I don't want to hear another word. I am quite tired of the whole business. We must face the facts as they are. Frederick must place William where he can, until such time as a school can be found to take him. It will, of course, be an added expense, and you cannot expect us to defray it . . ."

Pandora's heart turned over with a sickening fear. They meant to find some horrid little hellhole that would take William for next to nothing! "But the annuity?"

"Oh, that! My dear, *that* will scarcely suffice! No, there is a solution we have all overlooked. I believe the time has come for Courtney to leave Oxford and take up his responsibilities."

"You cannot ask that of him! He will have exams——"

"My dear Pandora, you know as well as anyone that Courtney cares not one jot for examinations!" Octavia rose gracefully, as though bored with the conversation. "Much better that he leaves now. Frederick can probably find him some employment of a clerical nature in the City, and the money thus saved can be put to other uses. You, naturally, may remain here until Courtney is able to make some kind of home for you. Come, darling." She held out a hand for her daughter, who had been gazing from one to the other with a wide-eyed, almost morbid interest.

It was on the tip of Pandora's tongue to blurt out that nothing would induce her to stay—that she meant to leave at once, taking William with her—but she was so filled with impotent rage that she could not bring herself to speak. Not caring if Octavia took her silence for acquiescence, she turned on her heel and left the room, climbed the bare unprepossessing flight of stairs leading to the nursery floor with hands clenched rigidly at her sides and a painful lump blocking her throat.

It was more than anyone could be expected to endure! To be any longer beholden to Octavia . . . to have the deplorable Frederick ordering their lives—this was bad enough; but infinitely more distressing to bear was the way Octavia talked about Papa as though he were not her father at all, but some frightful stranger. The woman who had begun the rumours had lost a son in the unfortunate accident and might be forgiven for hating Papa, but how could Octavia believe such a thing of him?

Yet dearly as she had loved her father, Pandora could not but deplore his carelessness in leaving them without home or direction. He was ever a man of erratic humours, spare of figure, red-haired, with a quick flaring temper that could dissolve as quickly into laughter. He had loved their mother with a passionate mercurial love which had reached out to embrace his children—his brigade major avowed that he was as black-humoured as ten devils when they were not with him—but Mama was used to say in fun that they were never in the least doubt as to their importance in relation to the regiment. His beloved guns came before all else; his men, who loved and feared him in equal measure, he regarded as his stern charge and responsibility and consequently watched over them with scrupulous care, while his family came a poor third. Though he refuted the accusation as a gross calumny, with a great show of indignation, there was a grain of truth in it nonetheless. Yet his enthusiasm was such that they were all carried along in its wake.

It had been Mama, gay, biddable Mama, who had provided some degree of stability; had insisted upon the house in Lisbon as a home to which they could return from time to time; had compelled her volatile husband to at least look the future in the face so far as to make a will. But when Mama had taken a Fever and died with such alarming suddenness, he had been blind and dead to all advice, had disposed of the Lisbon house, packed Courtney off home to Oxford, and had assumed that she and William would continue to live their lives very much as before. Pandora had no quarrel with this decision. The army was almost the only life she knew. But her father

13

was quieter, more withdrawn, and they were no longer carried along on the former plain of excitement. It seemed that she grew up, almost overnight, trying, as best she could, to fill the unbearable gap left by her mother's death.

"Dora!" The hissed whisper came to her from above. She blinked quickly several times to clear her eyes and looked up to see William hanging over the banister rail, his face pale with ill-suppressed agitation, so that his freckles, more marked than his sister's, were starkly etched. "Come on up quickly before that old nanny goat Prosset catches me! I am charged not to leave my room, and I'm to have no supper."

Pandora took the last few stairs at a run and bundled him inside, closing the door softly behind her.

"It's no more than you deserve, abominable boy! And kindly do not call Miss Prosset names." Her pent-up anger found release at last. "Why I don't box your ears, I cannot think! Quite apart from breaking your promise to me, you have put Octavia all on end—and this time there will be no smoothing her down! Whatever can have possessed you to use that wretched catapult again, let alone aim so glaringly abroad that you must needs hit your cousin?"

"There was nothing wrong with my aim," William maintained stoutly, his mouth tight with indignation. "I don't see that I can be blamed because that bird-witted widgeon Eliza chose to run across my path just as I let fly!" He met Pandora's eye and had the grace to flush guiltily. "Yes, I know I promised not to, but you see," he wheedled, "I had forgot to remove it from my coat pocket, and when I saw that crow sitting on the branch just waiting to be potted, it was in my hand before I thought." His enthusiasm could not long be stemmed. "If I'd had Pa's gun I wouldn't have missed, I can tell you!"

The sight of his sturdy body planted pugnaciously on thin bare legs exposed by his too-short nightshirt filled her with a great suffocating wave of love.

"Well, we have that much to be thankful for at least," she said on a choked laugh, and sat down abruptly on the edge of William's hard truckle bed. The sparsely furnished room set in the rafters was very much like the one allotted to her. Hardly a place to call home, she thought. Not that lack of comfort troubled them greatly—army life had long since accustomed them to laying down their heads in far worse conditions—but, compared with Octavia's luxurious boudoir, it seemed to Pandora just one more pointer to her meanness.

Her pensive manner brought a shuffling of feet and a slightly shamefaced "I didn't mean to make more trouble for you, Dora," and when she didn't reply at once, "Is Octavia still in a blue fit? She screamed at me so much, I thought she'd die!" and regretfully "But she didn't. I expect she'll go on about sending me away again now."

He sat on the bed and slipped a hand into Pandora's. "I shouldn't mind going away to school, you know—oh, I should miss you, of course, but I would much liefer be with a crowd of other boys than be obliged to stay here and share Eliza's lessons and be bored by Miss Prosset."

But not some awful school of Frederick's choosing, vowed Pandora, hearing the wistful note in his voice. She hugged him fiercely, and stood up. "We shall have to see. I had better go now before Miss Prosset catches me, but I will try to smuggle you some food up later."

There was little opportunity to broach the subject of William again that night. The Hamiltons were seldom at home in the evening and had never formed the habit of taking Pandora out with them.

She did try to talk to Octavia, visiting her room as she was preparing to leave for a ball, apparently fully recovered from the earlier severe shock to her nerves. Her mind already on the evening ahead, she brushed aside Pandora's opening question.

"Tomorrow," she said, accepting the wrap placed about her shoulders by the waiting lady's maid and drifting to the door. "We will settle William's future tomorrow."

The words, invading her attempts to sleep, assumed an ominous significance as the night wore on. She ought to write to Courtney, but experience told her that he would fail to see what all the fuss was about. Better, perhaps, to seek an interview with Mr. Lewis at the earliest opportunity. And if she could only find a suitable position . . .

The next morning, matters came to a head. William bore the punishment meted out to him by Frederick with a stoicism that filled Pandora with pride even as she protested at its severity.

"My dear sister," came the pompous reply, "it is clear that you understand little of the corrective processes so necessary to the adequate formation of a young boy's character. It is to be hoped that we have not already dallied too long in William's case!"

Pandora looked into Frederick's smooth, self-important face and recognised the futility of attempting to remonstrate.

She went straight to her room and took her best bonnet from the shelf in the tiny closet.

"It's a powerful *grand* house, miss!" breathed the diminutive Cassie, her trepidation very evident as she added: "You don't truly mean for to go inside?"

Pandora stared up at the windows glinting back at her like so many haughty eyes in the strong sunlight. She felt the first twings of misgivings. Viewed from the opposite pavement, the house in St. James's Square was indeed quite intimidatingly grand. Perhaps it would have been better to see Mr. Lewis first. But now that she had gone to the trouble of discovering from Binns where the Duke of Heron lived, it would be craven to cry off at the first qualm.

"Of course I am going in," she declared with a good deal of resolution, stepping out across the smooth kidney stones of the Square with all the swaggering bravado of a Johnny Raw marching to his first encounter with the enemy. "And you must come with me, Cassie." She heard the abigail's involuntary gasp, and said bracingly, "Don't be afraid. You need come no further than the vestibule!"

At first it seemed that they would be denied admittance even that far. The liveried porter eyed her disparagingly from a great height, his disapproval making itself felt. But the mention of Lady Margerson's name appeared to exercise a beneficial effect, and soon Pandora was following a soft-footed servant across the marble-lozenged hallway, past a pair of towering Corinthian columns which flanked the central stairway, drawing the eye upward to behold the delicately curving wrought-iron balconies which made such an impressive feature of the half-landing.

But Pandora, grown suddenly aware of the enormity of

the step she was taking, was too preoccupied with a frantic last-minute rehearsal of what she would say, to appreciate the architectural splendours wrought by Robert Adam upon the Duke of Heron's town house. One scared glance had been sufficient to induce panic, to persuade her that she ought never to have come.

Too late now to wish that she had paid more attention to what Lady Margerson, in her maddeningly indeterminate fashion, had said. Too late for regrets of any kind, in fact, for the lackey was throwing open a pair of doors. She collected her thoughts, smoothed down her best grey crepe dress, took a deep steadying breath, and stepped into the room as he announced in an expressionless monotone: "Miss Pandora Carlyon!"

"Good God!" came a soft derisive murmur from within.

She had been expecting a modest back parlour, as befitted the nature of her mission, but found herself instead in an exquisite little saloon, entirely circular—a library, she deduced, since it was lined from floor to ceiling with bookshelves, except for a beautiful bow window which occupied about one-quarter of its circumference. The ceiling, a masterpiece of intricate plasterwork, mirrored exactly the design of the carpet beneath her feet.

A gentleman, tall and willow-slim, his excellent shoulders displaying to advantage the unwrinkled perfection of blue superfine in a way that would have driven Courtney wild with envy, stood apparently absorbed before one of the bookshelves.

"Oh!" Convinced that she had been shown in error to the wrong room, Pandora swung round to find the doors already closing behind her, and was thrown into confusion. "Forgive me . . . I . . . *Oh, Gemini*!"

For the gentleman had turned slowly, book in hand—and she had no difficulty whatever in recognising the classical features and long inquisitorial nose of the gentleman who had so very nearly run her down in Brook Street on the previous day. He, however, gave no indication whatever of remembering her as he subjected her once again to that comprehensive raking examination.

"Miss Carlyon?" The lazy voice held a faint query.

Pandora, still desperately coming to terms with the situation, said blankly, "*You* are the Duke of Heron?"

"I have that honour, ma'am." He inclined his distinguished head and fell unhelpfully silent once more.

It was like struggling from the depths of some terrible nightmare only to find that it was not a dream at all, but dreadful reality. Thrown into fresh confusion, she blurted out, "I had expected a much older man . . ."

"I am desolated to disappoint you." There was an undercurrent of sarcasm in the softly spoken politeness. "Now, if you would oblige me by coming to the point? I need hardly state that I am not in the habit of receiving unaccompanied females. In your case an exception was made as I am given to understand that you bear an important message from Lady Margerson?"

Pandora sensed his disbelief and felt the blood surging into her face as she realised he had got quite the wrong impression.

"Well . . . that is not precisely true," she stammered, made nervous by the derisive curl of his lip. She smoothed the palms of her hands surreptitiously against her skirts. "That is to say, Lady Margerson is not precisely aware that I am here . . . at this moment, you know . . . though it was her idea in the first place . . . following upon your talk with her the other evening . . ." She saw his brow lift and hurried on. "About the position? Well, you did suggest, did you not, that she might find you someone? And I know it was her intention that we should meet first, only . . . my situation is such that I could not wait. In short, I decided to try my luck at first hand—"

"Enough!" He cut her short and stepped forward to pull the bell. "I have heard more than enough," he said with soft cutting sarcasm, "and shall own myself very much astonished if Lady Margerson has ever laid eyes upon you!"

The doors opened to reveal the impassive footman who had admitted her.

"Miss Carlyon is leaving," said the Duke austerely, and

turned away with a curt dismissive nod to resume his perusal of the shelves.

Pandora stood irresolute, staring at the arrogant back with mounting indignation. Perhaps she had made a sad botch of the interview, but she had expected to be accorded common politeness at the very least. To be thus accused and summarily dismissed seemed so grossly unfair that before she could bite on her tongue she had told him so in her clear light voice that trembled only the veriest bit from the force of her grievance.

"I daresay it was wrong of me to come here as I did. I have been abroad until very recently and am not quite accustomed to London ways and the conventions governing such matters. If I am in error, then you are fully justified in telling me so."

Pandora addressed her complaint to that particular area of those unyielding shoulders where his high-standing collar met a carefully contrived swirl of light brown hair. There was no immediately discernible reaction, but she rather thought that his neck would be stiff and red as fire if she could but see it. Aware that with every word she was damning her chances, she had by now come too far to turn back.

"But though you are at perfect liberty to term me ignorant," she concluded indignantly, "what I am *not* is . . . is encroaching, or brass-faced . . . or any of those other things you are so obviously imagining, and if you had only been a little patient instead of flying up into the boughs, I could have shown you Lady Margerson's letter . . ." She began to fumble in her reticule.

The Duke, his hand arrested in the act of withdrawing a book, appeared to sigh as he slid it back into place and came to tower over her, his tawny eyes blazing under the lazy lids with an intensity of emotion which she found impossible to fathom. Mastering a tendency to flinch, she looked back at him, her own gaze unblinking, and after what seemed an interminable interval he grunted, waved the waiting footman away with an impatient gesture, and swung away to a desk set deep in the window recess. Here he flung himself into a chair and sprawled, legs outstretched, drumming the desktop with the fingers of one slim hand.

He did not ask Pandora to sit; indeed, it occurred to her to wonder if he had forgotten her presence entirely. But she had grown up well-used to the odd peremptory ways of men in positions of command, so the Duke's manner did not trouble her unduly. What did unnerve her was his magnificence, for he was not quite like anyone she had ever encountered in her short but eventful life. And, irrationally, she blamed Lady Margerson for giving her quite the wrong impression, for he could not be a day over five and thirty!

The drumming ceased abruptly.

"How old are you, Miss Carlyon?"

The drawled question took her unawares. "Nineteen years," she said, "and a half." And then, with scrupulous correctness, "Almost."

The sardonic lines about his mouth deepened fractionally. He sat forward, elbows resting on the desktop, his slender firm-set chin lightly propped on folded hands. He bent a particularly acute eye upon her.

"And what makes you think you possess the . . . qualities I should demand in anyone chosen to fill this somewhat unusual position?"

"I have travelled a lot—and I speak fluent French," Pandora said promptly, mastering her surprise at his unexpected turnabout, and feeling that she was at last on firmer ground. "And Portuguese," she threw in for good measure.

"Portuguese." He seemed to choke a little on the word. "French?"

"Well, surely French must be a prime consideration . . . if the children are not to feel homesick?"

"The children? Of course. How silly of me," he murmured faintly.

"Oh, and I had almost forgot again . . ." She thrust at him the letter she had been clutching. "If I had given you this when I first arrived, I daresay we should not have fallen to brangling," she concluded magnanimously.

This time there was no mistaking that he sighed; it was a deep sound, betokening resignation.

"You had better sit down, Miss Carlyon," he said, regarding her balefully. "This is obviously going to take longer than I thought."

Pandora glanced around, and finding only a frivolously gilded spindle-legged chair close by, she drew it forward and perched nervously upon it, feeling totally out of sympathy with its mood in her sober dress. She had taken a great deal of trouble with her appearance. Neatness, she was sure (though her only experience of governesses was Miss Prosset, whom she had little wish to emulate), must be of considerable importance if one wished to make a good impression. Her hair had been the greatest problem; she had spent quite ten minutes with a damp brush quelling her straying locks into submission and braiding them neatly so that she might cram the neat black bonnet over them. She wiggled her face experimentally; she had an uncomfortable feeling that one or two strands had escaped and were even now lying against her cheek. Oh, well!

The Duke did not linger over the contents of the letter. Having read it through, he opened his fingers and allowed it to flutter to the desk.

"Very affecting," he drawled. "But it tells me little I wish to know, save that Lady Margerson obviously cherishes a tendresse for you, which I find intriguing. However"—his voice hardened as he rocked back in his chair—"your reasons for coming here this morning intrigue me even more. What did you hope to achieve, I wonder? For unless you possess talents heretofore unrevealed, I confess your strategy confounds me utterly."

Pandora knew in that moment that any hopes she might have entertained were no more than wishful thinking—and quite unexpectedly, she was glad. She did not belong in this exquisite room in this exquisite house, could not hope to match wits with this incomprehensible man; nor any longer did she wish to try.

But before she left, she would say her piece.

She rose with great dignity—a gesture somewhat

marred by her misfortune in knocking over the little gilt chair as she did so. She set it straight with fingers that shook, not missing the weary irony in the Duke's voice as he adjured her to let it be, and turned to face him.

"My lord Duke," she began with scrupulous politeness. "My reasons for coming here this morning are now quite immaterial, because I no longer wish to be considered for any position you might have at your disposal. I was a fool to persevere"—a touch of bitterness crept in here—"when you have made it abundantly clear from the first that you had not the least intention of taking my application seriously, which I must say I find quite odiously ungracious in you!" Her glance held his with a desperate defiance. "I daresay you will not understand how humiliating it is to be obliged to endure such insufferably high-handed behaviour in the hope of securing employment. It is an experience which must be quite beyond the comprehension of someone who has no doubt been able to command every luxury from the cradle . . ."

She had expected to be cut down before now, but the Duke's face had assumed a curiously blank expression, which was somehow more disturbing than open anger. It compelled her to rush to her conclusion before her courage failed her.

"I have not, of course, had your advantages, but neither has it been my misfortune until recently to have to make my own way in the world, and I am very conscious of having little to offer by way of experience, but"—she drew a steady breath—"had I a hundred impeccable references to lay before you at this moment, I would see myself at blue blazes rather than be employed by anyone as . . . as arrogantly unfeeling as you!"

The silence which followed had the breath-holding quality of those final moments on the battlefield when both commanders attempt to stretch their opponents' nerves to snapping point before ordering the bombardment to begin. Ample time for Pandora to reflect upon her probable fate. Could one, she wondered a little wildly, be locked up for insulting a peer of the realm in his own library?

If only he would say something—anything! She stole a glance at him and was not encouraged. An apology seemed somehow inadequate in the circumstances—and anyway, she didn't feel in the least sorry. Perhaps one should just leave? . . . She took a couple of tentative steps backward, and his chair came down with a crash that made her flinch. She rushed nervously into speech.

"With your leave, my lord Duke, I will go now. I do hope you will find a governess who meets with your requirements, though I pity her with all my heart—as I pity those poor children placed in your care!"

With this final thrust she dipped a hasty curtsy and, turning on her heel, walked stiff-backed to the door. She had not taken more than a dozen paces when he began to laugh.

It was such an unexpected, such an unfeeling sound, that for an instant her step faltered. Then she went on. Let him ridicule her if it pleased him. She would not be drawn again, though angry tears blocked her throat.

The doors opened silently at her coming. She passed through, head high, and as they closed behind her, the sound of his mocking laughter still echoed in her ears.

The Duke of Heron continued to sit for several moments after the door closed behind his contentious visitor, a faint smile lingering around his mouth—not the cynical, contemptuous curling of the lip which Pandora would have found all too familiar, but a smile of pure amusement which warmed his eyes and betrayed his appreciation of the ridiculous.

Miss Pandora Carlyon—aptly named, for a more disruptive young baggage he had seldom come across. He ought to have shown her the door at once, of course, but who could have guessed at the fire and eloquence so fiercely nurtured within that unprepossessing bosom? His lips quirked afresh at the memory. The set of her chin should have warned him, and her eyes—disconcertingly direct eyes, he decided in retrospect.

And then there was the curious matter of her connection with Lady Margerson, the nature of which could only be hazarded. What *was* clear, however, was that the old lady's vague meanderings had implanted several wildly misconceived notions in the young girl's mind.

He supposed he might have disabused her, but it had been such an entertaining little episode, alleviating, if only for a short time, the boredom that so frequently plagued him.

3

Out in the square a hack had just set down its fare. The driver was preparing to move off when he heard himself being hailed, and turned in time to see a rake-thin slip of a girl break into a run, one hand clasped to her bonnet, an abigail close on her heels.

"Please . . . I wish to go to the Strand!"

Eyes glittering with unshed tears challenged him with a fierceness that dared him to refuse. The abigail was biting her lip in a worried fashion and saying nothing. He shrugged good-naturedly and bade them "Hop in," and was rewarded with an unexpected lopsided grin.

The offices of Messrs. Althrop, Pickering, and Lewis, when found, exuded an air of shabby gentility. A cadaverous-looking clerk turned pale astonished eyes upon her and left his high stool in order to inform Mr. Lewis of her arrival. By the time he returned moments later with instructions to usher her into that gentleman's sanctum, Pandora, still smarting from the Duke's cavalier treatment, was left in little doubt that she had once more incurred masculine disapproval. She told Cassie to wait, and followed in his frosty wake.

The elderly lawyer rose to greet her with a guarded politeness which persuaded her that he, too, shared his clerk's opinion of young ladies who were so coming as to intrude themselves into so hallowed a domain.

He shuffled the papers on his desk for an unconscionable time before placing his fingertips together in a prayerful way.

"Believe me, my dear Miss Carlyon," he assured her, blinking over a pair of uncertainly perched spectacles as she explained the purpose of her visit, "you had much better leave the managing of your affairs to myself and Mr. Hamilton until such time as your brother is able to take them in hand."

Pandora was in no mood to be so easily routed. "I have every confidence in your judgement, sir, but . . ." She clasped her reticule resolutely. "Forgive my presumption, but are you well acquainted with Mr. Hamilton?"

The lawyer blinked more rapidly. "Not intimately, no. In fact, I believe I have met the gentleman but once. . . ."

Once, in Pandora's opinion, was more than sufficient. "My father dubbed him a 'whited sepulchre,'" she said frankly, "and I cannot think that he would ever have countenanced his having the least say in the ordering of William's education." She explained to him quickly what Frederick had in mind. "So that is why I have come to you, so that you may tell me exactly how Papa left things. Courtney is not the most communicative of people, nor is he at all businesslike," she added with sisterly candour, "and whenever I have attempted to clarify our situation with him, he has been incorrigibly vague. But you see"—she leaned forward in her earnestness—"it is of the greatest importance that I know how matters stand before I actually take steps to leave the Hamiltons."

Pandora saw his shaggy eyebrows wobble alarmingly. "Oh, it was very good of you to have prevailed upon them to take us in when we first arrived in London with nowhere to stay, but it is not the best of arrangements, you know, and now that I have had time to adjust, I see that I must make a push to stand on my own feet. So you will help me, won't you?" She smiled at him.

Mr. Lewis was looking more than ever bemused. "Really, I don't see . . . I am not at all sure . . ." He began again. "Dear me, this is all most difficult . . ."

"Because I am young and female?" she returned as quick as light.

"You are certainly a most forthright young lady," he acknowledged with a dry clearing of the throat. And, meeting her eyes, "Very like your late father, if I may say so."

"Thank you!" Her smile became a grin. "I take that as a great compliment." She sat back with an expectant air, and the lawyer shuffled his papers once more, took off his spectacles, and began to polish them with unusual vigour.

"Well, now, as to your inheritance, Miss Carlyon—all is simplicity itself. The amount is not great—but I doubt that will come as any surprise to you?" He replaced the spectacles with elaborate care, and peered at the sheet of paper under his hand. "It is in the form of an annuity, to be administered by me until your brother Courtney attains the age of twenty-five—the said annuity to be apportioned as to seven-eighths divided in equal parts between your two brothers, and one-eighth part to your good self . . ." His voice wavered between apology and embarrassment, but Pandora's brow remained untroubled.

"It is as I expected," she assured him. "The boys have their way to make in the world, after all—and Papa knew that they would never see me wanting. And so long as there is enough to send William to a good school . . . I had hoped for Charterhouse?"

Mr. Lewis, in whose eyes there had now dawned considerable respect, grew pensive. "Ah-h . . . as to that . . ."

Pandora's spirits plummetted. "You think they would not take him?" she asked bluntly, and saw that she had embarrassed him once more.

"No, no, nothing of the kind, dear young lady! More simply, I fear that it may be beyond our means."

"Even with my eighth thrown in?"

His shaggy brows shot up, but he only said, "Even then, ma'am," adding with a certain diffidence: "But perhaps . . . if you would leave the matter in my hands?"

"Yes?"

"Well, it occurs to me that now is not the ideal time to place William in school. But it might be possible to find someone—a cleric, perhaps, or a retired schoolmaster— who would be prepared to take William into his home and tutor him until the autumn . . . and then we can see about school. What do you think?"

Pandora chewed her lip in furious thought. It was not precisely what she had hoped for, but: "Just so long as we can be sure that this tutor will be kind to William?" she said.

"Naturally, my dear young lady. I shall give the matter my personal attention." Was there a twinkle in his eye? If so, it was quickly gone. "Now, er . . . I hope you will not think me presumptuous, but you spoke of leaving Mrs. Hamilton's . . . 'standing on your own feet' was, I believe, the phrase you used." Mr. Lewis looked at her in a troubled way. "Are you sure that this is wise? A young lady on her own . . ." He shook his head.

"Oh, you need not worry about me," she told him cheerfully. "Once William is settled, I mean to work to support myself."

"I see," said the lawyer with extreme dryness. "And do you have anything definite in view?"

Pandora, remembering her recent disastrous interview, flushed a little, but she met his glance squarely. "Not as yet, but I have every confidence that I shall find a post—as companion, perhaps, or governess. . . ."

"My dear Miss Carlyon, I do beg you to think carefully before you take this step. Life with Mrs. Hamilton may have its drawbacks, but she is, with the exception of your brothers, the nearest thing to family that you can own to."

"Maybe so, Mr. Lewis, but if I am to be a drudge, I had far rather be paid for my services. And that way, you see, I may save up until I am able to make a home for my brothers—nothing elaborate, of course, but a place where they may come and go as they please, without feeling beholden."

Mr. Lewis opened his mouth to demolish this roseate dream, but the light of enthusiastic determination in Pandora's eyes was such that he could not bring himself to quench it. He contented himself with an equivocal murmur.

"Well, well . . . we shall see. Should I hear of anything suitable, you may be sure I will inform you of it."

Pandora arrived back in Brook Street to find everyone from home. Binns informed her that Miss Prosset had succumbed to one of her bad headaches, and in consequence Madam had taken Miss Eliza out visiting with her, while William, left to his own devices, was last seen sloping off in the direction of the park.

Pandora stifled a momentary unease at this last piece of news and dwelt instead upon the heady prospect of finding herself, if only for a short time, in sole possession of her surroundings. Fast on the heels of this thought came the remembrance that she hadn't eaten since breakfast, a state of affairs soon rectified by Cook, who had a warm regard for this half-sister of her mistress, who, she had been heard to mutter in the safe confines of her kitchen, was worth ten of certain other persons who should be nameless.

Her pangs of hunger assuaged, Pandora gathered up Frederick's discarded newspaper and carried it along to the drawing room, where a cheerfully leaping fire had been lit to take the chill off the spring afternoon. With reckless abandon she kicked off her shoes and went round collecting up all the cushions scattered about the room, piling them indiscriminately upon Octavia's sofa and plumping down among them, resolved to sample for a while the hedonistic world of the pampered.

But her innate dislike of prolonged inactivity, be it physical or mental, soon stirred her into reaching for the newspaper. She scanned the columns of advertisements eagerly, but could find nothing which remotely met her needs. For the first time she began to regret the outspokenness that had undoubtedly damned her in the Duke of Heron's eyes. Drat him!

Recognition of her own shortcomings, however, did not prevent her from spending several satisfying minutes devising ways and means of bringing about his discomfiture and eventual downfall. She was in the throes of one such deliciously irreverent daydream when Binns came to shatter her mood by announcing in reverential tones that the object of her reverie was below and wishful for an audience.

Pandora sat up with a squeak. The blood drained from her face and then flooded back as guilt suffused her. She gripped the back of the sofa with convulsive fingers while her mind raced. Perhaps he had brought the constable in order to have her committed to prison? No, that would be too absurd! Wouldn't it?

"I can't possibly see him, Binns! Did you not tell him that Mrs. Hamilton was out?"

"Yes, miss." The butler paused, and then, with the air of one bursting with important tidings: "But his grace asked most expressly for you."

"Oh Gemini!" she said faintly.

She leaned her arms along the sofa back and sank her chin on to her hands, fixing Binns with a pensive unblinking stare that hid blind panic. Every instinct was urging her to seek the haven of her cramped but safe quarters up in the rafters. No matter how one viewed the Duke's summary visitation, that he had come at all, his speedy discovery of her direction, seemed little short of ominous.

Binns, very conscious of the impropriety of keeping so august a personage kicking his heels below, cleared his throat apologetically, making Pandora jump.

Heavens! She would have to make a decision—retreat or stand her ground?

"Oh well!" She moved her shoulders in rueful acceptance and gave the butler a smile that was pure bravado. "I may as well get it over with. He can't eat me, after all."

"Just so, miss." In the relief of knowing that he would not be called upon to deny the Duke admittance, Binns failed to find anything odd in this observation. "Then with your permission I will ask his grace to step up right away."

"Thank you," she said politely, and continued to kneel among the cushions long after he had left, lost in furious contemplation of how she should go on. The Duke would expect an apology, of course, for all that he had been quite as uncivil as she. It was grossly unfair, she reflected, but nonetheless true that his exalted position in society gave him licence to behave very much as he pleased, while her own circumstances precluded any like degree of self-indulgence.

It was only as Pandora stood up to make ready for her ordeal that she remembered her shoes, so carelessly discarded. A frantic search yielded one, but the second continued to elude her, and all too soon Binns was back, throwing the door open once more to announce in a voice that throbbed with pride: "His grace, the Duke of Heron."

She heard the quick impatient step and jerked upright, tucking an escaping strand of hair behind her ear as she did so and feeling distinctly disadvantaged balanced on her one properly clad foot precariously supported by its more disreputable fellow hastily drawn back under cover of her skirts.

The Duke came to a halt before her, a drab driving coat with many capes swirling about him, and her first coherent thought was of how completely he filled the room with his presence; her second, totally inconsequential, was that Octavia would be furious to have been denied the accolade of receiving personally into her house this acknowledged linchpin of society.

The thought brought a wicked little smile to her eye, a smile taken due note of by her high-in-the-instep visitor. Not a propitious start.

To cover her embarrassment, she returned his greeting politely and invited him to sit down, doing so herself and being careful to tuck her feet well back, tugged her dress down surreptitiously to ensure that they were out of sight. But not quite soon enough.

His mouth was quivering as he took the chair she indicated, the coat falling open to reveal gleaming hessians and immaculate buff calf-clingers. He folded his arms and seemed in no hurry to come to the purpose of his visit. The silence became almost palpable.

Perhaps, if she were to make her apology now? She was still wondering how best to word it when she succumbed instead to the irresistible pang of curiosity, the words tumbling out before she could stop them.

"Oh, I do *wish* I knew why you have come!"

Heron had been plagued by the very same question. He had expected to banish Miss Pandora Carlyon from his mind within moments of her departure, and was not best pleased when more than an hour later the memory of a pair of uncomfortably candid grey eyes still disturbed his concentration.

In the end he had damned himself for a fool, called for his curricle to be brought round, and driven to Lady Margerson's house. At that hour he had little expectation of finding her alone, and so it proved. However, a casually dropped word and she was beckoning him to her side to make him the recipient of her murmured confidences without his ever needing to ask a direct question.

"A charming gel, my dear Heron—pluck to the backbone, I give you my word on't." She threw him an arch smile. "I mean to give one of my little soirees as soon as I feel up to it, so that you may see for yourself. She ain't one of your society beauties, mind—in fact, she don't run to many of the social graces . . . never had the opportunity d'ye see. Been with the army most of her young life . . . but worth ten of these skitter-brained gels one sees around . . . and like to ruin her chances if something ain't done soon. . . ."

There had been much in similar vein, but he had managed to extricate himself at last, more intrigued than before, and without quite knowing why he should care one jot what Miss Carlyon thought of him, found himself presently drawing up before the Hamiltons' house in Brook Street.

Pandora, waiting upon his answer, watched him warily, wishing she might take the words back and begin again. She encountered his tawny eyes and found their irony unsettling. She opened her mouth to speak again and was forestalled.

"Miss Carlyon, it would seem that I may have misinterpreted the purpose of your visit this morning. Would I now be right in deducing that you came in order that you might make application for a post as governess to my recently acquired French wards?"

She could scarcely believe what she was hearing. It couldn't be—it surely couldn't be—that *he* was apologising to *her*? She gulped.

"Yes, of course. What other purpose could I possibly have had?"

"What indeed!" The words held a curious ambivalence. "Tell me, ma'am—do I really strike you as the kind of man who would put himself to the trouble of interviewing prospective governesses? Even when they come impeccably recommended?" Her obvious puzzlement provoked a faint exasperation. "Dammit, I wouldn't even know what to look for!"

"Then I don't understand . . ."

"At last we reach some measure of agreement," he said dryly, "for no more do I. Or rather"—he rose, took a turn about the room, and swung round to face her—"perhaps I do. Did Lady Margerson specifically indicate that I was in need of a governess?"

"Yes, of course! At least . . ." Pandora bit her lip, remembering her lack of concentration. "Well, my attention may have wandered just a little, but she must have said something of the kind, for she knew I was desirous of seeking just such a position—"

"Why?" he interrupted her.

"I beg your pardon?"

He came close to the sofa—overwhelmingly close—looking down at her with that degree of intensity which she found so disconcerting.

"Why are you desirous of becoming a governess—a job for which, in my opinion, you are ill-suited? Do you have no family to support you?"

Pandora flushed, nettled by his tone. "No, sir, I do not. My parents are both dead—"

"Yes, yes, I know all about that. Also that you have brothers, one younger than yourself, and you don't get on with your sister, which doesn't surprise me from what little—what *very* little—I know of her . . . or of you." He was frowning. "But surely there is someone other than Mrs. Hamilton to whom you can turn?"

Pandora, momentarily diverted by the thought that he must be omniscient, soon realised that he had been discussing her with Lady Margerson. She was not at all sure that she liked being talked about behind her back, and wondered, not for the first time, why he should have bothered. She made her tone deliberately matter-of-fact.

"I fear not, sir. You see, my parents were both only children, and their parents, too, are dead."

"I see."

"In any case, I had much rather be independent." It was surprisingly difficult, she discovered, to assert oneself with true conviction while craning one's neck at such an uncomfortable angle. "I do wish you would sit down again," she said with obvious feeling.

A smile passed fleetingly across his face, but he made no immediate move to comply.

"Was I mistaken in what Lady Margerson said, then?" she persevered in some despair. "Do you not require a governess, after all?"

"I haven't the slightest idea," he murmured. "You see, my wards have not yet arrived. But I very much hope that they will come equipped with all the attendants necessary to their needs."

"Oh!" Pandora thought him shockingly unfeeling, but forbore to say so. "Then . . ."

The Duke's expression scarcely altered, yet from under those lazy lids his eyes glinted at her in such a way that in other circumstances she might have suspected him of laughing at her.

"My dear Miss Carlyon, I do sympathise, believe me. I am only too aware that Lady Margerson's ramblings can become tediously protracted, so that if one's attention wanders for even a short while, one can miss the whole nub of the matter." He was standing with his back to the window, and the sun made a kind of halo about his head, which sat ill with that unholy glint in his eye. She was gripped by a sudden and quite illogical presentiment.

"The nub, in this case," he concluded casually, "being that her ladyship's quest—self-instigated, I do assure you—is to discover for me the perfect wife."

4

For a moment the aura of sunlight about his head shimmered. Pandora could feel the blood draining out of her face, but still that tawny-eyed look held her. She felt trapped and took refuge in bluster.

"And you thought . . . you actually thought that I had come to . . . that I was . . . Oh!" She was in grave danger of becoming incoherent. "I think that is quite beastly! How could you?"

"You are harsh with me, Miss Carlyon." He did not sound in the least repentant. "But pray strive to appreciate the nature of my predicament. A strange young lady —very *forceful* young lady"—he emphasised the word with obvious relish, and she blushed—"inveigles her way into my house, into my very library—"

"I did not inveigle!" she protested.

"—and offers herself, apparently with Lady M.'s blessing, as the perfect embodiment of some unspecified desire upon my part . . . What am I supposed to think?"

What indeed! Oh, what a coil! "Does Lady Margerson know?" she asked in a small voice, the blush now creeping right down to her toes.

"I saw no reason to enlighten her. It would simply have added to the confusion."

Well, that was something, at least. "I just didn't stop to think! But I see now how misleading my behaviour must have seemed, and . . . and idiotish. Small wonder that you were so . . ."

" 'Odiously ungracious' was, I believe, one of your more telling phrases!"

"Oh, good God!" she gasped, mortified beyond all

measure as the memory of all those other choice home-thrusts she had delivered in the white heat of her indignation rose like an unspoken reproach between them. Her eyes, no logner able to meet his, became engrossed in contemplation of her twisting fingers, now clasped convulsively in her lap. "I do beg your pardon, my lord Duke," she offered by way of apology. "I daresay I said rather more than I should."

"You did indeed, Miss Pandora Carlyon," he agreed pleasantly. "You have, if I may say so, a most colourful turn of vocabulary when roused. Offhand, I can think of no one, with the possible exception of my grandmother, who would have dared to rip me up in such a thoroughgoing fashion!"

"Oh no!"

"What is more to the point, I suspect you relished every word!"

This reading of her character came too close for comfort. She lifted her eyes to his once more and saw a gleam of somewhat malicious humour lurking in their depths. In desperation she sought to vindicate herself.

"It is a sad fault in me that in the heat of the moment I frequently say more than I mean." The gleam grew more pronounced, and she added with an extra lift of her chin, "But I have *said* that I am sorry!"

"And with that, I must be content, I suppose? Ah, well . . ." The Duke stepped back at last with a gesture of resignation. Pandora seized upon the opportunity to stand up, and in doing so, was reminded of her missing shoe.

"You are clearly a creature of impulse, my dear young lady," he continued, finding himself strangely loath to put an end to the interview. "Whether it be paying gratuitious calls upon unsuspecting gentlemen or stepping out under hooves of their horses . . ."

"So you did recognise me?" she cried.

He inclined his head briefly. "Or even," he drawled softly, his glance straying to something among the cushions scattered about the floor, "indulging a curious propensity for casting your footwear far and wide."

His mouth quivered as he beheld her confusion, and

then, disconcertingly he strode across the room, swooped suddenly, and straightened up, bearing aloft her errant shoe.

"This *is* yours, I believe?"

Pandora murmured embarrassed assent and held out a hand for it, but he continued to hold it just fractionally beyond her reach.

"No, no, young Cinderella. You must permit me." With a sweeping bow, he indicated the sofa she had so recently vacated.

By now convinced that he was at the very least eccentric, if not actually mad (a trait not uncommon among the nobility, so she had heard), and not wishful to make much of so trifling a matter, she resumed her place, feigning nonchalance as the Duke knelt before her and held out a hand authoritatively for her foot. After a moment's hesitation she thrust it out, wishing she might have managed to smooth out the wrinkles in her sensible cotton stockings first.

With a growing sense of unreality she watched the shapely fingers close round her heel, felt the cool firmness of his touch. The easy competence with which he accomplished his self-appointed task suggested that he was no stranger to such small intimacies. The notion further confused her. She murmured stifled thanks and gave the foot an experimental little tug, but the fingers still encompassing it held fast.

"A perfect fit," he commented sociably.

Pandora found this teasing quixotic mood more difficult to deal with than outright hauteur, perhaps because she was unused to such treatment. She schooled herself to meet his eyes with some measure of calm, though her pulse was jumping in the oddest way.

"Please, my lord Duke!" she pleaded. "Someone might come!"

The faint curl of his lip suggested that he cared nothing for the possibility.

"Lady Margerson would have the fairy tale played out to its accepted conclusion, did you know?" He seemed to wait intently for her answer.

"No! That is . . . You are talking in riddles, sir."

"Her ladyship holds the conviction that you would make me an admirable wife."

For a moment Pandora was bereft of speech. Her eyes widened in shocked disbelief.

"You don't agree?" His voice was now silk-soft.

She prized her tongue from the dry roof of her mouth. "I think it is the most shatterbrained notion I ever heard!" she said flatly—and then stopped, aware that once again she had spoken without care. She waited for the veil of hauteur to descend, the anger to make itself felt. But for the second time in their brief acquaintance he gave a great shout of laughter, which softened and transformed the classical features and brought a warmth to his eyes.

"That must surely put me in my place!"

She looked at him uncertainly, recognised the genuine good humour in his response, and gave him back a crooked half-grin.

"I *do* beg your pardon! My wretched tongue again. I only meant that I don't understand how Lady Margerson can for one moment have supposed that you would entertain such a . . ."

"Shatterbrained notion?" he supplied in a droll voice. "But then, her ladyship is an incurable romantic, you see, whereas"—a hint of the old mockery crept in—"you and I, my dear young lady, are essentially realists, are we not?"

She didn't feel at all like a realist as he patted her foot and gave it back to her. He appeared amused by the speed with which it was snatched away and disappeared out of sight beneath her skirts. He was about to rise when his glance was caught by the paper tossed aside upon the sofa, carefully folded back at the advertisement page.

"So? You are still set upon finding employment as a governess or some such?" he said. "Must you really pursue that particular road to independence? I cannot feel that it will answer."

Astonished that he should be interested enough to comment, she asked a little shyly, "Why ever not?"

His eyes mocked her. "Because, Miss Pandora Carlyon, you are not sufficiently subservient!"

Before she could form the words to refute this criticism, the door behind them flew open and William erupted into the room, excited, dishevelled, the words tumbling out in a rush.

"Dora, there is the most bang-up rig you ever saw down in the street . . . with a team of real prime goers! Do come and look. Binns says it belongs to a *Duke*, but I expect he was fudging me! I say!"

He stopped short upon beholding the somewhat intimate-seeming tableau before him. As Heron came unhurriedly to his feet, William took in the magnificently caped driving coat, the elegant garments beneath it, and his eyes grew round.

"I say!" he said again. "Is it yours, sir?"

Amused, the Duke nodded assent.

By now Pandora too had risen. Affection, aggravation, and relief were almost equally mingled in her breast as she viewed her brother's muddied nanekeens and crumpled shirt, and the streak of dirt across his face.

"Oh, William!"

He grinned unrepentantly. "Yes, I know, but I've had a perfectly splendid afternoon. I remembered there was to be a balloon ascent in Green Park, so I went along, and one of the gentlemen in charge—Mr. Oliver—let me help."

"You didn't make a nuisance of yourself, I hope," she said swiftly.

"Of course not. Mr. Oliver said I'd been tremendously useful to them. He reckoned I had a quick brain and that I might well make a considerable aeronaut myself one day if I will only apply my mind seriously to studying the principles of flight! And he wasn't bamming, either, because he actually offered to take me up sometime if only you will give your permission. You will, won't you, Dora?"

She gave a mock shudder. "You can't possibly expect me to answer a question like that now, you abominable little shag-rag! The only place I wish you to *fly* at present is upstairs to wash and tidy yourself before Miss Prosset catches sight of you." She saw that the Duke was watching with a kind of languid interest. "But first you shall let me make you known to the Duke of Heron. My lord Duke, this is my younger brother, William."

"How do you do, sir." William, not content with the usual formal bow, extended his hand in the friendliest fashion—and too late Pandora saw that it, like the rest of him, was streaked with dirt.

Heron regarded the hand pensively; then with a barely perceptible sigh he clasped it firmly and found himself in the (for him) novel position of coming under the frank scrutiny of a grubby schoolboy who possessed the same direct gaze and openness of manner that characterised his sister. The same freckles, too, only more so.

"I haven't met a real Duke before," William confided cheerfully. "We are pretty sure that Lord Wellington will be made one soon, of course—only that isn't quite the same thing, is it? As actually being born a 'top-of-the-trees' nobleman, I mean."

Pandora didn't know where to look, but Heron rose valiantly to the occasion, murmuring that he had never given the matter much thought, but he rather fancied that the man was more important than the title, which earned him an enthusiastic nod of approval.

"And Lord Wellington will make a splendid Duke," prophesied William, "for though he is a very jolly sort of person in general, when he is out of humour he can cut up as stiff as *anyone!*"

This masterly assessment of the great man's character brought a distinct chuckle from the Duke, who was enjoying himself more than he had thought possible. William, much encouraged, grinned and returned with the tenacity of the enthusiast to the subject closest to his heart at that moment.

"Do *you* know anything about balloons, sir?"

"The bare rudiments, only," Heron confessed, feeling this admission to be a sad let-down. "I fancy I read Cavallo's *History and Practice of Aerostation* in my youth," he added in mitigation.

"Well, that is something, I suppose, for it means you must have been interested once—but the *History* is sadly out-of-date now, you know. Mr. Oliver said he would be pleased to make me free of his own notes, which is splendid, for *he* knows a great deal. I daresay he wouldn't mind you seeing them too, if you would care to," he added magnanimously, "because it would be jolly useful to have someone else to converse with, and Frederick hasn't the least idea!" William concluded scathingly.

Pandora, all too aware that with very little encouragement William would be well astride his hobbyhorse and virtually impossible to halt, chivied him toward the door with the admonition that he must not expect other people to share his obsessions, and that his grace would think him positively rag-mannered, carrying on in that overfamiliar way, a charge that was stoutly refuted.

"I only wanted to know what the Duke thought about the future possibilities of being able to travel through the air—" came the eager voice.

"No, no! Not another word!" cried Pandora, and pushed him out of the door, closing it behind him and turning back to the Duke, red-faced and apologetic. He bade her think nothing of it.

"A bright boy," he prophesied on the ghost of a laugh. "He is obviously destined to go far."

She responded with her quick crooked smile. "Yes, but he does need proper guidance," she sighed, unaware of how much her worry showed. "In fact, William's future is my most pressing motive for wishing to leave here and find myself a paid position." And without quite knowing why, she found that she was telling him briefly of the situation in which they found themselves, how very unsatisfactory she felt it to be, and the way in which Mr. Lewis had promised to help.

"Mr. Lewis, of Althrop, Pickering, and Lewis?"

"Yes. Do you know him?" She sounded a little anxious. "I did have the feeling that I could trust him to do what was right."

"I am sure you can," Heron reassured her. "I don't

know the gentleman personally, but the firm is a much-respected one."

"Good. Because his idea did appear to have a lot of merit in it. And if only I can see William settled satisfactorily, I shall then be able to arrange my own life accordingly."

"Very resourceful," drawled the Duke. "That will be your army upbringing, no doubt?"

He was at once aware that he had said the wrong thing, for she pokered-up and replied distantly that he was at liberty to think what he chose.

"Curiously enough, I was not trying to be offensive," he said quietly.

"No," she agreed. "It is I who am by far too sensitive." There was a bleakness in her smile. "I daresay I shall grow a harder shell in time."

The Duke had been preparing to leave, but now he took out his snuffbox and tapped it thoughtfully with one slim finger. "Do you need to grow a shell?"

Pandora stood, head high, watching him. "Surely Lady Margerson has told you?"

His hand hovered for a moment more over the snuffbox before flicking it open. "She may well have done so, Miss Carlyon, but her ladyship does have a wonderful facility for saying a great deal without actually telling one anything, as you"—he inclined his head—"if I may say so, know to your cost!"

"My father was Colonel Carlyon," she said abruptly.

"Should that convey something to me?" he murmured, his eyes veiled by their heavy lids so that she could deduce little from his expression. He took a pinch of snuff with a deft, unhurried turn of the wrist, inhaled it, and snapped the case shut.

The Duke's apparently casual attitude caught Pandora on the raw and drove her onto the offensive. She could not quite keep the bitterness from her voice, or the slight tremor.

"If Octavia is to be believed, the whole of London knows about him!"

"Your sister errs, ma'am. If it has escaped my ears,

then most assuredly the whole of London does not know whatever they are supposed to know."

"Oh." Pandora bit her lip. "Well, there was an unfortunate incident . . . and some poor woman lost her son as a result of it . . . she is quite deranged with the shock and has been accusing Papa of the most dreadful things . . . and the rumours have spread . . ."

If she had expected to discompose him, she was quite out. The Duke regarded her steadily for a moment. His curiosity was aroused, but for once he forbore to gratify it, saying only in a matter-of-fact way, "That must be very distressing for you, my dear child. But people are frequently thoughtless, and more often than not, ill-informed. You would do well not to refine too much upon idle comment."

His words, as practical as they were kind, fell so unexpectedly upon her ears that for one awful moment it seemed certain that she would make a fool of herself. She turned away and stood smoothing her dress with trembling fingers, swallowing convulsively to free her throat. To give her time to recover, the Duke stood looking down into the fire for a few moments and then walked to the door.

"Thank you," she said huskily, pulling herself together as he took his leave. "It is silly of me to mind so much when I know that Papa had nothing to be ashamed of. I would mind less, I think, if he were still alive."

Pandora had no wish to linger in the drawing room once the Duke had departed. Indeed, her one aim was to retire to the relative privacy of her own room before Octavia returned. Not that she had any expectation of the visit being kept from Octavia, but the angry inquisition which would most surely follow the disclosure was bound to be trying to the nerves, and she needed time to compose herself and marshal her thoughts into some kind of order.

In the bare garret room, the small cracked mirror on the shelf beside the window gave back her reflection with unflattering starkness. She loosed the pins which confined the less wilful strands of her hair, and, set free, it slithered to her shoulders, unrelentingly straight, making her face appear narrower than ever—a face which years spent in the open had weathered to a freckled unfashionable brown.

The purpose of the Duke's visit still mystified her, though already it was beginning to assume an aura of un-reality. She picked up her hairbrush and began to attack the offending tresses with more vigour than science. A rueful grin crooked the corner of her mouth; one thing was certain—he had not been slain by her incomparable beauty!

"I do not understand!" cried Octavia like a disagree-able echo of these reflections a short time later. "Why was Heron here? Binns said that he actually *asked for you!*" Her tone evinced outraged incredulity.

She had come bursting into Pandora's room without ceremony no more than minutes after returning home, quite unable to believe that fate could have played so cruel a jest upon her. She prowled restlessly back and forth, hampered by the lack of space, her manner petu-lant as she stopped now and then to finger Pandora's few possessions. She seized upon a brown velvet spencer which lay with the braid ripped off awaiting new trim-mings, eyed it with contempt, and dropped it back on the bed.

"I mean, what possible interest could Heron have in you?"

"None at all," Pandora acknowledged, unaccountably depressed to hear her own views so brutally confirmed. To put an end to the tiresome inquisition, she said with scant regard for accuracy, "His grace came merely to bring a message from Lady Margerson."

Octavia stared—and then gave a rather shrill titter. "That woman! I know she is considered a law unto her-self, but really! To be treating Heron as an errand boy?"

"Perhaps it is because she has known him from the cradle."

"Has she?" It was such tit-bits of information dredged from Pandora's somewhat imperfect recollections of what Lady Margerson had said which were an unremitting source of aggravation to Octavia Hamilton, that this insignificant girl whom she had thought to patronise as a poor relation had been able to lay claim to Lady Margerson's acquaintance, a distinction she herself had long coveted in vain. Her ladyship was odd, but though one might effect to ridicule her, she *did* move in first circles—a fact which was becoming more painfully obvious by the minute. Octavia had never meant to house Pandora and her odious little brother for so long; it was only when Lady Margerson had written to the girl shortly after her arrival in London and looked like to take her up that she had changed her mind. But to her increasing chagrin, and in spite of many broadly delivered hints, Pandora had not only failed to exploit the heaven-sent opportunity to serve her own ends, she had also resolutely resisted (quite maliciously, in Octavia's opinion) the least inclination or indeed, one might think, *obligation* to introduce her family to Lady Margerson. And as for this latest piece of work . . . Heron! A desire to wound made her spiteful.

"Lud! It really is the most absurd thing I ever heard! The town's most notorious rake, seeking audience with my little sister! How he must have laughed to see you!"

"Is he truly that?" Pandora was diverted from outright indignation by Octavia's description of the Duke.

"My dear child, is it not apparent?" Octavia's voice was shrill. "Why, his taste in women is exquisite—his mistresses high fliers every one! But although his generosity toward them is prodigious, it is also fickle, for none can sustain his fancy beyond a matter of weeks. I heard recently that he was badly crossed in love several years back by some little French émigrée—and has held women cheap ever since. With the exception of Lady Sarah Bingly, of course . . ." Her voice took on that note of vague envy which the mention of society's most accredited beauty always aroused. "If anyone can bring him to heel, she will."

46

"How awful," said Pandora. "I believe I feel quite sorry for him."

"Sorry!" Octavia almost shrieked the word. "You think Heron is to be pitied? When he may indulge his slightest whim? When not a door in London is barred to him? Not a mother with daughters to bestow who does not pursue his acquaintance in spite of his reputation? Lud, Pandora, no one but you could think to pity such a desirable rake! Or are you so innocent that you did not perceive at a glance the kind of man Heron is?"

"Of course I did!" Pandora retorted indignantly. "But what you have said only makes me more sorry for him than ever. I can think of nothing worse than to be fawned upon for what one has rather than for what one is."

"That is sanctimonious twaddle, my girl, and coming from you, it is almost laughable! Perhaps it will please you to know that there are some things even Heron can't plan for. It seems that he has had the émigrée's children foisted on to him—tis being said that perhaps he fathered them in the first place!" Octavia laughed. "Not that such talk will bother him any more than the children will. He is rich enough to buy an abbey and may have them cared for without making the least push to involve himself!"

When Octavia finally tired of baiting her and left, Pandora picked up the half-renovated spencer and began absently to ply her needle. She was not the innocent that Octavia had accused her of being. To be sure, Papa was used to tease her by calling her his little air dreamer, but one could not grow up among soldiers without learning a great deal about the basic realities of life.

So it was not the Duke's morals which troubled her, though she could not approve them; rather, though Octavia had poured scorn on her reasoning, she thought it very bad for anyone to be so indulged. She could think of nothing more guaranteed to induce a lack of purpose than being able to gratify one's least whim, and if what Octavia had said was true, it would seem that the pursuit of pleasure was the Duke's sole reason for existence.

And yet? She remembered how he had been with William—suffering his chatter, encouraging him in that amused, indulgent way he had. It was more than Frederick had deigned to do in all the weeks they had been here.

Surely such a man could not be entirely lost to the more worthwhile precepts of life?

5

The Duke of Heron, in happy ignorance of the judgement being passed upon him, drove home in excellent spirits. He had found the recent interlude amusing, even stimulating, after a fashion. Not that he had any expectation of meeting the Carlyons again. In spite of Lady Margerson's fond machinations, the plain fact was that they moved in very different worlds. Their paths were unlikely to converge—and today, though pleasant, had been no more than the gratification of a passing whim.

He was still smiling quietly to himself when he arrived home. There a letter awaited him. He noticed it the moment he entered the hall; opulently pink, it graced one of a pair of handsome ormolu tables set either side of the staircase. He surrendered his hat and shrugged off his driving coat, handing them into the charge of a waiting footman, before picking it up.

His name was penned in a careful immature hand. He fingered the letter pensively, as though reluctant to break the seal, and a faint exotic perfume assailed his nostrils. His eyes lifted in faint query to his butler, Pinkerton.

"The missive arrived not more than an hour since, your grace," said that most astute of servants, recognising in his master's demeanour the now familiar indications of waning passion. As he confided later to his grace's valet over a restoring glass of port, "Whosoever this particular barque of frailty might be, her days are numbered, Mr. Glyn, you mark my words!"

The Duke, meanwhile, removed to the Yellow Saloon, where he scanned the incoherent protestations of devotion scrawled across the scented page, their underlying note of desperation filling him with a vague contempt. Poor Irena—an exquisitely beautiful creature, but greedy. He had lost count of the trinkets he had lavished upon her, not begrudging her one of them until last evening. His reluctance to provide instantly an emerald necklace to complement the pair of earrings with which he had presented her two days previously had provoked teasing and then petulance. Finally her huge violet eyes had filled with tears—a grave error on her part, as his hasty departure had no doubt confirmed to her. Hence this rather grovelling plea for forgiveness.

Heron sighed. Well, she should have the necklace. It would serve as well as any other as a parting gift.

He was standing over the fireplace watching the last of the letter curling up the chimney when his secretary, Ambrose Varley, entered the room bearing a sheaf of documents. The pungent aroma of the smouldering scented paper rose like incense on the air. His eyes met the Duke's.

"A suitably symbolic valediction, Ambrose?"

"If you say so, sir," said the secretary politely.

"I felt sure you would approve," murmured Heron.

After almost two years in his grace's service, Mr. Varley was still unsure how to deal with the Duke's levity on such occasions. He was a studious young man with a gravity beyond his twenty-four years, his dress as neat, as inconspicuous as everything else about him. Yet, if asked, he would readily admit that he enjoyed his work. He might deplore the Duke's butterfly existence—his numerous erratic liaisons with ladies of "a certain kind," but it had not taken him long to discover that there was a great deal more to his employer than was immediately evident; and if occasionally he ripped one up or was overly sardonic, he was also scrupulously just, never bore malice, and could, when one least expected it, be quite disarmingly affable. One thing he was not, however, was predictable.

Mr. Varley said diffidently, "I wonder if I might ask your grace to favour me with a few minutes of your time?" The papers cradled in his arms rustled significantly.

"Business, dear boy? Ah, well—if you must." A faint sigh of resignation accompanied the words. "But in the library, I think. This room reeks of that damned perfume." Heron strolled to the door, indicating that his secretary should accompany him.

"Do I then burden you so heavily with work?" he mused a few moments later, perching on the corner of his desk and watching lazily, arms folded, as Mr. Varley set down his bundle of papers.

The young man demurred, looking apologetic. "It is the somewhat pressing matter of your wards, sir. The lawyers have now completed the necessary documents—and await your instructions. I have a letter here . . ." He riffled expertly through the correspondence.

"Have I ever told you, dear boy, what a prince among secretaries you are?"

The young man looked up, colouring slightly. "Your grace is most kind, but I cannot think that I am in any way—"

"You can hardly fail to have been made aware of the present speculation concerning *my wards*."

"I never heed gossip, sir." It was almost a reproach.

"Very commendable," said the Duke dryly. "But you must surely have wondered?" A perceptible deepening of colour in the young man's face betrayed the accuracy of this conjecture. "Yet never by word or sign of any kind throughout these dealings have you exhibited the least curiosity. I find that quite remarkable."

"I did not consider it to be any of my business, sir," replied the young man simply.

"I see."

A wry grimace touched Heron's mouth. Would that he could have viewed Mariette's indiscretions and their unhappy outcome with the same detachment. Poor foolish Mariette—estranging herself from those who truly loved her, throwing away all that he would have lavished upon her for the hope of a prize that was always beyond her reach. So ready to be seduced by the oh, so charming Duc de Berri, handsome nephew of the late French king; so sure that once she had borne his children, he must eventually marry her.

His heart still contracted as he imagined her despair upon discovering that she was but one of many, that the Duc had already, it was rumoured, contracted a marriage with an English clergyman's daughter. If only she had come back to Clearwater then! Instead, she had been summoned by the Comte de Lille, now head of the Bourbon dynasty in exile. He had been shocked to hear of her treatment at his nephew's hands, and remembering her family from happier days, insisted that she take up residence with her children at Hartwell in the Vale of Aylesbury, where he was endeavouring to maintain the vanished splendours of French court life in diminished circumstances.

It was from there that she had finally written to the Comtesse, begging for her forgiveness. From the letter it was clear that she was deeply unhappy, far from well, and worried about her children's future should anything happen to her. Not all at the Court, it seemed, were so charitable as the Comte, or so ready to accept the Duc's bastards with grace. Mariette begged that, should anything happen to her, Madame de Valière would adopt the children and care for them in memory of one who had forfeited the right to ask such a boon, but bitterly regretted her past wickedness.

Clearly his grandmother was too old and infirm to give any such undertaking, but just as clearly Heron could not bring himself to ignore so passionate a plea from one for whom he had once cared so deeply, nor could he deprive Grandmère of the solace that Mariette's children might bring to her remaining years. He must adopt the children himself.

Matters were precipitated by Mariette's unexpectedly sudden death, together with the imminent cessation of hostilities. Delicate negotiations ensued.

The Comte, whilst conscious of a family responsibility for the children, was not averse to the possibility of being relieved of their embarrassing presence before he returned to France as king. Their father had approved the arrangements with great cordiality, promising to keep himself in touch with them and do his part by them whenever so required. And so all was decided.

"Your grace?"

The Duke came out of his reverie to find Ambrose putting a letter into his hand. He cast a cursory glance over the spidery handwriting.

"Well? So far as I can tell it is a typical lawyer's communication of the kind I pay you to deal with. Is there something about this particular one which renders it an exception?"

Mr. Varley was beginning to wish he had left well alone.

"You will recall, sir, that a lady in the Comte de Lille's retinue has been caring for your late cousin's children since their mother's sad demise . . ."

"And?"

"Well, now that the Comte has been proclaimed King Louis XVIII, he must return to France. As you will see from that letter, he is to leave for London very shortly, and from there he will proceed to Paris—"

"Pray spare me the tedious detail of Louis's itinerary, Ambrose, and come to the point."

Mr. Varley heard the faint rasp of impatience and hurried on. "Very simply, then, sir. The lady concerned quite naturally wishes to leave with his majesty, and is somewhat anxiously awaiting your decision as to how soon you will be ready to accommodate the children."

Heron handed him the letter and stood up, an indefinable glitter in his eyes. "Then we must inconvenience the lady no further. I take it the nurseries at Clearwater are ready to receive the children?" Mr. Varley nodded. "Then I fail to see your difficulty."

"It is only that . . ." Mr. Varley rushed the words, and then hesitated, swallowed, and continued lamely, "It is only that I wondered if your grace might not, in the circumstances, consider going down to Hartwell yourself in order to escort your charges to Clearwater?"

There was a small uncomfortable silence.

"Did you, indeed?" said the Duke softly. "And whatever gave you the crass-brained notion that I might conceivably wish to play wet nurse to a brace of muling infants?"

"I thought . . . But no matter. I will of course arrange matters exactly as your grace pleases."

"Very magnanimous!"

Reproach was clearly evident in the way Mr. Varley collected up his documents and clutched them possessively to his chest. In turning to bow, he encountered the Duke's thin sardonic smile.

"Sometimes, Ambrose, I fear I am a sad disappointment to you," he murmured.

"Not in the least, your grace," said the young man stiffly. "It is no part of my function to question your grace's behaviour."

"Excellent!" Heron's expression softened into something approaching a boyish grin. "A very proper answer, in fact. Only, do come down out of the boughs, dear boy!" he urged, adding by way of mitigation: "You should know by now that I never act to please others!"

Inexplicably, the words put him in mind of Miss Carlyon and her young rip of a brother. As Mr. Varley was about to leave the room, he asked casually, "Ambrose, do you recall talk of a Colonel Carlyon—in connection with some kind of army scandal?"

Mr. Varley admitted to nothing beyond the vaguest of recollections.

"Would you like me to make enquiries, sir?"

"No, no," said the Duke, a little irked to find himself a prey to curiosity once more. "It is of no importance."

And this might well have ended the matter, but for William.

Their paths crossed two days later as the Duke drove home from an assignation made on the previous evening, which had proved a sad disappointment. He was consequently preoccupied and feeling not a little annoyed with himself when he first became aware of a small disconsolate figure some way ahead of him scuffing up the dust with unwilling feet.

He might not have spared the boy a second glance but for the distinctive quiff of fair hair which stood up in a vigorously aggressive manner from the crown of his head.

Driving smartly past William, he brought his team to a halt and turned to watch the child. He was a sorry sight, one knee gaping out of his trousers to expose an angry graze and his collar torn. If this were not enough, he also looked very much as though he had been rolling in a muddy field, and despite the lowered head, Heron was able to discern a distinct puffiness around one eye.

"That must have been quite a mill!" he observed conversationally as William drew level.

The boy's head jerked up with a curious mixture of guilt and defiance, one hand going up instinctively to shield his eye.

"One is moved to wonder," continued his grace, "how your opponent fared. I trust you gave a good account of yourself?"

"I made his nose bleed!"

The intense satisfaction in the confession surprised the Duke. He had not somehow equated William's character with physical violence.

Finding himself under scrutiny, William looked down, as though not aware until that moment of his general condition.

"Oh, lor!" he groaned in disgust. "Dora will *kill* me!"

The Duke's mouth twitched. "That would be a pity." He leaned down to offer the boy a hand. "You had better come home with me and we'll clean you up a bit. My man has an infallible panacea for black eyes."

William cheered up considerably at the prospect of riding in such a bang-up rig, but as his glance travelled over the spanking coachwork and what little he could see of the interior, he hung back, shaking his head.

"P'raps I hadn't better," he said regretfully. "I'm sure to make the seat dreadfully muddy."

The Duke discovered, somewhat to his surprise, that he was not proof against the look of yearning in a small boy's eyes. "That is of trifling account, my child." He was bland as he turned to his groom. "We are not so small-minded as to let a little mud cast us into the suds, are we, Grimble?"

The groom, more used to incurring the length of his grace's tongue should so much as a speck of dust sully any part of his elegant equipage, muttered agreement, only the faint twitching of a muscle in his cheek betraying the true nature of his feelings in the matter.

William needed no further urging. He seized the hand reached down to him, and if Heron noticed how he winced as he clambered up, he tactfully refrained from comment. Instead he allowed himself to be quizzed comprehensively upon the skills necessary to the expert handling of a team of high-couraged cattle, and was amused to find himself being critically appraised and congratulated as he demonstrated a few of the techniques which had made him such a distinguished member of the Four in Hand Club.

William was equally enthusiastic about the house in St. James's Square when they arrived. With all the aplomb of the seasoned traveller, he declared it to be miles beyond anything he had ever seen, and the several footmen standing about the hall were more than once obliged to adjust their expressions under the austere eye of his grace.

He seemed particularly taken with the staircase, and spent some moments in rapt contemplation of its soaring grandeur before Heron recalled him to the necessity of mounting it.

"Oh, yes, sir, of course," said William thoughtfully.

In the ducal bedchamber Mr. Glyn awaited them, dapper, hands neatly folded before him, and looking, as William confided to the Duke, "as prim as pie." However, with the prospect of cakes and cordial as an inducement, he needed little persuading to relinquish his clothes into the hands of this rather forbidding personage.

His grace's valet viewed the advent of a grubby small boy into his well-ordered life with severe misgivings. His grace had evinced some odd quirks in his time, but this was a new and disturbing departure.

But by the time William had submitted stoically to having his cuts and bruises anointed and his fast-swelling eye treated with an herbal compress, the ingredients of which were known only to himself, Mr. Glyn was obliged to acknowledge that he was a likeable, well-mannered child—if a shade too inquisitive for his liking.

Later, enveloped in one of his lordship's shirts, which came down to his ankles and provoked an outburst of giggling, William curled up in one of the deep comfortable armchairs in the Yellow Saloon to await the promised repast.

Mr. Varley, presently passing the door of the Yellow Saloon on his way to his own room, was surprised by the sound of childish laughter. He put his head round the door and was regaled by the spectacle of a small boy, somewhat battle-scarred, with two footmen in attendance, being plied with a mouth-watering array of pastries and cakes under the indulgent eye of the splendid Pinkerton, while the Duke lounged in an opposite armchair viewing the proceedings with equanimity.

"Yes, I know, Ambrose," he said, interpreting his secretary's reactions with uncanny omniscience. "Not my usual style, I agree. May I present Master William Carlyon, whose recent foray into the noble art of pugilism, notwithstanding that he gave a good account of himself, left his clothing in a somewhat disreputable condition. Glyn is endeavouring to rectify matters with his usual aplomb. Meanwhile, we thought refreshments would be in order."

"Very proper, sir," said Mr. Varley with commendable composure.

It was only when William sat back replete and everyone else had left the room that the Duke turned the conversation once again to the fight.

"Do you make a habit of indulging in bouts of fisticuffs?" he asked casually.

"Only if I must." William grinned with engaging honesty. "Courtney says I've no science at all. I just go tearing in, all arms and legs—mere flourishing he calls it, though it usually gets results. Fighting can be jolly satisfying sometimes, I suppose, but mostly I think it a shocking waste of effort."

Heron was amused and intrigued by this astonishingly mature observation. "But in this instance you felt . . . er, compelled to offer violence?" he persisted gently. "Your protagonist offered you an unacceptable insult, perhaps?"

"Not *me*! He might insult *me* until he turned puce, and I wouldn't care!" William, red-faced, was clearly labouring under some powerful emotion. At last it could be contained no longer. "Clive Broughton is a . . . a sniveling little *bagpipe*—all wind and bluster and no bottom whatever! He don't understand the first thing about *real courage* and . . . and duty, and going on when everything is against you!" He drew a deep painful breath betokening sore ribs and ended in disgust: "He blubbered like a baby when I gave him one in the breadbasket. Then he ran away!"

"Clearly a most despicable youth," observed Heron, to whom matters were suddenly becoming much clearer. "Defending the family honour, were you, child?" he added quietly.

William climbed down from the chair, managing in his ridiculous garb to achieve a quaint dignity that reminded the Duke irresistibly of the boy's sister.

"If you don't mind, my lord Duke, I would as lief not talk about it anymore," he said politely. "Thank you *very* much for . . . for the food and everything, but I think I ought to be going home now, or Dora will wonder where I am."

Heron regarded him steadily for a moment, then shrugged. "Very well, young stiff-rump!" He rang the bell, and a footman appeared on the instant. "Be so good as to discover from Mr. Glyn whether Master William's clothes are ready for him. No, better still, you go with him, William, and come back to me here when you are ready."

At the door William turned, diffident but determined. "I wonder, sir—might I ask you a favour?"

The Duke, wondering what he might be letting himself in for, signified assent.

"Can I slide down your banister, sir?" The words came out in a little rush. "Octavia won't let me near the one at

Brook Street . . . and anyway, your staircase has theirs beaten to flinders!"

Heron was laughing as the door closed behind William. Then he grew thoughtful, and finally he sought out his secretary.

"Tell me, Ambrose—what opinion do you hold of Mr. Brearly?"

"The present incumbent of Chedwell?" Mr. Varley, unsure what to make of the question, couched his answer in general terms. "When I have encountered him on my visits to Clearwater, I have always found him to be an exceedingly pleasant, intelligent gentleman."

"One cannot always say as much of a clergyman," drawled Heron. "He has a growing family, I believe?"

"Oh, yes. I am not sure how many children there are—"

"Their exact number is quite immaterial, dear boy. What interests me is whether Brearly is a suitable person to undertake the care and instruction of a singularly bright little boy."

Mr. Varley was betrayed into momentary surprise. "Were you thinking of young Carlyon, sir?"

"He is in need of just such a tutor," said the Duke reflectively. Then, making up his mind: "Perhaps you will oblige me by communicating to Mr. Brearly that I should appreciate it if he could see his way clear to accepting the boy as a boarding pupil for a few months. The letter can go down to Chedwell at once, by one of the grooms."

"Yes, sir."

By now Mr. Varley's curiosity was stretched to the limit. It was so unlike his grace to interest himself in an obscure family like the Carlyons—let alone take to indulging the whims of a small boy. His immediate conclusion had been that William's sister must be a regular stunner. But this notion was dispelled by Pinkerton, who, when discreetly quizzed, had volunteered the information that the young lady of that name who had called upon the Duke several days since in Mr. Varley's absence, though a pleasant ladylike person, had been sadly plain. The mystery was vexing—most vexing. Furthermore, from the glint in the Duke's eye, he suspicioned that his grace was well aware of the confusion in his secretary's breast and was enjoying the situation hugely.

"And while you are about it," he said now, strolling to the door, "write also to Mr. Lewis of Althrop, Pickering, and Lewis, to inform him that a tutor has been found for young Master William. You had better give him Brearly's direction. No doubt Mr. Lewis will wish to convey the news to Miss Carlyon. If so, I have no objection, so long as my name is kept out of the proceedings."

"But, sir . . . ?"

Heron turned, his hand on the door, waiting for Mr. Varley to complete his query.

"Sir, should we not perhaps wait until we have Mr. Brearly's consent?"

"Why?" There was a touch of whimsicality in the soft reply. "Do you fear that he may refuse me?"

6

Pandora had been shy of facing Lady Margerson. Although assured by the Duke that he had not revealed her indiscretion, her conscience would not be easy. But when she at last entered her ladyship's drawing room, resolved upon making a clean breast of things, she was scarcely given time to draw breath.

Lady Margerson sat before her writing desk with indecision, not to say total bewilderment, writ large throughout every rippling fold of her ample form. She turned as Pandora was announced, uttering a cry of such undisguised relief as to make her visitor blink.

"My love . . . you could not have come more opportunely! See, here are all these invitations to be written, and I do not know which way to turn! Pritchard—my companion, you know—vowed that she would have them done in a trice, but we had not gone beyond making out a list of guests when . . . you will not believe it, she has succumbed to a bout of the influenza!"

Pandora hid a smile and commiserated with her ladyship over what she clearly regarded as the inconsiderate timing of her companion's indisposition.

"Oh, well, I daresay she could not help it," came the generous admission.

Pandora then offered, as was clearly expected of her (and indeed she did not mind), to take the unfortunate Pritchard's place.

Lady Margerson sighed and relinquished any pretence of making herself useful, retiring instead to her comfortable sofa, whence she was able to supervise Pandora's efforts quite adequately without the least exertion. "I had thought just a small soirée," she said complacently.

Pandora, settling to her task, took note of the pile of cards and the length of the list and wondered wryly what Lady Margerson would regard as a large gathering.

". . . I did put down dear Lady Sefton, did I not? And Emily Cowper? She was so very kind to me last month when I was indisposed. And the Tillertons? *She* is a trifle odd, but her husband is a charming man. . . ."

The nonstop commentary continued as Pandora wrote steadily in her very best script, pausing when necessary to reassure her ladyship over some newly imagined omission. It was in glancing down the list of names for the umpteenth time that one name stood out immediately above her own. She stopped writing for fear that her hand might shake—and made a pretence of mending the pen.

"Is . . . will the Duke of Heron attend, do you suppose?" she asked in what she hoped was a casual way.

"I shall be very much astonished if he does not!" A certain coyness entered Lady Margerson's voice. "He already knows a little about you, and is sufficiently intrigued to wish to know more."

"He is?" Pandora gulped, wondering how to tell the old lady politely that she had windmills in her head if that was what she thought—and decided that it couldn't be done. To attempt explanations now would also be fruitless. Lady Margerson's mind seemed unable to fasten on more than one idea at a time. The problem would have to be solved another way. "As to my own case," she began. "I really do not think that—" She got no further.

"It is no use your attempting to wriggle out of attending my little party, because I refuse to listen to any excuses!" Lady Margerson sounded unusually firm. "Why ever do you suppose I am putting myself to so much trouble? I am determined to introduce you into society a little. You have been in London for all of a month now, and since it appears that Mrs. Hamilton will do nothing for you, I must supply the deficiency. I am not quite without influence, you know."

"But, ma'am, I do not wish to be introduced to society."

"Of course you do! How else are you to meet with anyone in the least way eligible? No, no, only listen to me, my love," pleaded Lady Margerson. "I am well aware that we do not see eye to eye in this, but I have been giving the matter a great deal of thought, and it is quite clear to me that I shall never be able to look your poor dear mama in the face when we meet beyond the grave . . . Oh, you may smile, but I do most earnestly believe that we *shall* all meet again, you know . . ." She smiled with great sweetness. "And if I allow you to pursue this hubble-bubble notion of independence which you have taken into your head, without making a push to see you settled, then Arabella will be fully justified in cutting me dead! Oh, dear . . . well, you know what I mean."

Pandora did not know whether to laugh or cry. "Ma'am, indeed you are very *kind,* but——"

The door opened to admit her ladyship's footman bearing a card on a salver, which he presented to her.

"Heron!" she cried, beaming with pleasure. "Show him up at once, Carr. There, now!" She turned triumphantly to Pandora, who had risen in a panic and was already collecting up her reticule and gloves. "Could anything be more fortunate? Almost as if it had been ordained!" Much struck with this thought, she viewed her young friend's preparations for departure with dismay. "Wait, my dear child . . . can you not see that if only Heron can be persuaded to take an interest in you, others will soon follow. No, no, my dear, you shall not run away! I forbid it!" she wailed, as Pandora pulled her gloves on resolutely, lowering her voice as the familiar impatient tread could be heard outside. "Besides, only think how odd such behaviour must appear!"

The door opened.

"Ah, Robert! There you are. . . . Such a pleasant surprise! Pandora"——there was an unconscious pleading in her voice——"pray allow me to make you known to his grace, the Duke of Heron."

While the Duke bowed with scrupulous politeness, and

Pandora, almost rigid with embarrassment, curtsied and murmured something incomprehensible and would not meet his eyes, Lady Margerson chattered on nervously.

"I must tell you, Robert, that Miss Carlyon is the daughter of my late godchild, Arabella Wyndham. You will remember Sir Vernon Wyndham, Arabella's father, no doubt? Or was he before your time? A charming man . . . though a little unsteady, perhaps. As I recall, he showed a decided partiality for games of chance . . . but that was all a very long time ago. His wife was one of my dearest friends . . ."

She saw that the two young people were still standing, Heron, as always, very much at his ease, Pandora staring down at her hands and looking positively mulish! And as for that dress of grey muslin! The child was in mourning for her papa, of course, but that did not excuse a lack of style . . . cut with not the slightest attempt made to soften her almost boyish want of curves . . . not so much as a flounce or two! Lady Margerson could have cried with exasperation . . . and as for her nerves, they were all on end, for she knew that neither of the two could be relied upon to behave in a conventional fashion. "Oh, do please sit down!" she cried distractedly.

Heron's mouth quirked—and Pandora, no longer able to resist the temptation, stole a look at him and was caught in the act. It seemed to her that there was mockery in the smiling eyes, the curling lip.

"Miss Carlyon." He indicated a chair and came forward to hand her into it.

She tightened her grip on her reticule.

"Thank you," she said. "But I was on the point of leaving." She turned to Lady Margerson, hardening her heart against that lady's beseeching look. "I will come and finish your cards tomorrow, ma'am."

"Oh, but if you will only wait just a little. The Duke never stays above a few minutes, do you, Robert?"

"Never," he agreed, and Pandora could hear the amusement in his voice. "I came . . . er, merely to enquire whether you mean to attend Eliza Chorley's reception for the Czar's sister this coming week, and if so, whether I may have the privilege of escorting you?"

Lady Margerson's look of puzzlement was imperfectly concealed as she fluttered her assent, but Pandora was too distraught to heed it.

The Duke noticed, however, and without giving her time to comment, continued smoothly. "For my part, I would not willingly go within a mile of the Grand Duchess—she has the manners of a fishwife, and I have yet to discern any redeeming quality in her. However, Eliza is simply doing what is expected of her, and one can scarcely hold her accountable for the Grand Duchess of Oldenburg's shortcomings."

"No indeed. But they do say that the Czar himself is a charming man . . . though he is not expected for several weeks yet, of course." Out of the corner of her eye Lady Margerson saw that Pandora was making a move. She said in a last desperate throw, "Well, then, my love, if you must go, I am sure that Robert would be delighted to drive you home." She looked meaningfully at the Duke, who bowed and agreed that he would be happy to put himself at Miss Carlyon's disposal.

But Pandora, by now hot with fury and embarrassment, had reached the limit of her endurance. She pressed a swift kiss on the old lady's cheek, sketched a curtsy to the Duke, and moved to the door.

"I should not dream of inconveniencing his grace," she said lightly. "Besides, it is such a fine afternoon that I have been quite looking forward to the walk home."

She had not gone more than a few paces down the road when she heard his firm footsteps following her. He came abreast, his fingers closing inexorably round her arm, so that perforce she must struggle or come to a halt. He turned her to face him.

"Why did you run away?" he demanded.

"Why did you come after me?" she returned, quick as light.

He observed that although her eyes were bright accusing points of light, her voice sounded oddly stifled.

"To drive you home. Why else?" The pressure of his

fingers increased as he attempted to lead her back toward the waiting curricle, but she resisted his efforts.

"No. Thank you, my lord Duke, but I don't wish to drive anywhere with you."

"Impertinent baggage!" he said mildly. "I'll have you know that you are being accorded a singular honour."

"And should be suitably grateful? Is that what you are saying?" Pandora strove to speak calmly. "Well, I am very sorry, sir, but I cannot avail myself of your kind offer. Lady Margerson may have advanced all kinds of persuasive arguments on my behalf, but I promise you I was not party to them, nor"—and here her voice shook slightly—"do I in the least crave the sort of notoriety that being 'taken up' by you would afford me!"

"The devil!" Heron exclaimed on an abrupt laugh, and then, cuttingly: "You flatter me, ma'am. I doubt whether even my most pressing attentions could achieve that much for you!"

She flinched, blinked several times in rapid succession, and averted her gaze—and he immediately wished the words unsaid.

There followed an uneasy silence.

What *was* he doing here? Heron wondered in some exasperation. Young ladies of unimpeachable virtue —especially very young ladies who favoured unfashionable short-poked bonnets and dresses of insipid hue and little cut—were emphatically not his style; the more so when they were sharp-tongued withal. Yet, upon returning William to Brook Street, the stab of disappointment he had experienced upon being told that Miss Carlyon was not at home had taken him straight round to Lady Margerson's house with so feeble a motivation to explain his visit that she was probably puzzling over it yet!

He found himself studying the delicate line of jaw now tilted a little away from him—a delicacy curiously at odds with the quality of enduring strength which characterised the rest of the face.

He began to grow impatient. Common sense dictated that he should abandon her to her chosen fate. Yet her continuing, unyielding silence baffled and infuriated him. Rejection was for him a novel experience—and one for which he did not care.

And then he heard a sniff, so faint as to be scarcely audible, but a sniff nonetheless. Prosaic, vaguely comical even, it affected him as a display of tears could never have done. His voice was faintly chiding.

"Miss Carlyon, you cannot be so paper-sculled as to suppose that I came after you at Lady Margerson's bidding?" When she did not immediately reply, he put a finger under her chin and forced her head round until she must meet his eyes. "*Is* that what you are thinking?"

A solitary tear rolled down her cheek, and she brushed it away with an impatient gesture. "I don't know," she admitted frankly. "I do know it is what she hoped for . . . your interest, that is. She said as much just before you arrived. It is supposed to open all sorts of doors for me!"

Heron mentally cursed the old lady's heavy-handedness. "Lady Margerson may occasionally want for subtlety," he said dryly, "but her instincts are usually reliable, and I believe she does have your good at heart."

"Oh, I know she does, and I assure you that I hold her in the warmest regard!" In her earnestness Pandora quite forgot to remain distant. "But that only makes it worse, don't you see? She will keep trying to make of me something that I am not!"

"And what is that, pray?"

"Well, *you* are certainly not paper-sculled, so you must know the answer to that!"

"Must I?" he said softly, but his eyes were smiling. "Suppose you refresh my memory as we drive back to Brook Street?"

Still she hesitated.

His smile grew quizzical, but there was no hint of mockery in it. "A truce, Miss Carlyon? And my word on it that this is no part of any deep-laid scheme."

"Are you quite sure that you wish to put yourself to so much trouble?" she asked, allowing herself in spite of all her best resolves to be led back to the curricle.

"If I did not wish it, I would not be here, ma'am," he

said with damping reproof, so that she submitted meekly as he lifted her with ease into the curricle. "I may say I had nothing like so much trouble accommodating your brother! There was the small problem of the mud, but once we had overcome that, he thought it the most tremendous treat!"

"Mud?" Pandora stared down into that inscrutable face. "You *are* talking about William?"

"Certainly. I have not as yet the honour to be acquainted with your elder brother." She saw the glint of a smile once more. "And lest you fear William may have importuned me, let me hasten to add that I offered to take him up, not more than three hours since. So you may remove that unbecoming frown, Miss Carlyon."

Upon which remark he excused himself and went to speak to his groom, leaving Pandora to make of his words what she would. After puzzling the matter for a few minutes, however, she abandoned the exercise in favour of unreserved admiration of the Duke's curricle.

Truly it was a most elegant equipage, its huge yellow wheels mirrored in the black polished coachwork. The interior was richly padded with buff-coloured leather and had deliciously squashy seats that felt as soft and warm to the touch of her exploring fingers as the texture of a particular blue silk dress of her mama's that she remembered from long ago.

From her perch high above the splendid team of bays she could see the Duke instructing his groom, who looked a surly fellow, for all that he had a sure touch with the restive horses—the condition of their coats bore testament to his care of them.

A moment later, the curricle dipped and swayed, as the Duke sprang lightly up beside her, took up the ribbons, and called, "Right, Grimble—let 'em go!"

In those first moments, with the Duke fully occupied, she gave herself up to each heady sensation as it presented itself—the sun on her back and the faint scent of blossom drifting on the air; the sumptuous ease of travelling in first style—the almost detached pleasure she derived from watching the skill with which the Duke

68

handled his team. For the first time since she had come to London, Pandora's spirits began to soar.

"You are very quiet, Miss Carlyon?" said the Duke at last.

"Um," she sighed, his voice barely impinging upon her consciousness. A moment later she heard a distinct chuckle, and realising how impolite she must appear, sat up hastily.

"Clearly you do not find the experience of riding with me entirely distasteful?"

Oh, her dratted tongue. But it was all Octavia's fault, she concluded sweepingly. If she had not gossiped so about Heron, her prejudice would have been less easily fuelled.

"As to what I said, my Lord Duke——" she began, but was not allowed to continue.

"Pray do not feel that you must apologise yet again, Miss Carlyon," he said with sudden weariness. "I confess that I find your reading of my character on such short acquaintance disconcertingly acute, but it hardly constitutes an embarrassment. You are not alone in deploring my morals, I promise you."

"Oh, but I don't!" She leaned forward, eager to make her point. "Deplore them, I mean. In fact, I know very little about you, and should not have said what I did on mere hearsay. And even if it *were* true, I am well aware that gentlemen regard such matters in quite a different light, and it is certainly not for me to . . . to . . ."

She dried up as he shot her a look of the most piercing enquiry, before returning once more to his preoccupation with the traffic.

"Pray do not stop there, ma'am," he said softly. "You behold me in a fever of anticipation!"

"No." Her voice was rueful. "You find me presumptuous, and you are right. My approval or disapproval can be of no possible interest to you. In fact, my lord Duke," she hazarded with great daring, "I suspect you don't give a fig for anyone's opinion!"

She watched the austere profile for an anxious moment. Then, to her relief, he laughed, albeit a trifle reluctantly.

"True enough. I have long since become inured to criticism. But clearly I must have a care. I'm not sure that I care to be dissected with such disturbing ease by a mere slip of a girl."

"I do not mean to do so, sir. I suppose that growing up within the regiment makes one acutely observant of others and what motivates them to behave as they do." She grinned self-consciously. "Now you will think me pretentious as well as presumptuous!"

He laughed again, with more genuine amusement this time. "Not in the least. I shall simply turn the tables by insisting that you tell me about yourself."

"Well, I can't think you would derive much satisfaction from that," she confessed, "because I feel bound to warn you that with very little coaxing I shall be deep in tedious reminiscence!"

And so it proved, except that he did not find it in the least tedious. A lively enthusiasm animated her voice, her face, making one quite forget her lack of looks. So vivid was her narrative that it evoked in Heron a surprisingly comprehensive picture of the life she had led until late with all its attendant joys and terrors. It was implicit in everything that she told him (and even more so in what she omitted to say) of the incredible hardships; of forced marches over impossible terrains in diabolical extremes of weather, often bivouacking in squalid conditions; the philosophically accepted horrors of battles and their aftermath . . .

"But it wasn't all marching and fighting battles," she hastened to assure him. "There was gaiety and laughter, too. Young as I was, I can remember our house in Lisbon being filled with officers . . . and there were such parties! And even on campaigns"—Pandora warmed to her theme—"there were times when the snow was so thick on the high Sierras that we would be confined to winter quarters in some Spanish village or town. I think those were the best times of all, with plenty of hunting by day, and at night the local señoras and señoritas would teach the officers how to click their castanets and dance the fandango, and the officers of the Light division would find a barn or some such and give fine dramatic entertainments!" She stopped at last with an embarrassed laugh. "There! I said I would bore you!"

"Do I appear bored?" He noticed that she had said nothing of the tragedy that ended her grand adventure—and he did not press her. "Now, suppose you tell me about these notions Lady Margerson cherishes for your advancement?"

"Heavens! I have talked more than enough about myself. You can't possibly wish to hear more!" Pandora caught sight of his expression and said hastily, "Oh, very well! But I cannot imagine why you should. The thing is, I had rather hoped her ladyship would abandon her efforts, because it does make life very difficult. And yet I know how unhappy she is about my wishing to earn my living, and would much prefer that I permit her to introduce me into society so that I may make a respectable marriage."

The Duke glanced down at her. "Is the idea so repugnant to you? I had supposed it to be the all-engrossing ambition of most young ladies—urged on by their mothers!" He spoke with feeling, not remembering her own lack of parental guidance until the words were out, but she seemed too wrapped in consideration to have heeded his momentary insensitivity.

" 'Repugnance' is perhaps too strong a word," she mused, "but I confess that I have an actue abhorrence of people who parade under false colours, and that is how I should regard my own behaviour were I to encourage Lady Margerson's aspirations, well meant though they undoubtedly are." Pandora paused before adding wryly: "Does that make me sound a shocking humbugger?"

"No, just idiotish," said the Duke. "But go on."

"You are unfair, sir," she said, striving for lightness. "Not long since, you were pleased to call me a realist, and that is exactly what I am attempting to be. I have no genteel background to commend me—rather the reverse, for one can hardly account a life spent following the drum an advantage. And I have no money. I daresay it is indelicate to speak of money, but I don't have much moral sensibility either . . ." She heard again that faint chuckle, which encouraged her to continue. "So, since I am neither witty nor beautiful, nor even particularly mannered, and have the added encumbrance of two brothers, one of whom will certainly need my support and protection for some years to come, perhaps you will be good enough to explain to me just what I *do* have to offer which might commend me to any prospective suitor who is neither shortsighted nor a congenital idiot?"

Heron brought the curricle to a halt and turned to face her. "Do you really hold yourself in such contempt, Miss Carlyon?"

"By no means! I have no quarrel with my situation—I am simply facing facts. Society would laugh at my pretensions, and they would be right!"

"Humbug!" he retorted. "What you have just treated me to is a grossly biased inventory of what you consider to be your shortcomings, none of which, of themselves, need preclude you from taking the kind of steps proposed by Lady Margerson." He fixed her with an uncomfortably discerning eye. "What you have omitted from your reckoning is any mention of those qualities which would count in your favour should a suitable applicant for your hand come along."

Pandora looked at him in astonishment. "Do I have any such qualities?"

He sat back, the reins loosely clasped in his strong slender hands, smiling faintly at her reaction. "One might begin with a certain modesty that you should think the matter in any doubt!" he drawled. "Added to that, I would hazard that you are generous by nature, overimpulsive—as I know from experience! And probably compassionate. You are also incurably truthful . . ." His smile deepened. "Though whether that can be accounted a virtue, I am not sure! Finally, you would appear to possess a particular brand of courage . . ."

"Oh!" She could feel her cheeks turning bright red.

"Qualities, on the whole, that many a gentleman might consider of more real worth than those by which you set such store—William notwithstanding!"

He had flustered her—and found it an agreeable experience. While she was still collecting herself, he added reflectively, "In fact, Miss Carlyon, it is not so much a question of whether society might find *you* wanting, but rather, I suspect, that you would find us a frippery lot! One day I shall take you to Hyde Park during the Grand Strut so that you may observe at close quarters how the rich and the fashionable take the air," he concluded, setting the horses in motion once more.

This calm assumption that he meant to pursue an acquaintance, however slight, so comprehensively deprived Pandora of speech that she could think of nothing to say. He really was an extraordinary man! In the course of reflecting upon their earlier conversation, however, she recalled something which had puzzled her.

"About William, sir?" she ventured. "I am not quite clear . . . you spoke of mud? Had he, then, been involved in some kind of accident?"

He did not answer at once. When he did, there was a curious inflection in his voice. "Not an accident, precisely."

Pandora's heart sank. "Had he . . . had he been fighting?"

"I really don't think you should expect me to answer that, Miss Carlyon. It is for William to explain to you himself."

"He had been fighting," she said flatly. "What is more, I know why—and I know with whom!"

"Then, being a sensible girl, you will not need me to advise you to make as little of it as possible." His voice had that calm, matter-of-fact tone which he had used previously when speaking of their troubles. "Pride and the defence of honour come high in William's scale of values, I think. And a boy of that age is absurdly sensitive. It would be so easy to belittle what he did!"

"As if I would!" she exclaimed. And then, feeling that she had appeared ungracious: "But thank you for realising it. You seem to know a great deal about little boys."

He glanced down at her, amused. "I *was* a boy myself once, Miss Carlyon—though farther back than I care to

73

remember!" She responded with a gurgle of laughter, and he nodded his approval. "That's much better. Tell me, has that lawyer of yours found a tutor yet?"

"No. But then, he has scarcely had time to do so." She sighed. "I confess I shall be easier in my mind when William is settled."

"Certainly. A boy of his age and natural ability needs to be kept occupied. Let us hope Mr. Lewis will discover someone of equally lively intellect to direct him."

"Yes indeed."

Her attention was taken by a man hobbling toward them, supported on a crudely fashioned crutch. His coat had a military look about it, though it was faded beyond recognition. One empty breeches leg fastened up bore mute witness to the price he had paid fighting for his country.

She must have uttered some sound, for Heron's glance followed hers.

"Poor devil," he said. "The first of many. I expect the streets will be full of them before long—fit for little beyond begging, their deeds forgotten before the smoke has had time to clear from the battlefield."

His words, so casually uttered, smote Pandora as she recalled how many such she had watched throwing themselves into the thick of the fight—cheerful, unquestioning —simple men who understood little beyond the instinctive obedience to command. Poor devils indeed!

But as this one drew close, there was something about him . . .

"Oh, please, my lord Duke, may we stop—just for a moment?"

Heron obliged her with a kind of amused resignation, curious to know what she would be about next. What she did in fact was to lean down from the curricle with a perilous disregard for safety, waving frantically.

"Josiah Blakewell, it *is* you! I was very nearly sure!"

"Miss Pandora? Well, blister me!" The man halted his painful progress to look up at her, his weathered face losing a little of its worn, dispirited aspect. His weary eyes took in the smart equipage, her elegant companion, and some of the initial pleasure faded from his voice. "Well, miss—you're looking fit and prosperous, and no mistake."

Pandora turned swiftly to the Duke, unsure quite how to correct the misconstruction that Josiah had attached to finding her in his company.

"Sergeant Blakewell is one of ours," she explained.

"*Was*, Miss Pandora," the man corrected her bleakly. "You should know—no place in the troop for a one-legged cripple."

"Oh, Josiah! I am sad to see you so reduced! How did it happen?"

"Same engagement the Colonel got his, only maybe he was the lucky one, God rest him. The doc did what he could to patch me up, but it was clear I wouldn't be good for much, so they shipped me home on the first available transport. *Home!*" He choked on the word. "I reckon my Alice'd be better off without me. I am nothing but a drag on her and the kids."

Pandora was unprepared for the sudden impotent rage that welled up in her. She had long since learned to accept with a kind of sympathetic fatalism the more distressing consequences of war, but she had never given a thought to what happened to the maimed and used-up dross of battles once they were sent home. Now, here in London, with the sun shining and everyone in spring finery already rejoicing and making preparations to celebrate a glorious victory, she was face to face with cold reality—and found it totally unacceptable.

Blindly, because she could think of nothing else to do, she fumbled in her reticule for what little money was there. The Duke's hand closed over hers, staying it. There was a faint rattle of coins, and the glint of gold shimmered in her palm, and she looked up in swift gratitude, seeing his face as a blur.

It seemed at first that Josiah would refuse the money. His surly embarrassment was indicative of a man not yet accustomed to accepting charity as his lot.

"Oh, please Josiah—take it! For your family if not for yourself—just to tide you over, you know." And as he still hunched on his crutch, looking stubborn: "You wouldn't have refused it from Pa!" she accused.

He drew himself up and put the money in his pocket, his eyes sweeping them both with a kind of angry pride. "You're a good lass, Miss Pandora, so I'll take your kindness in the spirit it's meant—and because of the feeling I had for the Colonel. And God bless you!"

She begged for his address, which he gave most reluctantly before stomping away.

Heron regarded the tense young girl beside him, her profile taut with the effort of containing her emotions. Without a word he picked up the ribbons and gave his horses the office to start.

They were already in Brook Street when she said with suppressed violence, "Sergeant Blakewell was one of our *best* gunners! Dependable as a rock, Pa was used to say. He doesn't deserve to end like that! Better he *had* been killed . . . there is at least a certain dignity in dying for your country!"

"I suspect the sergeant would agree with you there. But Fate, in her capricious way, does not always deal with us as we would choose."

The cool objectivity of his reasoning, far from offering comfort, only fuelled her anger the more.

"Oh, how easy it is for you to sit there uttering platitudes," she cried, "when you haven't the remotest idea what it's all about! When have you ever lacked for anything, let alone suffered the privation and miseries of men like Josiah, with nothing at the end of it but ingratitude and hopelessness! If I had your resources, I would . . . I would . . ." She searched recklessly for words. "Oh, I don't know what I might do, but I wouldn't be so smug!"

The horses jibbed, and Heron realised that he was gripping the ribbons much too tightly. He adjusted his hands, angry with her rather for making him careless of his skill than because of the injustice of her accusations. He sensed rather than saw her slump back against the squabs, and even before she spoke, he knew that she was silently weeping.

"*I am so very sorry!*" The words came out in a choked

whisper. "It was an unforgivable thing to say . . . and after your great generosity, too!"

"A few coins, Miss Carlyon," he said in precise tones, flicked on the raw by this unwitting reminder of how little the gesture had meant to him, "hardly constitute an excess of generosity."

A tiny gasp was the only acknowledgement of his censorious put-down. He hardened his heart and drove on. Presently he heard her blow her nose and was aware of the faint creak and movement of the leathers as she sat upright once more. But she made no further attempt at apology, or speech of any kind.

Pandora had in effect acknowledged the utter futility of attempting to find words to explain the confusion of emotions the sight of Josiah had unleashed. She did not understand herself how the injustice of Josiah's fate and her grief over the death of her father had become inextricably linked with a sudden overwhelming homesickness for the life that had gone forever. And even could she have put it into words, there was little expectation of his caring or wishing to understand. Why, after all, should he?

The more she considered the matter, the more she convinced herself that he would probably be quite glad to be presented with some valid excuse for not pursuing her acquaintance further, which was a pity, because in spite of their differences, she realised too late that she had rather enjoyed her exchanges with him. A sigh escaped her. They were almost home.

Heron heard the sigh. It was so full of weary resignation that he could take it no longer. But before he could speak, she was sitting forward, her mood completely altered, as her attention was caught by two young men about to ascend the steps of the Hamiltons' house.

The younger was a fashionable sprig in yellow pantaloons, a yellow spotted handkerchief tied in an elaborate bow over high shirt points. His companion, a tall lanky young man, wore the blue braided dolman of a hussar, but with the red facings and sash and the elegant helmet of the Royal Horse Artillery.

"Courtney!" Pandora cried. "Oh, I don't believe it—and Captain Greville!"

They looked up at the sound of her voice, and the younger of the two came bounding down the steps, his handsome face lighting up. He swung her from the curricle almost before it had stopped moving, whirling her off her feet in a laughing embrace, talking all the while, parrying her questions with questions of his own.

"But why are you here? You haven't been rusticated?"

"Devil a bit!" You're looking a bit hag-ridden, Dora. Not feeling quite the thing?"

"Oh, never mind me! Why aren't you at your studies?"

"Don't nag, little sister! You shall know all presently. Meanwhile, you are being deuced impolite to Hugo!"

"Oh, Gemini!" Pandora extricated herself from her brother's arms and turned to the fair handsome Artillery man with the twinkling eyes, who took both her hands in his and held her away from him, declaring that she was grown into quite the young lady, which caused her to blush rosily.

The Duke, forgotten in all the excitement, watched their meeting and found it curiously enlightening. On the Captain's side there was the teasing affectionate familiarity born of a long acquaintance, and nothing more. But on hers? He had seen that look in a young woman's eyes too often to mistake it now. Whether she was aware of it herself, he knew not, but there was no mistaking that Miss Pandora Carlyon was head over ears in love with the gallant Captain!

As if he had declared his conclusion aloud, she looked up at that moment, guilt written large submerging the joy as she belatedly remembered his existence.

"My lord Duke—" she began, stepping forward.

But he was in no mood for introductions and polite conversation.

"You are clearly much in demand, ma'am." He nodded curtly and picked up the reins. "I will bid you good day."

7

Pandora led the way to the breakfast room, where she could be reasonably certain of their being able to talk undisturbed. She was conscious of questions burning to be asked, and painfully aware that her eyes must be blotched from crying. She was quite irrationally furious with Courtney for arriving unannounced and for bringing Hugo Greville just when she must be looking at her worst. Not, she reflected in a brave attempt at philosophy, that Hugo could ever be brought to consider her in a romantic way.

Hugo had always been there—or so it seemed; always special, not quite a brother, but more than just a friend. His princess, he had called her from the day seven years ago when he had arrived in Lisbon straight from the Royal Military Academy at Woolwich, a very young, very dashing officer with laughing blue eyes. He had stolen her twelve-year-old heart clean away.

"Well, princess," he said now as he closed the door, and no amount of cold common sense could entirely disperse the little ripples of happiness that radiated through her to hear herself so called once more. "You keep exalted company these days, it seems. A Duke, no less!"

"Oh, but he isn't . . ."

"Never mind what he isn't, my girl!" put in Courtney with a brotherly lack of tact. "It don't take much wit to see what he *is*! Which means that you've got a mite of explaining to do, by George! Lord, that fellow must have been all of thirty-five—and up to no good, either, I shouldn't wonder."

Courtney's notion that his grace might be secretly lusting after her sent Pandora into a paroxysm of mirth. He looked decidedly put out.

"You may laugh, sister mine, but you're just a babe in the ways of the world. Wouldn't know a loose fish if you met one, I daresay!"

"And you would, I suppose?" she gasped amid fresh whoops of laughter. "Oh, Courtney, how I wish I could see his grace the Duke of Heron's face if he heard himself described as a loose fish! And by a mere stripling!"

"Heron, did you say?" The slur on his manhood overlooked, Courtney's eye brightened, his mouth dropped open. "Lord, I wish I'd known! They say he's complete to a shade, you know—rivals Brummell at his best!"

It was clear that he was much struck by his sister's acquaintance with such a Nonpareil, and when she scoffed at the importance attached to such considerations, he replied loftily that she could not be expected to understand.

It was left to Captain Greville, his amusement at their good-natured squabbles tempered by concern, to say quietly, "Leaving aside the matter of his grace's sartorial excellence for the moment, could we return to the matter of his reputation? I don't know how you came to be in his company, princess, but—"

"Heavens! What a fuss! Do stop being ridiculous, both of you!" Pandora spoke lightly, not entirely displeased to find Hugo so concerned. "It is all perfectly proper," she said with a simple adherence to the truth. "The Duke is Lady Margerson's friend—you know, Courtney, I wrote to you about Lady Margerson . . . Mama's godmother? It was entirely at her behest that he was escorting me home." Octavia's words came back to her. She gave a rueful shrug. "Well, honestly, look at me—you surely cannot suppose that the Duke would find me to his taste?"

"That's true enough," said Courtney with a grin, as Hugo made gallant protest. "And now I come to think about it, you weren't exactly looking the picture of a maiden wooed in his company! In fact, I rather think you had been crying."

"Oh that!" She explained briefly about meeting Josiah and how much it had upset her.

"Sergeant Blakewell will come about," said Hugo bracingly. "He's not the kind to brood for long on his ills." He looked keenly at Pandora. "Nor is it like you to let such things get you down."

"No." She wished she could explain her feelings rationally, but feared that she would make as sad a botch of it as she had to the Duke earlier, since she didn't wholly understand them herself. While she was still debating, Courtney claimed her attention, and something in his manner, an air of urgency, of nervous excitement ill-concealed, recalled to her mind the unexpectedness of his arrival.

"My turn to play the inquisitor now, brother dear," she said. "If you haven't been rusticated, would you mind telling me why you are here—and looking as guilty as a cat that's swallowed someone's pet mouse?"

The two young men exchanged glances.

"Well, the thing is, Dora—I've quit!" The words came out in a rush of bravado. "I'm going to do what I've always wanted to do—join the regiment."

Pandora stared, saw the stubborn set of his chin, and was bewildered. "But why now—when Boney is beat? Oh, Courtney, you promised you would finish your studies!"

"I know! But something has come up . . . and, well, you see . . ."

"I'm afraid the fault is mine, princess." Hugo was apologetic, though he looked anything but. "I had been visiting my parents, and I bumped into Courtney quite by chance in the middle of Oxford."

"Hugo's off to America, Dora! Now that we've put a stop to Boney, there's a strong contingent of troops being sent out to clear up that affair too! America, Dora! Only think of it!"

"I *am* thinking." Pandora felt that her head was spinning. "But surely you cannot go—just like that? What about your training . . . you know it is customary for all our officers."

"Well, actually," said Hugo. "I am on my way now to

Woolwich to report, and if Courtney cares to come along, I might be able to pull a string or two . . ."

"If you can't, then I shall join some other regiment!"

This defiant announcement brought a shocked: "Courtney! You wouldn't?"

"Oh, I doubt it will come to that." Hugo's grin was laconic. "After all, he isn't the usual green would-be hero, is he? Knows a deuced lot already. Been around guns most of his young life—father's son and all that! By the by, did you know that Wellington had made a point of citing your father's last engagement in his recent despatches? Said he'd seldom seen anything to equal the sight of Colonel Carlyon charging out of the mist sword in hand at the head of young Craig's battery to scatter the French when they had three companies of our third Foot cut off in perilous conditions—his horses stretched like fire-breathing greyhounds, the guns bounding behind them like weightless toys in headlong career, and the mounted gunners, heads bent low, weapons at the ready. He referred to it, I believe, as an act of conspicuous bravery carried out without regard for personal safety, and said that in losing his life, the Colonel had undoubtedly averted a massacre!"

Pandora clapped her hands. "Oh, that is wonderful news, isn't it, Courtney? Dear old Nosey! *That* will make a few people eat their words!"

"It's splendid," agreed Courtney. "And don't think I'm any less pleased than you, Dora, but . . . well, there isn't much time, and if I'm to be ready, I shall have to purchase my commission and find myself a good mount, and . . . oh, well, you know!" He was the coaxing, wheedling boy she remembered from their childhood days. He almost always could get round her. "I've been to see that paltry lawyer fellow—"

"Mr. Lewis isn't paltry!"

"He's a regular slow top! Jawing on about responsibility. He don't approve, I could tell that at a glance—and he ain't prepared to advance one jot more than my present allowance, which is all but used up. In any case, it wouldn't be anywhere near enough!" Courtney grinned sheepishly. "I wondered . . . that jewellery of Mama's . . . you always said it would serve for emergencies."

Pandora bit her lip and went to stare out of the window. It was true. She had said it, and it would be awful to blight Courtney's dreams by denying him this chance—but she didn't much want him to go off to America, either, certainly not with such a woeful lack of experience. And besides . . .

"Oh, come on, Dora—be a trump! I have tried, you know, but studying ain't in my line. *This* is what I've always wanted. And America! It'll be the most tremendous adventure!"

He sounded exactly like William! Pandora's objections melted away, and she reluctantly abandoned her own dreams of how she had intended to use the money from the jewellery to set up a home for them all. The way things were shaping, there would be no one to make a home for!

She turned with a bright smile. "Very well. We'll see what can be done in the morning."

"I knew it! Didn't I say she was the greatest gun ever!" Courtney whirled her off the floor, spinning with her until she cried for mercy. "The best sister a fellow ever had!"

Captain Greville, watching Pandora's face intently, had guessed more or less accurately at the struggle preceding her decision. It made him say with more than usual warmth, "She is indeed a sister in a million. I only wish that she were mine!"

He could not know how his words wounded—how Pandora longed to have him more than a brother. With her back toward him, she was vouchsafed precious moments in which to conceal her feelings before turning to laugh at him over her shoulder.

"Thank you, Hugo, but two are more than sufficient for my needs! And anyway," she concluded with pleasing conviction, "I almost count you one!"

The door burst open to admit William, his animated face already showing clear evidence of his recent conflict.

"Binns said you were here!" he crowed with delight. "Are you staying? I say, Captain Hugo. You too!"

Courtney strolled across and put a hand under his brother's chin, turning the boy's face to the light. "Still not learned to put up a guard, I see. That's quite a shiner, young Will. Be closed by morning—black and blue into the bargain, I shouldn't wonder. Wouldn't you say so, Hugo?"

"More than likely." Hugo grinned sympathetically.

"No it won't!" William retorted. "Because the Duke's man put something on it and he *swore* by it!"

"The Duke?" Courtney raised his eyebrows, and even his sister stared.

"Did he actually take you back to Heron House, then?"

"Yes. And what's more, I had a perfectly splendid time!"

Pandora had uttered the question before realising how it must give rise to fresh speculation about the Duke's involvement in their affairs, but William forestalled comment by launching upon an enthusiastic account of his afternoon's adventures, which were only curtailed when Captain Greville interposed to say regretfully that they must be going if he was to keep his appointment at Woolwich.

Mention of Woolwich and the fact that Courtney was going too necessitated fresh explanations for William's benefit.

"But you'll come back here afterward, Court?"

Courtney said there wasn't a doubt of it, so long as Octavia didn't object to him shaking down in his room for a couple of nights.

"I shouldn't think she'd even notice," said William scathingly.

Before Pandora went to bed that night, she took down from the closet shelf the soft leather bag which she had guarded with such care since her mother's death. She tipped everything onto the bed and spread it out. A pretty garnet brooch and matching bracelet, a string of pearls; nothing of any value, she decided, except for the necklace. This she drew toward her, tracing the delicate flower settings of the diamonds with loving fingers, recalling how her mother had treasured it as a sole link with her own mother, who had been given it by her husband as a wedding gift. Candlelight lent the stones warmth and brilliance.

Acting on impulse, she lifted it from the bed of crimson velvet on which it lay and fastened it round her neck, standing up, peering in the tiny mirror to see her shadowed face looking almost alluring above the glowing circlet. Just for an instant she imagined herself in a beautiful gown, her head piled high with pale golden curls. . . . Would Hugo Greville feel differently about her if he could see her like that? She concluded that it was unlikely, and removed the necklace, putting it carefully back in its case.

Messrs. Rundell and Bridge's on the following morning exuded an aura of discreet luxury sufficient to make Pandora hesitate on the threshold. Had not Courtney been at her side, ebullient with expectation, she must have shrunk from entering, but upon the outcome of this transaction rested all his hopes, and she could not fail him now. This was where the necklace had been made for her grandfather, so it had seemed the logical place to bring it. She stepped resolutely toward the very grand gentleman who awaited her.

The said gentleman, an obsequious smile fading from his face as he took in at a glance the undoubted insignificance of the would-be clients, delegated them without hesitation to one of his underlings, who, taking his tone from the other, did not trouble to offer the lady a chair. Pandora misliked his manner and was put very much on her mettle as she explained the nature of her business.

The young man was on the point of cold outright rejection when a door at the rear of the showroom opened and a voice drawled, "My thanks for your trouble, Bridge— this emerald trinket will answer my purpose excellently."

Pandora uttered a small gasp and hastily turned so that her back was toward the door whence the voice came. But she had reckoned without the Duke's instant recognition of Courtney, which in turn led him to look more closely at the trim back so firmly presented to him. The salesman's air of cold disdain spoke for itself.

"Miss Carlyon? May I be of some assistance?"

She knew that he was at her shoulder, though she had not heard him approach across the thick carpet. Turning now to look up at him, she saw that he was frowning, which she took to denote disapproval. No doubt he too thought she had no place in such a grand emporium. Aggravation made her greeting correspondingly formal as she declined his offer.

She was, however, obliged to introduce Courtney to him—Courtney, who had the looks in the family and of whom she was so patently proud, was visibly impressed by his grace, forgot his earlier misgivings, and showed a maddening disposition to be friendly, regaling the Duke with an eager account of his prospective good fortune and imminent departure.

"Thing is, though . . . a bit short of the ready," he informed Heron with the same ingenuous frankness that seemed to characterise the whole family. "Obliged to pop Grandmother Wyndham's necklace in order to purchase my commission."

Heron's amused glance moved to Pandora's face, suffused with mortification, and thence unhurriedly to the necklace where it lay on the counter pad.

"May I?" He lifted it to the light, the petal-like settings lying glittering on his palm. "A charming piece." He allowed it to slip through his fingers back onto the counter, and turned his keen glance on Pandora. "Must you really part with it?"

She tilted her chin, answering obliquely, "There seems little point in my keeping it, sir. I doubt that diamonds would ever sit well on me."

There was a fleeting expression in his eyes that she could not read. Then he said casually, "In that case, I have no doubt that Mr. Bridge will be pleased to give you a handsome price for it."

Well aware of the weight his words must carry, he nodded to that rather bemused gentleman, touched his hat to Pandora and her brother, and strolled to the door, which the head salesman had rushed to open for him.

A short time later, Pandora too was out in the street, clutching her reticule in a rather dazed way, still hardly able to credit the treasure it contained—enough to fit Courtney out in first style, and with so much to spare that already her mind was teeming with possibilities. It was Courtney who finally brought her back to earth, reminding her that he had very little time in which to accomplish all that must be done.

They hurried back to Brook Street, where Hugo Greville awaited them, being ably entertained by William, but his relief upon seeing Courtney betrayed his impatience to be off.

"Come along, my boy. I can tell by your face that you have the ready, and I heard of a good steady mount only this morning—should suit you admirably if only we are in time to snap it up!" He turned his charming rueful smile upon Pandora. "Sorry, princess, but you of all people don't need to have matters explained to you."

"No indeed. I only wish I might be going with you!" She made a quick dismissive gesture. "I know. It isn't possible, and it was a stupid thing to say." She smiled. "Go along, now, both of you. I won't hold you up a moment longer."

She shooed them out just as the summons came from Octavia's room demanding to know what was going on, Frederick having delivered an account which she found it impossible to credit.

"I'll deal with Octavia," Pandora said, confident in her newfound wealth of being equal to anything. And when the letter bearing good news from Mr. Lewis was delivered later that morning, it seemed to set a seal upon the day.

The Duke, meanwhile—the delivery of the emerald necklace to the fair but unlamented Irena accomplished—proceeded to a house in Curzon Street, where he was presently admitted to a first-floor apartment by a manservant of uncertain age and melancholy countenance who informed his grace in hushed tones that his master was at his toilet.

"What—past midday and not about yet? No matter, Jenkinson, I'll announce myself."

He discovered the Honourable FitzWilliam Humbert Chessington seated at his table in a discreetly shaded dressing room, regarding his image mournfully in the mirror. Drooping eyelids lifted momentarily to acknowledge his friend's arrival before returning once more to contemplation of his own not-unpleasing countenance.

Heron crossed to the window, intent upon throwing back the half-drawn curtains.

"No, no—not any further, I beg of you, Robert . . . not until I am feeling more the thing. D'you know, only yesterday I discovered three new wrinkles—yes, three, I swear it! Just there, do you see?"

Heron's shout of laughter demonstrated a distinct lack of sensitivity. He rattled the curtain back along its pole, ignoring his friend's pronounced wince, and proceeded to stretch out in a comfortable hide armchair, surveying him lazily.

"On the toddle last night, were we?"

"Certainly not," came the pained reply. "I was at Amelia Meldon's levee—and a demned fatiguing affair it proved to be. You were quite right to eschew it. After only two hours I was quite done in!" A crumpled cravat fluttered to the floor to add to a fast-growing pile, and he selected a newly starched one.

Heron chuckled. "If I didn't know you so well, Fitz, I would be tempted to think you a very paltry creature."

A faint gleam lit Mr. Chessington's eyes. "So I am, dear old fellow. Deuced paltry." Alarm flickered momentarily. "You haven't come to make me do anything energetic?"

"Rest easy. I hope I know my limitations."

Jenkinson glided into the room bearing Mr. Chessington's best blue superfine, and for the next few minutes an absorbed silence prevailed as the efforts of master and servant combined to fitting it to the satisfaction of both. A faint sigh proclaimed the task accomplished.

"Is that brother of yours still in town, Fitz?"

"Ned?" There was a note of surprise in the young exquisite's voice. "Wasn't aware that you craved brother Ned's company."

"I don't. I merely wish to pick his brains—concerning a certain colonel who was involved in some minor scandal."

Fitz shrugged. "Oh, well—if it's an army affair, then Ned's your man. He bores on about such matters for hours!" He sat for a moment more, his hand hovering uncertainly over the crisply falling intricacies of his cravat. Then he sighed and stood up. "I suppose you are driving? If you care to take me as far as Brooks's, no doubt we shall find him there holding forth as usual upon the encounter in which he acquired the ball in his leg!

"Y'know, it ain't like you to interest yourself in army scandals, Robert," he continued as they drove.

"True. But my curiosity has been aroused—and must be satisfied."

"Ah!" Fitz nodded sagely. "There's a woman in this somewhere, I'll wager."

Heron cast him an amused look. "Now, why should you suppose that?"

"Because only two things can be guaranteed to engage your interest to such an extent—and I doubt it's horses in this instance!" He returned Heron's glance with unexpected keenness. "Do I know her?"

"I very much doubt it. And you may remove that knowing look from your face, Fitz," said the Duke, without taking his eyes from the road. "I don't lust after this lady—in truth, she is little more than a girl, and not a particularly well-endowed one at that." He favoured Mr. Chessington with a deliberately brief summary of his encounters with Miss Carlyon.

"Pandora?" A frown creased the young exquisite's brow. "Got it! Greek mythology! Ain't she the one who—?"

"Loosed from her box all the ills that plague mankind." Heron's mouth quirked as he completed the fable. "Quite so. But in this case—though Miss Carlyon certainly exhibits a genius for precipitating the unexpected, one could never, I believe, suspect her of mischievous intent!"

"Nonetheless . . ." Mr. Chessington shook his head. "It don't auger well. Give her the go-by, dear boy. Much the best thing."

At Brooks's, they found Captain Lord Edward Chessington eagerly imparting the news just brought from Bordeaux by a friend. Following upon the surrender of Paris to the Russian and Prussian troops, Napoleon had already abdicated and fled to Elba, but apparently the fighting was not yet at an end. Bayonne was still under siege, and in a wanton disinclination to make peace, poor General Hay had been killed and Sir John Hope taken prisoner.

As Hay had been his lordship's immediate chief, it was some time before he could be brought to discuss the matter of Colonel Carlyon.

"What? Fancy your knowing about that little affair!" Edward, leaning upon an elegant ebony cane, limped gracefully across to sit beside Heron. "Didn't know such tales carried this far—an unfortunate incident, y'know, but no more so than many another. Campaigns are littered with 'em! Somewhere in the Pyrenees, as I remember . . . wasn't actually on the spot myself at the time, but we all heard about it soon enough. It was the old story—atrocious weather! Rain. The ground a deuced quagmire . . . the nine-pounders bogged down on one side of a ravine, and the rest not in a much better way . . . Soult's troops entrenched along a ridge across the river, barring the way . . . and the whole lot shrouded in mist."

Edward tapped one gleaming boot tip thoughtfully with his stick. "Well, the long and short of it was that Carlyon rode off to confer with other senior officers, and a message was sent back that the guns were to bombard the ridge while the engineers attempted to get a small force of our fellows across the river unnoticed. There was a fair bit of confusion, and the message, as interpreted by a regular johnny raw in charge of one of the batteries, was that the French were crossing the river and he was to stop 'em.

"I daresay you can imagine the rest." Edward lifted a laconic glance to Heron. "Fortunately the mist saved most of the men, and Carlyon arrived back in time to prevent what might have been the most bloody awful carnage!"

"And accepted full responsibility," finished the Duke.

"Naturally. Like I said, these things happen. Even old Nosey, who has little love for the artillery, was fairly sanguine about the whole thing. But then, he did have the greatest respect for Carlyon. I believe he made a point of saying so in a recent despatch."

"Well, my thanks to you," said the Duke, rising to take his leave.

Lord Edward grinned. "Pleasure, my dear Heron. Shouldn't have thought it the kind of thing to take your interest, but then, you delight in surprising us occasionally." He squinted up at Heron, his voice deepening to a drawl. "You have recently acquired a brace of French brats, I hear. Most diverting!" He chuckled. "One is not sure whether congratulations or commiserations are in order!"

8

Time was now passing almost too quickly for Pandora. No sooner had she bid farewell to Courtney, who looked quite heartbreakingly young and handsome in his new regimentals, with Papa's sword at his side, than the moment came to prepare for William's departure, too.

Her elation upon first reading the letter from Mr. Lewis was tempered almost at once by the realisation that, if the clerical gentleman he had found proved acceptable, William would not only be leaving her charge, but also would be going farther away than she cared to contemplate.

A second letter followed swiftly upon the first, this time addressed to Pandora from the clerical gentleman himself and couched in such pleasant kindly terms that she was instantly reassured. Mr. Brearly explained that he was obliged to visit London the following week upon a small matter of business, and that if convenient he would be happy to take William with him when he returned home. His visit would also (and this found particular favour with Pandora) enable Miss Carlyon to satisfy herself that he was a fit person to have the care of her brother.

William looked forward to his new life with all his usual optimism, the only cloud on his horizon, apart from leaving Pandora, being a fear that he might lose contact with his friend Mr. Oliver.

"I 'spect I had better return his notes, which is a great pity, because they are fearfully interesting! Do come with me to meet Mr. Oliver, Dora," he urged, "because you never have, and he would very much like to meet you. I've told him all about you!"

Pandora wondered, laughing, what there was to tell.

"Oh, heaps!" William grinned. "What a jolly person you are to be with, for one thing—comfortable, you know, not in the least like most fellows' sisters!"

She was much moved by the unexpected encomium from this most undemonstrative of brothers, and though her manner was teasing, there was a sudden hollow in her chest as she realised how much she would miss his cheery company.

"Besides," he continued with an ingenuousness that quite restored her spirits, "if you come, you would be able to tell Mr. Oliver that you are agreeable to letting me go up with him, and *then* we might manage to fit in an ascent before I leave!"

William's aeronaut friend was not at all as Pandora had imagined him. A shy, gangling young man, he pumped her hand in an excess of nervous zeal and spent the first few minutes of their meeting apologising for the state of his tiny room, gazing round with a kind of vague helplessness at the piles of books and papers which overflowed every available space, and finally clearing a chair for her with an impulsive sweeping gesture.

"If you do not object, Miss Carolyn, I should very much like to keep in touch with William. He has an astonishing capacity for understanding . . . a true feeling for aeronautics . . . quite rare, you know, in one so young! Should be nurtured . . . can't tell you how glad I am that he's going to receive more adequate tuition at last. . . ." The words died away and Mr. Oliver turned pink at what he was sure must seem very much like presumptuous criticism, but Pandora quickly put him at ease by agreeing with him wholeheartedly. They parted on the best of terms, it being decided that Mr. Oliver would call upon William whenever he found himself at all close to Chedwell Rectory, and that though an ascent was not possible at present, Willaim should be accommodated at the very first opportunity.

"It's a great pity that you couldn't have met the Duke of Heron," said William, shaking hands as they left. "*He* is jolly interested in ballooning, too, isn't he, Dora? We had a long talk about it. In fact, I expect he'd be quite pleased if you were to call upon him—bring him up-to-date, you know. He did say his knowledge was a bit behindhand."

Pandora had no such faith in his grace's burning thirst for knowledge, and endeavoured to convey the fact as tactfully as she could, lest the young man be misled. But a faint glint in his eyes told her that she need not have worried.

Octavia had been ill-tempered from the day Mr. Lewis' letter had first arrived. It had, she said, come as a great shock to her nerves to learn the news.

"I had thought you would be relieved to be rid of William," said Pandora mildly.

"That is hardly the point. What I do not care for is the sly way in which you have gone behind our backs!" Octavia's voice had quivered with grievance. "Frederick has been to a great deal of trouble, I might tell you, and had all but settled with the headmaster of a small school near Islington to accept William upon the most reasonable terms. . . ."

Pandora could imagine the kind of school it would be, and blessed Mr. Lewis for his excellent timing.

"He will be made to look exceedingly foolish if he must now tell the man he no longer requires the place! I cannot understand why you should prefer some impoverished cleric whom no one has ever seen, and who will probably fleece you and allow William to do as he pleases!" she concluded angrily. "But then, you all seem to think you may do as you please—irresponsible to a degree, Courtney most of all! I hope you may none of you live to rue your thoughtless ways!"

Since it was clear that her hopes were quite the reverse, the only positive outcome of this diatribe was to make Pandora resolve to quit Brook Street the moment William was settled. Now that her finances were less desperate, she could afford to moderate her ideas somewhat. Perhaps Lady Margerson would take her in for a short time—just until her mind was made up.

Any lingering qualms that she might have entertained regarding William's future were dispelled within moments of meeting Mr. Brearly, who managed to encompass in his large genial frame exactly the right degree of wisdom and firmness necessary for dealing with small boys. Even Octavia, who had officiously insisted upon being present, could not deny as much, though it was clear she found his pleasant leavening of humour an ominous sign.

William took to his prospective tutor on the instant and was soon being regaled with a comprehensive account of the Brearly family's doings at Chedwell Rectory guaranteed to dispel any hint of apprehension he might harbour. Pandora warmed to the bluff clergyman. There were, it seemed, apart from the rector and his wife, two boys, one a year older than William, and one younger—and two little girls.

"Oh, girls!" scoffed her brother with his wry lopsided grin, and was sharply reproved by Octavia.

But Mr. Brearly's eyes only twinkled the more deeply from within deep laughter creases. "Yes, I know, my boy—but they are necessary to our lives, you know! And though perhaps I may be guilty of partiality, I think you will find Liza and Amelia not too tiresome! In fact, we all rub along very comfortably together, and I am sure you will soon feel yourself one of us." A chuckle rumbled deep in his chest. "I daresay you will not wish to be working all the time!" he concluded as he left, having arranged the time at which he would collect William on the following morning. "In which case my boys can find you some excellent country to explore round about."

These last few hours with her brother suddenly seemed very precious to Pandora, but he was so full of all Mr. Brearly had told him and was so cheerful that she finally resigned herself to the probability that he would miss her far less than she would miss him.

In consequence, she accompanied the travellers to the coaching inn upon the following morning determined to maintain a phlegmatic mien, but at the last it was William who grew pensive. The sight of him, looking pale and earnest amid all the noise and bustle of the inn yard, undid all her resolution. She gathered him into a swift convulsive hug and adjured him shakily to mind all that Mr. Brearly told him—and to write.

This last was urged without much hope, but "I will see that he does, ma'am," said the clergyman, taking her hand in a comforting clasp just before they departed. He would also, he assured her, keep her informed as to how William did, and she must feel herself welcome to visit them at any time.

She waved after the fast-blurring outline of the coach until it lumbered from view. Then she blew her nose and summoned a hack. There was something she had been making up her mind to for several days now; it would help her to stop brooding if she accomplished it at once.

The driver of the hack looked somewhat taken aback when she directed him to the address Josiah had given her. The reason became apparent when they reached the long row of depressingly dingy houses, among which one stood out by reason of the extra care lavished upon it.

Mrs. Blakewell was a brisk woman veiling a certain despair behind eyes that were sharply questioning as they took in the slim, neatly clad form of her visitor and the waiting hack.

Pandora explained who she was and asked if she might speak with Sergeant Blakewell.

"This way." There was a brusqueness in the woman's voice as she ushered Pandora into a sparsely furnished kitchen where, at a well-scrubbed table, two little girls and a boy laboured at their books under the unyielding supervision of their father, who was more used to dealing with soldiers.

He came clumsily to his feet, chair scraping back, his words equally rasping as he demanded to know why his wife had not shown Miss Pandora into the parlour.

"Why should I? Are you ashamed to let the Colonel's daughter see how we live?"

"Alice!"

Pandora had heard that ominous growl many times. Very much aware that the children were staring with interest, she smiled at them and, stripping off her gloves said lightly, "Why indeed, ma'am? The sergeant and I have been in too many tight corners together for us to be standing on ceremony now!"

Her words, quietly practical, had the desired effect. Mrs. Blakewell sounded slightly less grudging as, having shooed the children outside to play, she said, "You'll sit down and take some refreshment, Miss Carlyon? We haven't a lot to offer . . ."

"Thank you, but I cannot stay." Pandora explained about William, and how she did not know her way about London, hence the waiting hack. "I will come another time, if I may. For now, there is an idea I wish to put to Josiah." Without further preamble she took a small purse from her reticule and laid it on the table.

The atmosphere at once prickled with resentment. Before anything could be said, however, she continued crisply: "I am not offering you charity—in fact, I am not offering you anything at all." She looked squarely at the sergeant. "I have a little money to spare—not much, but I would like it to be spent usefully. It occurred to me, Josiah, that a lot of our men will be coming home soon—some of them in much worse case than you. So . . . well, I thought perhaps that if you had this set aside"—she put a hand on the purse—"you could advance them a little, just to tide them over." She smiled nervously, as though appealing for their understanding. "After all, you are more likely to know who is in genuine need than I."

There was a silence.

"It isn't fair, tempting us with all that money!" Mrs. Blakewell looked Pandora fiercely in the eye. "How do you know we won't use it for ourselves?"

Pandora stood up and put on her gloves. "If I had thought that, ma'am, I would not have come in the first place."

The Duke of Heron, on his way back from Clearwater, had reached the outskirts of London when he found his way suddenly barred by some kind of altercation. The road ahead was blocked by several vehicles, and a crowd had formed to cheer on the adversaries and proffer advice.

"Devil take it! There is no room to turn. See what you can do, Grimble."

The Duke's man stood up, craning his neck to size up the situation before clambering down. "Appears to me that a waggon has got itself mangled with some young swell in a Stanhope!" he pronounced dourly.

A voice rose clearly above the rest.

"No, no, you stupid man! Can you not see that it is quite futile to lash at the poor creature? You will never make a horse heed you in that way!"

The Duke stiffened, frowned, and then unhurriedly handed over the ribbons. "On reflection, Grimble, perhaps I will investigate for myself."

"As you please, your grace," said Grimble, whose own ears had not been slow to pick up Miss Carlyon's impulsive tones. "I thought as you might," he added beneath his breath.

Heron arrived upon the scene in time to behold Pandora, amid much expostulation and head-shaking and mutters that "She'll be trampled into the ground . . . a slip of a thing like her, an' serve 'er right, pushin 'erself in . . . she's no business to be there at all," reaching up to grasp at the rein where it was buckled to the bit on the heavy waggon horse, which had become inextricably entangled with a pair of nervy blood mares being ill-managed by a very young, very haughty gentleman in a smart Stanhope gig, against all the advice of a tight-lipped groom.

Pandora had supporters in the crowd—a vociferous minority, generous with their advice, urging her on with enthusiasm.

"Watch out for 'is near side, my lovely . . . break your leg, 'e will, gal, if 'e lashes out!"

"Never mind that old nag! It's them fancy prancers as'll do for 'er! Take no more'n a puff of wind to blow her away!"

"Get you back where you belong, gal, and leave the job to them as knows how!"

"I would gladly do so if I could see the least evidence of there being any such person," Pandora returned crisply, and continued her chosen task of soothing the old cart horse, talking to it in a calm way, exerting a firm steady pressure on the rein to make him attend—a task made more difficult by the owner of the Stanhope, who was fast losing what little control he retained over his own horses and his temper.

When someone presently leaped up beside him and wrenched the reins from his clasp, he turned in a fury, but his expostulations died away as he beheld the austerely handsome profile presented to him by the usurper of the reins, who was already issuing a number of terse authoritative instructions to the groom and those who ventured too close.

"G-good God! Heron!" he stammered. And in an effort to appear nonchalant, "Devilish tricky situation, what? G-good of your grace to honour me . . . beg you won't heed this rabble!"

"I don't," said Heron curtly. "But there'll be no peace for anyone if something isn't done—and I can't abide to see fine cattle having their mouths sawn to pieces!"

The young gentleman's groom concealed a smirk as his master's mouth dropped open. But the Duke's attention was already elsewhere.

"You obviously know what you are about, Miss Carlyon. Can you contain that animal a few moments longer—just where you have him now?"

Pandora raised a flushed face, astonished to hear Heron's voice. Her answer was confident.

"Yes, sir. He is already much calmer."

In a very short space of time the combined efforts of Pandora, the groom, and the Duke had the two vehicles separated, and the crowd, seeing the drama at an end, began to drift away.

"Well, Miss Carlyon, your impulsiveness seems destined to lead you into contentious situations!"

"If you mean, sir, that I deplore stupidity and must intervene when I see it, then I don't deny it. It was, after all, no more than you did yourself!"

They stood in the dusty street facing one another. The waggon had gone, the haughty young man had driven away, much chastened after a dressing-down that must have rankled more had it not been delivered by such a Nonpareil. Only the Duke's curricle remained—and the hack in which Pandora had been travelling. The driver moved restlessly on his box, his voice weary.

"Beggin' your pardon, miss, but are you wishful to continue your journey? Only I can't wait here all day."

"Oh, Gemini! I had quite forgotten!" Pandora turned to the Duke. "Forgive me, sir, but I must go. This poor man has been held up quite long enough—"

"Then let us detain him no longer."

Before she could divine his intent, he had crossed the road, paid the man off, and returned to offer her his arm, indicating his curricle, where Grimble waited impassively. She ignored the proffered arm.

"Really, my lord Duke," she exclaimed, "you take a great deal too much upon yourself."

"Do I?" He seemed surprised by the accusation. "Forgive me, but my duty seemed plain. I do not know how you came to be here"—he looked about him with vague distaste—"but clearly I could not leave you to proceed, unaccompanied, in a common hack—"

"I don't see why," she retorted with spirit, detecting a rebuke in the drawled observation. "I was managing very well without your help."

"Perhaps so," he agreed. "But would you not much rather ride home in comfort with me?"

Her glance strayed involuntarily to the waiting curricle, and was quickly checked, but not quickly enough. "That is hardly to the point now," she persisted. "Since you have dismissed my conveyance, I have no choice."

"Very true. However, if you are set on a hack, Grimble can doubtless procure you another one."

"Now you are being silly." Pandora met his eyes, and against all resolution, her mouth began to quiver. "It would have been pleasant to be consulted," she maintained stoutly.

"My apologies, ma'am. I am not, you see, accustomed

to meeting with any objection. I will strive to remember in the future."

His humility was so patently bogus that a giggle escaped her, and she was lost.

"That is much better." With an approving smile he drew her hand into the curve of his arm and led her across to the curricle. "The rug, I think, don't you?" he said, tucking its fleecy softness about her legs against the chill breeze, watched by Grimble, whose opinion of her had been grudgingly modified after witnessing her competence in dealing with the horses.

"I expect you are wondering why you found me there," she ventured when they had gone a short distance.

"My dear girl, I would not presume to incur your displeasure by quizzing you further!"

Pandora decided to ignore the sarcasm. "I have been seeing William off on the stage," she continued, and told him about their good fortune in finding William so promising a tutor.

"He should be happy enough, at all events," said the Duke casually. "As it happens, Chedwell is quite close to an estate of mine, and I am very slightly acquainted with the Brearlys. They seem a pleasant, happy family."

"How extraordinary!" Pandora turned to him eagerly. "And you really think he will be well-received? I declare it is the impression I gained from Mr. Brearly, but to have it confirmed . . ." She sighed.

Heron glanced at her sidelong. "You will miss him, I expect?"

"Yes."

"And your other brother—Courtney, is it not? I trust all went well for him? He will be upon the high seas by now, I suppose, bound for adventure with his friend Captain Greville."

"As to that, I'm not sure. Courtney is the most dreadfully lax correspondent. But I did have a letter from Hugo only this morning, and he said that they were expecting to leave at any time, so perhaps they will have done so by now." Again she felt that terrible hollowing gulf of loss, but refused to give way to it, beyond saying passionately, "Oh, how I wish I might be going with them!"

"Do you?" He gave no sign of having noticed the extent to which she betrayed her feelings.

"It is very wrong of me. I must learn to be content with my lot," she said brightly. "Touching upon Courtney's affairs, sir, I must make you our thanks."

"Indeed? How so?"

"Well, Mr. Bridges paid far more for Grandmama's necklace than I had expected and I cannot help but think that your grace's interest . . . and recommendation must in some measure have accounted for his generosity."

"I fear you credit me with too much influence, ma'am."

"I don't think so. I would hazard that you are a much-valued customer," she concluded shrewdly. "And that being the case, he will have taken your comment as a hint that we should be treated in a manner pleasing to you."

"Very perspicacious!" he drawled.

"You must not think I am complaining," she said hastily, "for in consequence we were able to fit Courtney out very comfortably and I am left with far more than I ever dreamed possible."

"Well, don't go giving it away to every crippled soldier who happens along with a hard-luck story." The silence that followed was so pregnant with guilt that he glanced at her and found her pinkly blushing beneath her demure bonnet. "Oh, good God! I don't believe it!" As her chin took on its most stubborn aspect, he said more harshly than he intended, "You can't help them all, you know!"

"I do know," Pandora returned swiftly, making no mention of Sergeant Blakewell. "As it happens, I am not so ninnyhammered as you seem to think! In fact, I know exactly what I want to do with the money. At least," she amended less belligerently, "I know what I would like to do."

"Which is?"

There was still a touch of irony in his voice. Would he laugh at her if she told him? She had been going to broach the idea to Lady Margerson, but . . . perhaps the

Duke would be better placed to advise her. She decided to chance it.

"I wondered . . . whether it would be possible to take a small cottage somewhere not too far from Chedwell?" When no derision was immediately forthcoming, she continued with more confidence, "I shall have to see Mr. Lewis about it, of course, but I thought that if some of the money was invested . . . well, I am very good with my needle. It must be possible to earn some money by taking in sewing, and I could be near William . . ." Still he had said nothing. "It would be better than being a governess, surely? I'd have my independence."

"Were you intending to live alone in this cottage?" he asked with unexpected mildness.

"I suppose so." She frowned. "But . . . no one would take exception to that . . . in the country?"

"My dear girl, they are like to be just as sticky about such things in the country as here. More so, in fact. However, that is not an insurmountable obstacle."

His lack of opposition so surprised her that she could think of nothing to say. She had taken little heed of where they were going, and looked up in some surprise to find that they were approaching Hyde Park—she was even more surprised when the Duke turned his horses toward the gates.

"Sir?"

"One moment, Miss Carlyon." He successfully negotiated the manoeuvre, then gave her his attention. "My pardon. You were saying?"

"N-nothing. I was not expecting you to come this way, that is all."

He threw her something very like a boyish grin. "You are now a woman of substance, ma'am. I decided that it was time to show you how the fashionable disport themselves. It might dissuade you from wishing to bury yourself in the country."

"I think not." Pandora laughed, but for a while she was in serious danger of succumbing, for it seemed to her that there was a kind of magic about the park that afternoon.

She was used to seeing it in the morning or early afternoon, empty except for an occasional purposefully striding nursemaid, her charges preceding her in neat array, or maybe a sedate barouche might pass her by, or a party of riders taking the air.

But now, under trees bursting with new green, the Duke's curricle joined a slow-moving procession of gigs and high swaying phaetons, of lively curricles and graceful landaulets. In spite of the chill breeze, the walks and wide sweeps of grass were alive in the sunshine with the gentle shimmer of silk and muslin. Burnished curls gleamed beneath extravagant confections of swirling plumes and ruched ribbon, with many a lacy parasol to shield the more sensitive complexions.

Some ladies rode, some strolled about in the company of elegantly pantalooned dandies with tight blue coats and high starched collar points, and hessians that rivalled the sun for brilliance. The movement was intermittent as acquaintances were acknowledged and greetings exchanged.

Many a head turned to mark the approach of Heron's famous bays; many eyes widened in surprise as they beheld his unlikely companion.

"Egad!" drawled Mr. Chessington as he rode down the tan toward them with Sir Henry Dalrymple. "So that is Miss Carlyon!"

"Eh? Where?" Sir Henry, with a light in his eye and a reputation to uphold, glanced about him hopefully, and seeing Pandora for the first time, blinked. "Good Lord!"

"Gently, Harry!" murmured Fitz as the curricle came abreast of them, and introductions were effected.

Pandora could hardly tear her glance from the scene before her. "Does this happen every afternoon?" There was a note of awe in her voice that made them all smile.

"Every afternoon, ma'am," admitted Mr. Chessington with his gentle sleepy smile.

Sir Henry felt that more explanation was required. "You have seen nothing as yet, Miss Carlyon. When the weather grows warmer and the Season is at its peak, you will find twice as many people here."

"Gracious! And is this all you do—just walk about talking to one another?"

"Like exotic sheep," murmured Mr. Chessington.

"Certainly not," Heron reproved her. "If you watch more closely, you will observe that careful note is being taken of who is wearing what and, more to the point, who is conversing with whom—or *not* conversing, which is much more diverting!"

Pandora turned to stare at him suspiciously. "You *are* bamming me?" she accused him, sounding exactly like William.

"One does not make light of such matters, Miss Carlyon," he replied with convincing gravity, and was rewarded by an attractive gurgle of laughter—which was echoed in the eyes of her companions.

"How extraordinary!" she cried. "And what a shocking waste of time!"

"No, really, ma'am!" Sir Henry protested, though his eyes twinkled. "Would you deprive us of our harmless little amusements?"

On this they parted in a mood of high good humour.

"Well, now, Fitz," said Sir Henry when they were out of earshot, "do tell me about Robert's curious little friend."

Someone else was also showing unusual interest; in a carriage drawn up at the verge, a vision in peach-blush twilled silk had just bidden farewell to a friend who had shown something less than friendliness in the glee with which she imparted news of the Duke's companion to her.

Lady Sarah Bingly, the daughter of an impoverished earl, had married at eighteen a commoner with more wealth than wit. She was less than heartbroken when some years later Mr. Bingly had suffered a fatal fall in the hunting field while trying to emulate his betters. She had spent the required period of mourning abroad, since when she had exploited her beauty, her late husband's vast wealth, and her status as a widow to attain a much-envied position in fashionable London circles.

Now well into her thirty-seventh year (though she admitted to no more than two and thirty), she acknowledged that her looks would not serve her indefinitely. The time had come to take another husband. There had never been any doubt in her mind as to whom she would have, but although his grace of Heron exhibited a flattering preference for her company, she had until now quite failed to bring him to the sticking point.

The prospect of a rival, therefore, did not amuse her, though nothing in her manner betrayed the fact when presently she saw Heron's curricle approaching.

Pandora was much intrigued to meet the famous beauty whom Octavia craved to emulate. It was not difficult to see why. She, too, found herself momentarily envying the dark, smoothly burnished curls, the curvaceous figure, and the elegance of manner. She could not know how much conjecture seethed behind that charming facade.

Heron knew, however. He parried a look in those first moments that told him plainly how he would be quizzed later.

"I have not seen you for days, Robert!" Lady Sarah chided in an attractive husky voice.

He explained that he had been down to Clearwater.

"Of course. Your wards. You are too generous, my dear!" She wrinkled her exquisite nose. "I daresay you will be off to Paris in King Louis's wake," she continued, ignoring Pandora. "The children will have connections there, no doubt, if all is not destroyed?"

Heron shrugged. "I have no idea. I leave all such details to my secretary."

"How fortunate you are in the excellent Mr. Varley," she said archly. "I believe I shall go. London is growing quite tediously festive . . . white cockades everywhere, flags and bunting. And have you *seen* Carlton House? My dear . . . Prinny has got quite carried away! The whole place is festooned with *fleur-de-lis*! Heaven knows to what lengths he will go for the Czar's visit!" She turned her restless azure-blue eyes upon Pandora. "Do you not crave to visit Paris, Miss Carlyon? To see for yourself what changes the war has wrought. Of course, you cannot know how it was before. Why, I can scarcely remember myself!" she added with a tinkling laugh. "I was a mere babe when I was taken there!"

Pandora said stiffly, "I am not familiar with Paris, Lady Sarah, but I have seen enough of war to wish never to go anywhere simply to gloat over the miseries of a defeated people."

Lady Sarah's delicately arched brows rose in faint hauteur.

"Miss Carlyon has spent most of her life with the army, Sarah. We cannot expect her to see things quite as we do."

"How very interesting," she said, sounding bored, and then, as she caught sight of a friend, "Forgive me, I must go. *A bientôt,* Robert . . . Miss Carlyon."

"I daresay I should not have expressed myself so freely," said Pandora, still in the same stiff voice, as Heron picked up the reins without comment. "I fear I may have offended Lady Sarah."

"Nonsense," he said brusquely.

Perhaps he was right, she mused, feeling rebuked. Perhaps she was too insignificant to merit so much notice. The thought kept her silent for some time.

Heron was occupied with the traffic, but he was very much aware of the young woman beside him. In his mind's eye he saw that trim grey-clad figure sitting quietly erect, the narrow brim of her bonnet not quite concealing a purposeful thrust to the delicate jawline which so graphically evinced a determination not to be put down. It was impossible not to compare her with Sarah—the wild rose, its open-faced simplicity concealing prickles; and the flawless lily.

"Are you still set on your country cottage?" he asked as they turned the corner into Brook Street.

Pandora came out of her abstraction with a start. "Yes, of course."

"This afternoon has not, then, given your ambition a higher direction?"

"Good gracious, no." She paused fractionally. "If anything, it has confirmed me in my resolve."

"How so?"

Pandora smoothed each finger of her gloves carefully.

"Oh, come, sir! You, of all people, must recognise that I could never fit into that world."

"Gammon!" said the Duke as the curricle came to a halt outside the Hamilton house. Grimble climbed down and went to the horses' heads, and Heron moved aside to face Pandora with a curious light in his eyes. "You are talking, my dear Miss Carlyon, out of the top of your exceedingly unfashionable bonnet! Plain and unadorned you may be, but you are not without style, and I begin to suspect that you could hold your own in any company."

But she would only shake her head.

"So be it." He secured the reins and leaped lightly down, turning to swing her expertly to the ground, walking with her to the door.

"Thank you, sir." She gave him her hand. "I would ask you in, except . . ." She thought of Octavia possibly waiting to pounce on him.

"No matter," he said, with the same thought. But still he lingered, retaining her clasp, his thumb moving absently in a circular caressing motion over hers. "If you wish it, I will instruct my agent down at Clearwater to keep his ears open for a cottage."

There was an odd singing sensation in her veins, a kind of breathlessness as she said, "You are very kind, but I could not put you to so much trouble."

"No trouble."

He released her abruptly, but the sensation remained. He smiled faintly, flicked her cheek with one careless finger, and walked away. "No trouble at all."

9

Lady Margerson's "little evening," as she called it, passed off very satisfactorily. She was delighted by the way her protégée was received. Everything was working out splendidly, she told herself, blissfully unaware of what Pandora was planning.

It had not been Pandora's intention to deceive Lady Margerson, but circumstances had conspired to force her to act more quickly than she had expected.

Octavia was indeed at home on that day when the Duke brought Pandora back. She had, unfortunately, seen the carriage arrive at the door from the drawing-room window and rushed willy-nilly to change her gown, to chivy her maid into perfecting her coiffure, her heart fluttering with the expectation that *at last* she was to have the accolade of receiving the Nonpareil into her drawing room.

Her fury upon learning that he had driven away without so much as setting foot over the threshold knew no bounds. The entire household was privy to her opinion that Pandora was "*the most rag-mannered, selfish, ungrateful, and conniving little upstart that I have ever had the misfortune to know!*" There was much more in similar vein—about Pandora, about her brothers, their parents, their way of life—growing incoherent as it became punctuated with hysterical sobs, until finally hysteria won and she could no more.

Pandora heard her out in stony silence, then turned and left the room, went straightaway to pack her few belongings, and William's, and asked Binns in a strained voice to summon a hack. This he did with obvious distress, and within half an hour she was at Lady Margerson's door.

"But of course, dear child! You may stay as long as you please!" Lady Margerson, with the threat of William removed, was genuinely delighted to have her. "We shall deal most agreeably together, shall we not? And it will be so much more convenient," she added ambiguously, though Pandora knew very well what she meant.

She ought to have told her then of her intentions, but could not face an argument at that precise moment, and as time went on, the old lady was so happy, so full of her forthcoming soirée, that Pandora doubted she would even have attended her.

She managed to resist the more ambitious of Lady Margerson's plans for her, pleading her state of mourning as excuse, but as this found favour rather than otherwise with her ladyship's influential friends, she was invited, along with her patroness, to many of the more informal evenings, breakfasts, and such that proliferated as the Season progressed.

Nor did it escape the notice of the gossip-mongers that Pandora was seen with ever-growing frequency in the company of his grace the Duke of Heron. Sir Henry Dalrymple, quizzed by a friend about the "girl in grey," said with a fruity chuckle, "What? Don't y'know? *That*, my dear boy, is Heron's little puritan!" The description caught the imagination and soon it was being confided behind fans in discreet parlours and bandied about in the less-rarefied world of the clubs.

Pandora continued in happy ignorance of what was being said, seeing the Duke's interest in her as no more than a kindness, but appreciating it the more because she could talk to him about William. Lady Margerson uttered polite noises when she spoke of him, but clearly was not interested, whereas the Duke went so far as to ask after him, and she needed no further encouragement.

"I have *had* a letter," she told him one day when he called to take her out. "But I suspect that it was only accomplished with Mr. Brearly standing over him the whole time! Still, it is quite apparent that he is enjoying himself enormously! And Mr. Brearly keeps me informed of his progress, which he vows is prodigious." There was an unconscious wistfulness in her voice.

Heron looked down at her. "You are missing William badly still, are you not?"

"Foolish of me, isn't it?" She managed a smile. "You would suppose that with so many people being nice to me, I should be content."

"Would you like to visit him?"

The question was so unexpected, so abruptly asked, that she did not at once take his meaning.

"Mr. Brearly did assure me that I could do so, but . . ."

"I'll take you," Heron said. "We can get there and back easily in the day." And as she stared at him: "In fact, I had meant to broach it sooner. My agent writes that he has found a cottage that might suit you—if you are still interested?"

It was clear from her reaction that she was. He found himself pondering upon why he had been so reluctant to tell her. Would he miss her so greatly if she were to leave town? A ridiculous notion, he told himself firmly, and dismissed it from his mind.

A day was arranged for the end of the week, and Pandora's spirits rose accordingly.

The evening prior to the trip, they were invited to a musical entertainment at Lady Sarah Bingly's fashionable Mayfair house.

"There, now—what could be more fortunate?" exclaimed Lady Margerson, who had been more than a little surprised to receive the invitation. She did not care for the elegant young widow who wielded so much power in society, but there was no denying that to be noticed by her would greatly enhance Pandora's standing. She wondered fleetingly if Heron had arranged it, for she was not unaware of the relationship between them, or of Lady Sarah's expectations in that direction. It would be a relief to have Pandora satisfactorily bestowed, vowed Lady Margerson with a sigh. All this gadding about was proving a severe trial. She steeled herself to fresh enthusiasm.

"To be sure, it is not a ball, but even a musical evening

. . . well, my love, it is quite something to have been singled out! We must make a special effort. A new dress, I think . . . yes, certainly a new dress," she said more firmly as Pandora looked set to argue. "There was that very pretty lilac gauze we saw in Henriette Street last week. It would become you vastly! Oh, I can see it now, with a ruched bodice and knots of ribbon . . ."

"No, no, ma'am, I beg you!" Pandora stopped her with a trill of laughter. "No frills and furbelows. And no lilac gauze, either. Truly, it would *not* become me."

In the end they agreed upon lavender-grey silk with sufficient warmth of colour to be guaranteed not to turn the fading brown of her complexion to sallow. It was simply cut, with puffed sleeves, the high-waisted bodice ruched a little to please Lady Margerson and "just one flounce, my love . . . a narrow one an' you will . . . across the bosom. And, only this once, do say that you will allow my Monsieur Henri to have the arranging of your hair!"

How could Pandora refuse without appearing churlish? But it felt very strange to have someone dressing her hair. "So soft! So fair! Like the finest gossamer . . ." tutted Monsieur Henri, who was plump and garrulous and, she suspected, not French at all. "But of a straightness!"

He shook his head and doubted that he could achieve the style "à la greque" upon which he had built his hopes. After what seemed an unconscionable length of time, during which she wilted and he grew ever more voluble, he succeeded in piling the hair on top of her head, securing it there, and with the aid of crimping irons and much perseverance, perusaded it to fall in an artless cascade of curls. Pandora very much doubted that they would last the evening, but Lady Margerson was content, and Monsieur so overcome by his own artistry that she could not bring herself to disillusion either of them.

Heron, coming upon her in one of Lady Sarah's crowded drawing rooms, frowned and stood back.

"Good God! What *have* they done to you?" he exclaimed, employing his quizzing glass to view her better.

"Robert!" chided the gentle Mr. Chessington at his side.

Pandora liked Mr. Chessington enormously. His indolence rivalled Lady Margerson's and his droll humour made her laugh, as did his preoccupation with the niceties of dress. And sometimes she surprised in his eyes an expression which seemed to suggest that it was all quite, quite deliberate.

This evening he was peacock-fine against the Duke's severe black and white, resplendent in a blue coat with a huge collar and mother-of-pearl buttons, and a cravat of marvelous intricacy. He smiled sleepily and made her a leg.

"I beg you will not heed this rough fellow, ma'am. His manners, though in general quite distinguished, are apt to crumble upon the slightest provocation, as you have probably noticed. Permit me to inform you that you look charmingly."

"Thank you, sir." Pandora looked challengingly at the Duke.

"Did I say otherwise?" he murmured, unabashed. "The dress is well enough, charming, in fact, as Fitz has already remarked." His glance travelled upward. "But for the rest, I would rather have you as yourself."

"Plain and unadorned?" she suggested. He lifted an ironic brow. "You are right, of course, but I could no longer deny Lady Margerson that for which she has long been hankering—the opportunity to make me over to her liking!"

"Where *is* her ladyship?" he asked, amused approval glinting in his eyes.

"Gone already to the music saloon. I believe she wished to find a comfortable corner where she might doze unnoticed through the concert."

He laughed aloud at this, and, looking up, surprised a shaft of fury from Lady Sarah that came as something of a shock. In a moment it was gone and she was smiling, making her way toward them in an outrageously modish gown of sapphire-blue spider gauze over a slip of pale satin which clung to her figure, revealing the curve of her thigh as she moved. Her brilliant eyes, like jewels, echoed the shimmering gauze. He began to wonder whether he had not imagined that look.

"Come, everyone. It is time to take our places in the music room. The concert will begin in a short while." She spoke to the room at large, but it was Heron upon whose arm she hung as she led the way. "Did I tell you, Robert, that I have prevailed upon La Gianetti to perform this evening? She is in London, you know, to give a concert in honour of the Czar's visit, but she had vowed she would not perform elsewhere. Am I not clever?"

The Duke murmured something in reply, and Mr. Chessington gave Pandora one of his droll looks and offered her his arm as they followed.

"I wonder if that lady seated on the couch near the door is quite well," she said as the room began to clear. "I have been watching her on and off, and she has had recourse several times to her vinaigrette. Do you suppose one should mention her indisposition to Lady Sarah?"

"Ain't our affair, m'dear," advised Mr. Chessington. "The lady has a friend with her. Let well alone, I'd say."

The woman, dressed all in black, must in ordinary circumstances have been quite pretty in a rather faded way, but there was a gauntness in her face that Pandora had seen many times in the faces of men who had gone beyond the limit of what was supportable. The thought troubled her, but she did not wish to appear officious, and so said no more.

Ahead of them, Lady Sarah half-turned, her voice floating back. "Miss Carlyon? Ah, there you are. I was just saying to his grace how pleasant it will be for you to hear La Gianetti. You will not have had many such treats, I daresay, in your travels with the army!"

The effect of her words was as startling as it was unexpected. The woman in black, who had risen to join the stream of guests, let out an anguished moan and swayed on her feet, a small square of cambric pressed to her mouth. The people about her hesitated, moved back uncertainly, but already she was steadying herself, one hand grasping her companion's arm with a desperate strength, her eyes staring about her wildly until they came to rest on Pandora.

"It is you!" she gasped. "You are his daughter, are you not? That *murderer* who robbed me of my boy . . . my Jack!"

"No!"

Into the silence that followed came a rush of sound—exclamations, speculation—Heron saying sharply, "Sarah, for God's sake, stop this quickly"; the lady's companion urging in a distraught whisper: "Mrs. Ibbot, hush, do, dear! You mustn't make a scene . . . not here!" and turning in mute appeal to Lady Sarah, whose glance had moved briefly to observe Pandora's reactions.

She stood transfixed, her face ghastly beneath its fading tan, oblivious of everything, everyone, except this woman who had blackened her Papa's name and roused so much bitterness in her heart. Now, seeing her in all her grief, she could feel only a welling, throat-aching pity. Instinctively she stepped forward, hand outstretched.

"Ma'am, I do beg you will sit down!" Her voice was thick with unshed tears.

But her hand was dashed aside. "Don't touch me, do you hear? Don't even come near me!" Mrs. Ibbot's voice rose alarmingly and, as oblivion claimed her, it was Mr. Chessington who with unexpected presence of mind and agility caught and lifted her, laying her gently on the couch she had so recently quit.

It was all over in a matter of moments. Lady Sarah was everywhere, reassuring, soothing, urging people toward the door, while Pandora still stood.

"Are you all right?"

It was the Duke, his fingers digging into her arm, shaking her and sounding harsher than she had ever heard him. Mr. Chessington was moved to remonstrate, but his abrasiveness was exactly what Pandora needed.

She shuddered, drew a steadying breath, and nodded, the blankness in her eyes changing to concern as she saw that a small crowd of well-meaning people was pressing forward round the couch, arguing as to the rival merits of salts against burning feathers to rouse the inert figure.

"Oh, no!" she cried huskily, hurrying forward. "Please stand back so that the poor woman can breathe! My lord Duke . . ." She half-turned, appealing to him for help. "She must have air and complete quiet!"

Lady Sarah, coming back at that moment, was not best pleased to hear Robert's little nonentity giving what amounted to orders in *her* drawing room, but as the Duke, with Mr. Chessington's help, was already engaged in shepherding people toward the door, she was obliged once more to play the perfect hostess.

Soon, everyone had gone and the room was quiet. Only Pandora and the lady's companion remained, the latter staring at Pandora with open curiosity bordering on respect.

"Forgive me, ma'am, but we must be brief," Pandora said, low-voiced. "It will be for the best if I am not here when Mrs. Ibbot comes to her senses. You have her vinaigrette?"

"I do." The woman was fumbling in Mrs. Ibbot's reticule. "And there is some physic she carries with her . . . I think it contains laudanum for her nerves." Her eyes, regarding Pandora, begged for understanding. "Cordelia isn't a vindictive person, Miss Carlyon. She hasn't been herself since . . . well, you know! You'd think she'd be getting over it by now, but . . . you see, Jack was her youngest . . ."

"Ma'am, you don't have to explain . . ."

"No. Only I told her she ought not to come tonight . . . so many people! But Lady Sarah asked her especially. She thought it might do her good, the music, you know . . . it came as a surprise . . . her bothering about Cordelia's trouble, that is . . ."

There was a faint moan from the couch.

"Yes, yes . . . but do go to Mrs. Ibbot now. I will send one of the servants to you . . ."

Pandora turned quickly away and found that the Duke had come back into the room. She had not heard the door. He inclined his head.

"How is the lady?"

"Just about to regain consciousness. Please, can we go?" she pleaded. "I don't want her to find me here."

He uttered something remarkably like a snort of exasperation and took her arm. She was thankful for it. Now that the episode was over, the expended emotions took their toll. Her legs began to tremble. She stumbled and was at once lifted off her feet.

"Little fool!" he muttered, ignoring her protests. "You just had to involve yourself!" He carried her into a small anteroom and deposited her upon a ridiculously ornate sofa. "Don't move!" he said, and strode from the room.

Pandora had no desire to move. A cold sweat of faintness threatened to engulf her, and she bent, head down, until it passed, while in the far recesses of her mind she wondered why the Duke had sounded so angry. Perhaps Lady Sarah had taken her annoyance out on him! Somehow it didn't seem very important at that moment.

When he returned, she was still hunched over, immobile, her forehead propped on spread fingers, her elegant coiffure fast disintegrating into straggling disarray about her shoulders.

"Pandora?" Alarmed, he spoke her name sharply, without thinking. As he knelt beside her, she lifted a wan face to him.

"Sorry. Stupid of me . . ."

He said something indistinguishable and thrust a glass under her nose. "Drink it," he commanded.

"Must I?" Pandora managed a wry smile as the brandy fumes caught in her throat. "I'd as lief you didn't insist, sir. My stomach would most surely reject it, and I fear I am disgraced enough in your Lady Sarah's books for one evening as it is!" She sat up with great care—and sighed. "Besides, I am already feeling much more the thing." His face, very close to her own, looked curiously taut. "Why don't you drink it yourself?"

He uttered a short bark of laughter. "Perhaps you would like me to offer it to Mrs. Ibbot?"

"Thank you, but no—she has her own physic. Oh, dear, I promised that nice lady who is with her that I would send someone to them . . ."

The Duke stood up, tossed off the brandy, and set the glass down with great precision on a pretty *boulle* sofa table at her elbow.

"You are an exasperating girl!" he said, towering over her. "Not ten minutes since, that woman was treating you abominably, accusing your father of murder in front of everyone—and not only did you let her get away with it, you actually stayed behind to . . . to fuss over her like a deuced mother hen! Why, for pity's sake?"

"You have just said it, sir. *For pity's sake*." Pandora shrugged, her voice sounding suddenly tired. "Perhaps I overreacted in the first place. And Octavia's attitude fanned my bitterness toward that poor woman. But who, seeing her grief, could continue to hold her responsible because she needed to find someone to blame for what happened?"

The Duke could have said much, but looking at her, refrained. From the distance, faintly, came the soaring notes of a soprano.

"Do you want to stay . . . or go home?"

Pride dictated that she should brazen it out, but pride seemed suddenly unimportant.

"Oh, home, I think. It would be less embarrassing for everyone. But what about Lady Margerson?"

As if she had been summoned, there was a rustling, and her ladyship's flowing form filled the doorway, turbanned and draped in shawls. She extended her hands, and the whole edifice began to slide. The Duke rescued the shawls and rearranged them about her shoulders.

"My dear child! Such an unfortunate occurrence. I am sure you will not wish to stay . . . the shock to your nerves! The carriage is even now being summoned. . . ."

"But I don't want to spoil your evening, ma'am. Is not the singer supposed to be very fine?"

"She may be, for all that I am any judge." Lady Margerson leaned forward, wheezing slightly with the effort. "To tell the truth, my love," she confided, "her screeching gave me the headache within a very short time. The moment I discovered what had happened, I was glad to be away from it. Let us go home and be comfortable."

"By all means." Pandora laughed a little shakily, and as the Duke raised her to her feet, she lifted her eyes to him. "Will you make my apologies to Lady Sarah?"

He offered to accompany them, but she would not hear of it.

"Would you prefer not to go to Chedwell tomorrow?" he asked her quietly as Lady Margerson's carriage prepared to leave. "We can easily postpone the visit until next week."

"Heavens, no!" she exclaimed. "I am not so poor-spirited!"

When Lady Sarah came upon the Duke a short time later, he was sitting alone in the drawing room.

She remarked upon it as he stood up, exclaimed that he was missing La Gianetti, and attempted to take his arm.

He put her away, and there was a blankness to his voice that should have given her pause. "I have just seen Mrs. Ibbot and her friend to their carriage."

"Very noble of you!" she said with a brittle laugh.

"Lady Margerson left with Miss Carlyon a little earlier," he continued in an even tone. "All asked me to convey their apologies to you . . . in your absence."

"I came as soon as I could. I do have my other guests to consider." Sarah moved restlessly about the room, avoiding his eyes. "Well, perhaps it is for the best. Lord, what a coil!"

"I wasn't aware that you numbered anyone like Mrs. Ibbot among your acquaintances."

"I . . . She is something of a family connection." Sarah shrugged her beautiful shoulders. "I thought to take her out of herself, but I see now that it was a grave error!"

"It was indeed," he said, soft as silk.

"Well, what is done cannot be mended!" she exclaimed flippantly, swaying provocatively as she moved to the door. "Now, do stop being tedious, Robert, and come to the music room."

"Why did you do it, Sarah?"

Something in his tone stopped her. She swung round,

brows arched. "Do? My dear, what *am* I supposed to have done?"

"Spare me the air of innocence. You don't really take me for a flat." His voice had grown clipped; his eyes were chill as ice. "That scene was carefully contrived—and since I cannot suppose your object was to expose that poor demented woman, I can only imagine that you thought to discredit Miss Carlyon."

"*Your little puritan?*" She was betrayed into wild derision. "Lud! I vow I could laugh! Why ever should I wish to do such a thing?"

"Why indeed?" he drawled, and strolled to the door. "You had better return to your guests. Pray make them my excuses. Your music, I fear, holds insufficient charm to render my stay bearable."

10

Pandora had never before travelled any distance in such style or felt herself to be so cosseted, and she gave herself up to it with shocking ease. The sun was shining and her eyes were drawn constantly toward the window and upward to the clean-washed blue of the sky. The countryside was in its most glorious array as Heron's coach swept through town and village and out again onto roads where hedgerows gave way now and then to cottage gardens vibrant with colour. Red-roofed houses nestled among orchards busy shedding the last of their blossom in heavy snowy drifts, and on the distant Surrey hills great stretches of woodland showed thick and green.

She sighed blissfully, and the Duke threw her an indulgent look. By tacit agreement, no mention had been made of the previous evening's events, and she certainly appeared none the worse for them.

"We should reach Chedwell shortly before midday. I have arranged for luncheon to be prepared for us at Clearwater. I thought we might collect William first and take him with us, if you would like that?"

"Like it?" Pandora exclaimed. "I think it the kindest and most splendid of ideas! You are going to a great deal of trouble, sir—" This he denied with an air of lazy indifference that she was fast coming to know. She said anxiously, "You don't think—that is, Mrs. Brearly won't mind, will she? I know I thought it would be fun to surprise William, but . . ."

"With a family as large as hers appears to be," drawled his grace, "I doubt that one small boy will be much missed."

And so it proved. When the first excitement of their arrival was over, Mrs. Brearly, who was every bit as agreeable as her husband, said that of course William would be wanting to spend as much time as possible with his sister—and Mr. Brearly promptly excused him from his studies for the rest of the day.

The unreserved joy with which William flung himself upon her moved Pandora greatly and more than compensated for the shortcomings in his letter-writing. It took but a short time to establish that he was very much at home and was eager to show her everything there was to be seen, especially his room.

The Duke had been standing a little apart, a faint smile touching his lips as he watched brother and sister reunited, so alike in many essentials, so obviously one in spirit. When applied to, he assured them that luncheon would await their pleasure, but declined the honour of accompanying them on their voyage of discovery, electing instead to take a glass of Madeira with Mr. Brearly in his study.

William's room was just right, comfortably cluttered but airy, and spacious enough to house all those things a growing boy is prone to collect. Pandora had loved the rambling old rectory on sight. There was ample space for work and play, and a large garden ordered enough to look pleasant, but with many secret corners and an orchard full of trees just asking to be climbed. And from beyond the trees came the unmistakable sough of running water.

"You really are happy here, Will?" From her place on the window seat Pandora looked round from her contemplation of the garden. ·

"Yes, of course. If I can't be with you, I'd as soon be here as anywhere—in spite of the girls!" He gave her the lopsided grin she had so missed seeing.

She recalled Mr. Brearly's comments earlier.

"The boy still likes to wander off on his own a good deal, but it is in his nature to do so, and there is room enough here, in all conscience! William is a great thinker, Miss Carlyon—he often prefers to work things out on his own . . . and work them out he does, by George! But he gets on well with the others, too . . . there is no hint of standoffishness! I am well pleased with him."

Pandora stood up and held out a hand. "Come on. We had better not keep his grace waiting too long."

"I guess it was jolly lucky for me," William said, opening the door. "The Duke knowing about Mr. Brearly, I mean."

Pandora stopped in her tracks. "Oh, no, dear—you are mistaken. It was Mr. Lewis who found Mr. Brearly."

"Well, I know that's what we thought, Dora, but it was the Duke who first suggested the idea. Benny let it out— he's the one who's a bit younger than me," William explained with lofty superiority of his years. "He overheard his mother and father discussing my coming before it was ever arranged." He saw the consternation in her face. "Oh, lor! I expect I shouldn't have told you— though I can't see why. I mean, it isn't the sort of thing the Duke would need to keep secret, is it?"

"No," Pandora said slowly. "But perhaps you had better not say anything to *him* about it."

"Oh, I shan't blab, never fear!" he said cheerfully. "I say, I am looking forward to my luncheon. I can still remember that spread I had at St. James's Square. Just wait till you see Clearwater. Honestly, Dora, it is the most enormous house . . . and Heron owns everything for miles around!"

She began to realise what he meant as the carriage presently drove under a great stone arch with ironwork gates thrown wide in answer to a sharp blast on the horn, past a substantial gatehouse, and then seemingly for miles through rolling parkland, until at last a building could be seen on a slight rise in the distance. Eventually the driveway curved and the full West Front of the house came into view. She must have uttered some sound, for William paused in his chatter and grinned, while the Duke turned his head lazily to look at her.

With both pairs of eyes upon her, she felt obliged to say something. "So that is Clearwater," she managed, clearing her throat. "It is certainly . . . impressive!"

She thought he chuckled.

The stonework of the extensive facade, trapped in sunlight, glowed with a golden warmth which, as they drew nearer, highlighted the eight Corinthian pillars fronting the portico quite splendidly. The carriage had scarcely drawn to a halt when two footmen came running to open the door, let down the steps, assist her to alight.

In a daze she was led through a vestibule into a vast marble hall, where their echoing footsteps added to the feeling of unreality; they passed up grand stairways and down less grand ones and along spacious corridors lined with ancestral portraits whose subjects glared haughtily down at their intrusion.

Finally they came to a charming saloon of modest proportions furnished in shades of pale bronze pinks and soft yellowy greens. Here a table was laid with covers for three in the curve of a large window looking out over terraced gardens toward the shimmering expanse of water which gave the house its name.

William voiced unstinting approval, but his interest was plainly centred with hopeful expectation upon the table and the imminent arrival of food.

"And what of Miss Carlyon?" The Duke's voice brought her back from a rapt contemplation of the view.

"I think it is quite beautiful," she said simply.

"Yes, I suppose it is." He said it as though he had never before given the matter consideration. He came to stand beside her. *"Where every prospect pleases,"* he quoted softly, *"and only man is vile.* Isn't that how the hymn has it?"

"Oh, no! At least, the quotation is right, but . . ." She stopped, realised in time that she was being gently baited, and bit her lip on a rueful smile. And then the luncheon dishes began to arrive, providing a welcome distraction.

Pandora was grateful for William's uncomplicated chatter, which continued almost unabated throughout the meal, allowing her to pursue her teeming thoughts. She had grown used to the Duke's unusual, sometimes quixotic ways, but this latest revelation of William's was beyond anything! Why should he put himself out in such a way for a boy he scarcely knew?

She looked up and found herself under scrutiny.

"You are eating very little, Miss Carlyon. Pray allow me to tempt you to one of these pastries."

"Yes, do have one, Dora. They are truly scrumptious!" William, having eaten his way through two enormous helpings of a succulent beef pie with oysters, a selection of cold meats, and the pastries, had now turned his attention to a dish of sweetmeats.

"Oh, I meant to tell you," he said, selecting the choicest one and nibbling at it, "Mr. Oliver was down here last week. He was dreadfully downcast! He was bringing the balloon down in a field just beyond the village when he hit a crosswind . . ." He glanced at the Duke. "It can happen, you know, sir, when you get very close to the ground . . ."

"Disconcerting, I imagine," he murmured obligingly.

"Yes. But everything might have been all right if the valve hadn't stuck fast. He couldn't close it, you see, and with the gas escaping, the balloon wouldn't lift again. The upshot was, he crashed into the branches of a tree, and what is worse, the boat was quite badly damaged!"

"Oh, poor Mr. Oliver! I do hope he wasn't hurt!" exclaimed Pandora, and was instantly reassured. She cast a swift glance at Heron. "But really, dear, I don't believe his grace—"

"On the contrary, Miss Carlyon, you behold me a fascinated audience! Pray go on with your story, William."

"Well, that's it, really, except that I don't know how he'll go on now. His pockets are almost always to let, and I don't *think* he can afford to replace the balloon, which is a *great* tragedy, because he is jolly clever and quite dedicated. . . ." Again William's eyes strayed toward the Duke. "Of course, what Mr. Oliver really needs is a benefactor!"

"Oh, no!" cried Pandora, mortified beyond all measure.

"Well, why not?" he reasoned. "I should've thought you might like to help Mr. Oliver, sir—only you'd have to convince him that you were really interested, because he can get pretty stiff-rumped if he suspects anyone is trying to offer him Spanish coin!"

"William! That is enough!" Pandora implored. "You really must not plague his grace in this bully-ragging way!"

Heron rested his elbows on the table and laced his fingers together, tapping them reflectively against his chin. "And how do you suppose we could go about convincing Mr. Oliver of my genuine desire to be involved?"

"Well, *that* shouldn't be too difficult." William's hand hovered over the sweetmeat dish once more and, receiving the nod from his host, he took one. "I mean, you know the rudiments of the subject, and I could probably prime you if there's anything you don't quite twig. And only consider, if you *do* help him to build a new balloon, he will most likely offer to take you up in it!"

The Duke met Pandora's anguished embarrassment with blandness. "An irresistible inducement, naturally," he murmured.

She didn't know where to look.

"Manned flight is a fascinating subject, sir! One day I mean to conduct some experiments—on a small scale, you know . . ." Warming to his theme, William pushed aside his plate and leaned forward earnestly. "You see, if one could find some way of controlling speed and direction, the possibilities are endless! In battles, for instance, one could fly over the enemy and fire down on them, perhaps even drop missiles of some kind."

"And get fired on in return," said the Duke sceptically. "You'd be a sitting target, my boy."

"Yes, I know." William sighed. "But there has to be a way." He frowned. "What the boat really needs, of course, is an entirely different structure—do away with the balloon altogether and perhaps give it wings like a bird, and some kind of propelling mechanism, as Trevithick did in his engine."

"Would that not make it too heavy to lift off the ground?" Heron pressed him, intrigued by the boy's propensity for imaginative innovation.

"That's the part I don't fully understand as yet. You

see, it's not simply a question of air displacement."
William took a knife from the table and balanced it
thoughtfully on one fingertip. "There has to be some kind
of thrust you can control. But the idea of a flying machine
isn't new, you know," he said stubbornly, looking up.
"Leonardo da Vinci believed in it centuries ago!"

The Duke raised an ironic eyebrow. "I can see *you*
won't be following in the family footsteps. The artillery
would be much too tame."

"Oh, guns are well enough in their way—there's a deal
of skill to handling a nine-pounder effectively. But it isn't
exciting in the way discovering things is. Do you know
what I mean, sir?"

Heron said gravely that he thought he did.

"The engineers might be better, I suppose, but it don't
hold a candle to inventing things, and *that's* what I mean
to do."

Pandora was by now looking dazed. "You really mean
it! You have never said a word of this to me."

He half-grinned. "No . . . because you would have
thought I was dicked in the nob!"

"Oh, William, I wouldn't!" But she didn't sound too
certain.

This time there was no mistaking that the Duke
chuckled. "Well, young shaver, I can't offer you the kind
of excitement you crave, but perhaps you would care to
see my collection of sporting guns?"

William's eyes lit up. "I should think so! I'm a pretty
fair shot, though mostly it's with a catapult." He caught
Pandora's eye, and they both dissolved into giggles.

Unperturbed, the Duke summoned a footman and in-
structed him to take William to find Mr. Dawkins. "Mr.
Dawkins is my head gamekeeper. If he is not too busy, he
has my permission to take you out to try for a rabbit or
two."

It was very quiet when he had gone.

"I don't know where he gets it all from," Pandora said
faintly. "At least it explains all those strange little models
I saw scattered about his room!"

"I should like to see them sometime."

He really sounded as though he meant it. She toyed with her glass and finally plucked up her courage. "You are being very kind to William."

Heron pushed his chair away and walked round to stand behind her. She pushed her glass away and came to her feet rather hurriedly.

"Nonsense. I enjoy his chatter. Perhaps you had better address your appreciation to Dawkins. He is like to be thoroughly interrogated and put through his paces for the next hour or so!"

"I wasn't thinking simply of your present generosity," she continued, breathless but resolute, trying not to feel intimidated by his closeness.

"Ah!" he said softly, and she could feel the stillness in him. "Someone has been talking out of turn."

"Not intentionally." Pandora thought he sounded angry and hastened to explain how she had found out. "If it is indeed true, my lord Duke . . . and I am sure I don't know why you should put yourself to so much trouble, then I do not know how to—" She was not allowed to finish.

"My dear Miss Carlyon, you make too much of it. I merely caught a glimpse of a fine enquiring mind and thought it a pity that it might be squandered for the want of a little effort."

She knew that she was making too much of it, that he wanted the subject dropped. Yet, irrationally, she also felt piqued by his attitude and could not keep her resentment from showing.

"You appear to understand William better than I do, for all that we are so close!"

"Not really," he said, but less sharply. "I would hazard that one seldom recognises evidence of genius in one's nearest and dearest."

"Genius?" Pandora's grudge was forgotten. "You really think that . . . about William?"

"I think," said the Duke, "that we have already devoted more time than enough to William's affairs. There is, or had you forgotten, another purpose to your visit today."

"The cottage! Yes, of course. May I see it now?"

"What an impulsive creature you are!" he murmured. "I had thought to wait until we have returned your brother to the rectory. You did say that you would prefer him to remain in ignorance until the matter is settled?"

"I certainly don't want to raise his hopes unduly," she agreed.

"Then we have time to spare. I wonder . . ."—he gave her a speculative look—"would you care to visit my grandmother?"

She stared at him. "You mean . . . the French Comtesse? The one you rescued at the time of the Revolution?"

"I infer that Lady Margerson has been indulging in one of her customary flights of fancy," he drawled.

"It was a very courageous act," Pandora insisted boldly.

"It was a ridiculous escapade," he said with dampening matter-of-factness. "But when one is absurdly young . . ." He shrugged.

"And she is still alive?"

There was a touch of whimsy in his smile. "Very much so, though age and infirmity now tie her to the suite of rooms she occupies in the East Wing. In consequence, she sees few people other than her companion."

"Poor lady!" said Pandora with swift sympathy. "I should very much like to meet her if you think she would not mind."

"You won't find her easy," he warned, but got no further, for at his side, Pandora uttered a small gasp.

They had been walking as they spoke, and had come at last to the long gallery, the sheer scale of which invariably caught at the throat upon first beholding its grandiose splendours, and made one wonder at the mind which had conceived it.

Seven gracefully arched Venetian windows ran the length of the room, giving breathtaking views of the rising woodland and dipping valleys beyond the lake. Here and there, sunlight bounced in splintered fragments of brilliance from a domed roof, suggesting hidden pavilions, and in the far distance rose the spire of Chedwell church.

The gallery itself could not be wholly taken in at a glance, but as the eye was inevitably drawn to the windows, the spaces between the windows made an instant dramatic impact, for each housed a pier table of solid marble encrusted with ormolu whose scrolled legs were linked by swags and loops of heavily gilded flowers and fruit, and above each table rose a tall mirror similarly embellished, from the tops of which the gilded masks of goddesses and satyrs stared down with sightless eyes.

It was, thought Pandora in a daze, indigestibly magnificent and must be more than a little daunting to live with.

The Duke enjoyed the stunned look on her face for a few moments before releasing her from the room's spell. "The fourth Duke was much influenced by the Palladian movement," he explained. "It was, I believe, on returning from a tour of Italy that he commissioned a man by the name of Kent to design Clearwater. This gallery is generally considered to be among his finest achievements. Aficionados of architecture travel from miles away to gaze and admire! Do you find it to your liking?"

The question came upon Pandora unexpectedly. She wished he hadn't asked, bit her lip, and said guardedly, "It is . . . very fine . . . quite overwhelming, in fact."

She thought his lips twitched, but couldn't be sure.

"A tactful reply, Miss Carlyon. I'm bound to say I have always found it a trifle rich for my palate."

A small giggle, born of relief, escaped her. "Like eating too many sweetmeats!"

He laughed aloud. "Exactly so! That sounds much more like the practical young woman I have come to know." They moved on, and after a moment he recalled what he had been about to say. "You may find Grandmère a little strange. She is very old now, of course, but still governed by the pride that is her heritage. She is in general remarkably alert, but every now and then her mind clouds and she slips into the past, so don't be alarmed if she suddenly grows confused. She may mention Mariette . . ."

Something in his voice intrigued Pandora. "Is . . . was Mariette the child of the lady you brought out of France with the Comtesse?"

"Yes."

His answer was so abrupt that she feared her curiosity had angered him and was destined to remain unsatisfied. Then, just as abruptly, he seemed to recollect the need for further explanation. So it was that he related to her in simple, unemotional terms the events spanning Mariette's brief tragic life, and Pandora thought it one of the saddest stories she had ever heard. She would have liked to know more, but his manner did not encourage questions. But because she knew what it was to be orphaned, her heart went out immediately to the two babies, so pitiably deprived, so that she was moved to ask in some trepidation if she might see them while she was here.

The Duke appeared to find the request surprising, but was disposed to indulge her, observing with faint irony that he supposed it was inevitable that she would be curious to see the children to whom she had once hoped to become governess. This reminder of their first meeting was undoubtedly meant to disconcert her, but Pandora was by now so bemused by the constant change of scene and the sheer distance which they must be covering that the thrust fell somewhat short of its mark.

By the time they reached the Comtesse's suite, she was breathless from keeping up with his pressing stride. "One can only suppose," she gasped, "that any visitors you have must be forever losing their direction!"

"They do," he said with a laconic grin. "Frequently."

"And I shouldn't wonder if they expire from starvation or simple exhaustion long before they can be located!" she added with feeling.

He laughed. "Not so, for we make a point of sending out regular search parties. I believe we have never yet lost a guest, though I cannot vouchsafe as much for their valets."

"What a shocking admission of partiality!"

"Is it? But then, one must draw the line somewhere, after all."

They were still laughing when they reached the Comtesse's suite; Pandora felt quite giddy with it. At the door they were met by Madame Daubenay, sour-faced companion to the Comtesse. She eyed Pandora with ill-concealed disapproval and informed his grace in chilling tones that her charge was not enjoying one of her better days. The implication was plain, but Heron could more than match her in coldness, and within moments her jealously protective attitude had crumpled into reluctant compliance.

But the laughter was over. A mood of sullenness prevailed as they followed Madame Daubenay through yet more rooms—saloons that might well have graced a French palace of some bygone age, Pandora decided weakly, as her senses were assailed yet again: thick Aubusson under her feet; rich tapestries and much gilding everywhere one looked; a faint indefinable perfume that lingered on the air; and finally, a sumptuous little boudoir draped and swathed in white and gold, and dominated by the portrait of a girl, misty, ethereal, and very beautiful. Mariette.

The Comtesse de Valière sat bolt upright in a carved ebony chair. Thin veined hands, curled rigidly round each other, were pressed against the frail shell of a body draped in folds of black bombazine. She looked, thought Pandora, incredibly old, her face, which must once have possessed a delicate beauty, now heavily crisscrossed with lines, eyes closed, mouth as small and vulnerable as a baby's—and the whole surmounted by an incongruously ornate wig.

But their presence had been noted. Without warning, eyelids hidden deep in the crevices snapped open to reveal tiny black eyes as bright and inquisitive as a blackbird's, their febrile darkness seeming almost shocking in the waxy transparency of the Comtesse's face.

"Grandmère." The Duke bent to kiss the puckered cheek with infinite gentleness, and introduced Pandora.

The darting eyes took in every detail of Pandora's unequivocal plainness. Then she greeted her formally in French, her voice unexpectedly strong and authoritative.

"For shame, *ma petite*," Heron reproved her. "Miss Carlyon is well aware that you speak English. It is unworthy of you to pretend otherwise."

But Pandora was undismayed. She might well have been overawed by this extraordinary lady had she not glimpsed a wicked twinkle lurking in those bird-bright eyes.

"I don't mind in the least, sir, if Madame wishes to converse in her given language," she said, "so long as she will bear with my attempt to match her!"

A cackle of laughter greeted this sally. The old lady leaned forward, beckoning with a stiff-jointed finger, motioning her to a footstool.

"Come. Sit close, where I may hear you better, and you, Robert"—she gestured vaguely with the hand—"you may go away. Miss Carlyon and I will talk."

He lifted an interrogatory eyebrow at Pandora. When she smiled confidently, he walked to the door. "Ten minutes," he said.

"You also, Daubenay. Go, go!"

The companion went reluctantly, casting Pandora a look of dislike. It was very quiet in the room when she had gone, but the air was charged with the vibrance that exuded from that tiny rigid figure in the chair. Occasionally there was a faint rasp in her breathing, and Pandora knew that those sharp eyes were on her still.

"Well, little sparrow," she said at last. "You will tell me now all about yourself, for I find it quite extraordinary that Robert should know such a one as you!"

Was this, then, where the Duke had acquired his habit of inquisitorial directness? Pandora hid a smile and gave the old lady a brief account of her life, seeing even as she did so how quickly the Comtesse's capacity for concentration faded. Her eyes grew vague; the hands shook slightly.

"You do not know how matters go on at court, I suppose?"

The voice, less authoritative, broke in upon her. Pandora managed to conceal the little frisson of shock that ran through her, and replied, as normally as she was able, that she did not.

"A pity. One must beware of spies, you understand. My grandson does not believe that there are spies. He knows nothing of how matters stand at court. But Mariette is there, and I worry about her."

Pandora drew a steadying breath. "I am sure that you need feel no concern, madame," she said, cautiously feeling her way. "His grace would never allow the least harm to befall you . . . or Mariette."

There was a moment of silence. Then: "Mariette is dead," said the Comtesse harshly.

Pandora let her breath go very slowly. "Yes, madame."

For a moment the wizened face seemed to crumple even more. The stiff hands gripping the chair arms with surprising strength looked bloodless—paper-thin skin over white bones. There was fierce pride in the Comtesse's eyes, but behind that pride Pandora sensed an almost insupportable fear.

"Sometimes, Miss Carlyon, my mind . . . cannot hold to its course." The words came out as if dragged from her, and Pandora felt an overwhelming pity. "Sometimes I am aware of it, but cannot prevent it . . . and sometimes it . . . can happen quite without warning, and . . . I am . . . afraid . . ."

In a gesture born of instinct, Pandora held out her hand, and after a moment the old lady relinquished the support of one chair arm to clasp it convulsively.

"You will not tell Robert?" It was an anguished plea. "I would not like him to learn of such a weakness in me!"

"He would not think it a weakness, madame. He loves you!"

"Yes, but I would not want his pity, you understand? We have always valued our pride." Her breath quivered. "Daubenay thinks that I am losing my reason—"

"Oh, no!"

"She has not voiced her opinion, but it is in her eyes . . ."

The cruel old bitch, thought Pandora. Aloud she said, "You are too much alone here, madame. It is not extraordinary that your mind wanders." She leaned forward impulsively. "Soon I shall be living quite close, and I promise that I will come up to visit you often. Perhaps we can even find a way to get you out into the garden during the summer weather."

"Ah!" The old lady's head moved tremulously, making the curls of her wig bounce. "You are a good child! I was not aware that Robert could show so much sense. I have told him many times that he needs a wife who will give him an heir, but when did a boy ever heed his elders?"

This picture of the Duke might have amused Pandora had she not been totally embarrassed by the misconstruction that the Comtesse was putting upon their relationship, without knowing how to tell her that she was quite out in her expectations.

Her moist eyes lifting briefly to the portrait, she continued. "He cannot grieve forever. You are not beautiful, but *tant pis* . . ." She gave a little shrug. "You have much goodness in your face . . . and a caring heart, and this is more important. As for that other one"—a touch of scorn here—"she wants only to advance herself!"

That other one? Could she mean Lady Sarah? With a jolt, Pandora realised that she had probably visited Clearwater more than once. The thought disturbed her more than it ought. The old lady was still rambling on, but her concentration was beginning to fade again.

"Louis loved me, you know . . . but he married the Austrian . . . and her foolishness led him to . . . led him to . . ." At this point her reason refused to accept the unacceptable truth and she wandered off into vague mutterings.

Pandora sat on quietly with the fragile papery hand enfolded in hers, its faint erratic pulse at odds with her own heart's thudding as she turned over the strange conversation in her mind.

Her eyes lifted involuntarily to the portrait. It must have been painted when Mariette was about seventeen; the artist had caught a hint of recklessness in the beautiful eyes—a certain willfulness about the full lower lip. But there was generosity, too, in her smile, and oh, she was lovely! Perhaps the violence in which she had been conceived had left its mark upon her character, yet it was small wonder that the Duke had loved her. Pandora's heart hollowed at the thought of him losing her in such a tragic way. But she had paid a bitter price, poor lady— and now Heron must watch her children grow up in his home.

"Pandora?" It was an urgent whisper.

She came to with a start, to find him bending over her—and was confused.

"Why are you crying?" he demanded tersely. "If this is Grandmère's doing . . ."

"No, indeed! I promise you it is not so! I was simply lost in thought—air dreaming, my father was used to call it." She was unable to move without disturbing the Comtesse, and so said a little defiantly, "We had a most interesting talk, your grandmother and I."

He was regarding her in a very odd way. His eyes moved to take in the two clasped hands and then came back to her face, given an almost childish vulnerability by the tears that spiked her lashes, a tremulous mouth, and those damned freckles. One tear rolled down her cheek, and he lifted a slim finger to wipe it away.

"So why the tears?" he murmured.

The door opened and Madame Daubenay came in. She took in the small tableau at a glance, the clasped hands, the unwarranted intimacy, and her mouth thinned.

"The children are outside, your grace," she said, her voice as thin as her mouth. "Do you wish them to enter . . . or be sent away?"

The Duke looked up, annoyed by the interruption. It was on his lips to dismiss them, when he caught Pandora's eye.

"The blue saloon," he said. "We will come in a few minutes."

"*Laissez donc!*" said the authoritative voice. The bright eyes were open, keen once more. The fingers stirred in Pandora's hand and released themselves. "Bring them in, Daubenay, bring them in!"

Heron's eyebrow lifted resignedly as a young nursemaid

136

entered carrying a baby in the curve of her arm and leading by the hand a very tiny boy with a mass of tight gold curls.

"This, Miss Carlyon, is Eduard de Choille and his sister, Yvette," said the Comtesse. "Make your bow, Eduard."

The boy, dressed in cream silk skirts and small clothes, could not have been above two years, but he bowed with the self-possession of a much older child, though his eyes slid a little nervously toward the Duke.

"Bonjour, Edward," said Pandora, crouching to put herself on a level with him and smiling at him encouragingly. The baby was not asleep. It lay gurgling quite happily in the nurse's arms, and she was obliged to stifle a sudden longing to reach out and take it from her.

"These are Mariette's children, Miss Carlyon. We spoke of Mariette, did we not?"

Pandora held her breath, but the eyes that met hers were clear and coherent.

"She would have been proud of them, don't you think?"

Pandora sighed, and smilingly agreed.

"How did you find Grandmère?" the Duke asked as they left the suite. "Madame Daubenay is worried about her."

"There is nothing wrong with your grandmother, my lord Duke, except old age . . . and loneliness." The sharpness of accusation in her voice brought her a searching stare. She met it pugnaciously. "Well, how would you like to be incarcerated in that . . . that exquisite prison, with only a sour-faced gorgon for company? I'm not surprised her mind wanders to happier times!"

"You are forthright as ever, Miss Carlyon," he drawled.

She walked a little quicker. "Well, you did ask me, sir," she insisted. "And I might as well confess while I am about it that I have given the Comtesse my word that when I am living down here . . . allowing that the cottage is within my means, that is," she added belatedly, "I shall visit her regularly!"

She did not say "so there!" but might well have done so. When her declaration met with silence, she stole a look at _him_ and found him pensive.

"I am sorry if you are not pleased," she said, feeling unaccountably deflated.

He looked up then, though she still found his expression hard to read. "My dear Miss Carlyon," he said. "If you would not find it a trouble, I shall be very much in your debt."

They found William returned from his foray into the covers, his freckled face glowing with animation and claiming to have "bagged" three rabbits.

"And Mr. Dawson said I might take them back with me for Mrs. Brearly. He said I had a keen eye and a right cool head on my shoulders!" he declared, and was returned to the rectory proudly bearing his spoils and with the happy prospect of rabbit pie to come.

The Duke then directed his coachman to a small group of cottages beyond the village, where his agent awaited them. There was one cottage set a little way apart from the rest—squat and comfortable-looking, with a tiny garden spilling over with colour at the front, and just visible to the rear a slightly larger patch with at least two fruit trees.

The front door admitted them straight into a sitting room sparsely but adequately furnished. A further room led off this, separating it from the kitchen. At the top of a staircase that creaked in several places were two reasonable bedchambers together with a cupboard-sized room which might just take a bed and a small chest.

Pandora, with a dreamy look in her eye, was already seeing it with new covers to the chairs and bright curtains at the windows and, if she could afford it, a few extra pieces of furniture. Anxiously she asked about the rent, and the agent, looking blandly at the Duke, quoted a sum that was well within her means. But she had not missed that look, and much as she wanted the cottage, she had to be sure.

"William said that you owned all the land for miles around, my lord Duke," she said, feeling her way with some trepidation. "So I expect that this cottage belongs to you. I hope . . . that is, I don't know anything about rents . . ." The Duke was ominously expressionless, and she began to flounder. "But I very much want . . . I wouldn't wish to be treated differently from anyone else!"

The agent made a choking sound which he quickly turned to a cough.

Heron, hardly able to stand upright against the low ceiling, and already irked by Pandora's enthusiasm for her surroundings, felt the old exasperation rising. Coming here as they had, directly upon leaving Clearwater, one might reasonably have expected her to draw unfavourable conclusions, but not a bit of it! Not content with babbling on about setting a polished table in the window and adorning it with a jug of flowers from the garden, she now had the temerity to accuse him of overgenerosity!

"Am I to infer, ma'am, that you actually find this insignificant hovel to your liking?" he demanded in his most dampening manner.

"Yes, of course," she answered readily. "It is exactly what I should like, only——"

"Then it is yours. To my mind the rent seems excessive, but I leave that sort of thing to Parker here. There remains only the question of someone to lend you respectability . . ." He glanced pointedly at the agent, who obliged him by stating that there was a pleasant body, the relict of the underkeeper, Briggs, who had, his grace might remember, suffered a fatal mishap not two months since. "She is staying with her sister at present, your grace, but she has expressed her willingness to fulfil any duties as might be required of her in return for a roof over her head . . . if Miss Carlyon is agreeable?"

"Well, it all seems very silly and unnecessary," said Pandora, not daring to protest further. "But if I must, then I am sure Mrs. Briggs will suit admirably."

11

It was June, and London was in the grip of celebration fever. The Czar Alexander and King Frederick of Prussia had arrived together with other dignitaries, and the crowds were treated to processions and illuminations, and innumerable state banquets were prepared for the distinguished guests. A gathering throng, of ladies in particular, lined Piccadilly at all hours, hoping for a glimpse of the handsome Emperor of Russia each time he moved from the Pulteney Hotel, where he had elected to stay with his sister, the Grand Duchess Catherine of Oldenburg.

"Prinny is beside himself!" Sir Henry told Mr. Chessington during one of the many balls being held to add to the festivities. "And I'm bound to say, though I seldom find myself in sympathy with our Regent these days, Alexander has treated him deuced shabbily, spurning the apartments prepared for him at St. James's, declining to attend the Carlton House banquet on his first night here—it don't auger well, Fitz!"

"It's the sister's doing, of course." Mr. Chessington lifted his quizzing glass to observe the gyrations of the waltzers circling the ballroom floor. "Y'know, Harry, I'm not at all sure that I approve this new craze. I mean, just take a look at young Thorley there—damn me if he ain't cuddling his partner!" He shuddered delicately and returned to his theme. "Lady Hertford vows that the Grand Duchess has primed her brother to plague Prinny with questions about his rift with the deplorable Caroline!"

"Vastly entertaining, though, ain't it?" Sir Henry grinned. "Even bluff King Frederick had 'em turning Clarence House upside down to find him a camp bed!

The state bed didn't please his Spartan soul! Heigh-ho. One's heart almost bleeds for our bedevilled Prince!"

Pandora was also entertained by the spectacle, but more genuinely so. She had deferred her remove to the country in order to enjoy it to the full, and when writing an account of it to William, she allowed her enthusiasm free rein: "The cows in Green Park are frightened by the constant 'Huzzas' and won't give milk and all the washer-women are up to their elbows in suds washing for kings and princes, and have no time for ordinary mortals! The most popular by far among the visitors is dear old General Blucher—he is treated as an Absolute Hero and is mobbed everywhere he goes! Yesterday I was watching as the crowd removed the horses from his carriage so that they could pull him about the streets themselves, when he noticed me and greeted me most warmly. He was clearly quite overwhelmed by his reception, but the old soldier in him was very evident as his eyes twinkled and he confessed with that rumbling laugh of his, 'But, ah, my dear Miss Pandora: What a city London would be to sack, heh?' Only consider—so like him! There are more and more soldiers among the crowds these days—some maimed, some just looking lost, poor things! Which reminds me, Will—I have seen Sergeant Blakewell again. He is looking much more the thing and is getting about quite nimbly on his crutches. . . ."

The sergeant had arrived on Lady Margerson's door-step one morning while her ladyship was still abed. He had regained much of his old jauntiness, the well-drilled air of order that had made him such a splendid soldier. Pandora took him into the small front saloon and per-suaded him to sit down, which he did, perching at attention on the very edge of one of the pink velvet chairs, plainly ill-at-ease amid so much elegance.

He had come, he said, to render her an account of the moneys she had left with him. "And much appreciated it was, if I may say so, Miss Pandora. There's been many a lad through London these past weeks as will bless your name forever."

"But that is nonsense," she said. "It was so very little!"

"Little is much, ma'am, when you have nothing to begin with. See, now, I have written it all down for you so that you may know where and how the money was spent."

"Oh, Josiah! Now you are being foolish," she exclaimed. "As if I needed to know."

"Alice insisted, and she was right, begging your pardon, Miss Pandora," he said with a brisk little nod. "I like to be all beforehand with things. That way everyone knows where they stand."

Pandora took the list that he pressed into her hand and glanced down it swiftly, seeing several names that she knew. "Goodness, what a lot! Are they still coming?"

"They've hardly begun to come yet, ma'am. Most have families awaiting their return, of course—they're the lucky ones." He sniffed. "It's the ones recruited from the gutters—they squander their arrears of pay in the nearest public house, and it's back into the gutter they go, with no one like my Alice to lift them out of the mops. Maimed or whole, it's all the same." The sergeant looked Pandora squarely in the eye. "Small recompense, wouldn't you say, for men—dross though they be—who've helped us to this fine victory we're all so busy celebrating?"

"It all seemed so different out there, didn't it?" she said. "A grand adventure."

"Oh, it was that, right enough, miss."

She sighed. "Why does life have to be so unfair, Josiah?"

"Well, now, Miss Pandora, I reckon a philosopher would tell you that it's all part of the Grand Design, and that we must trust the Good Lord to change things if and when he sees fit." The sergeant bent to pick up his crutch, fitted it under his oxter, and came nimbly erect. "Myself, I think we might have to give him a bit of a hand."

"Josiah!"

He gave her a wry grin. "Oh, I'm not plotting a revolution! My Alice wouldn't stand for that, for all that she gets mad as fire! But I've had a lot of time for thinking lately. You'd be surprised what notions you take into your head when there's nothing better to fix your mind to—

142

and what I say is, things'll have to change, and change sharpish, or it might well end in bloodshed . . . and we don't want to end up like the Frogs, do we?"

"No." Pandora fingered the list, trying hard to come to a decision. Josiah had made the money go a very long way, and it wasn't all used up yet. She looked round the pretty saloon and thought about the little table she had set her heart on for the cottage; it was, at this moment, reposing in the window of a shop tucked away behind Bond Street. She had finished the curtains and covers, and the table was to be her last extravagance. The money for it was in her reticule now, Josiah having caught her on the point of going out. But it *was* an extravagance.

The sergeant coughed, recalling her to the fact that he was waiting to take his leave. On an impulse she seized her reticule and took out the money.

"Put that with what you have left," she said before she could change her mind. "No, please—it will be the last I can give you. You see, I'm leaving town at the end of the week . . . to live in the country, so I would like it to be a kind of farewell gesture."

Lady Margerson was finding it hard to come to terms with Pandora's decision. Nor, it must be said, was her dismay solely on Pandora's account, for she had begun to find it a most agreeable luxury having the child to wait upon her every need. Pritchard was getting old and a trifle deaf—and anyway, Pandora was so willing! Of course, were she to become betrothed, one would put such considerations aside, but . . .

"Bury yourself in the country, my love," she wailed upon first hearing the news. "But why? Are you not happy here with me?"

"Dear ma'am, of course I am. You have been kindness itself."

"Well, then . . ."

"It was never my intention to impose myself on you forever."

This brought swift reassurance from her ladyship. It would not be forever. She was convinced of it. Why, she

143

could name any one of several young men who had begun to show a definite interest . . . oh, yes, Pandora might smile, but it *was* so. Sir Henry had called twice within the past week, and Mr. Chessington three times (though one could hold out little hope of *his* being considered in the light of a suitor!). But Mr. Navensby, now . . . ten thousand a year, someone had told her . . . and though she had never been quite clear as to the source of his income, he was a personable enough gentleman and could not be discounted. . . . Except that if Pandora insisted upon this idiotish venture . . . "Really, my love, I cannot imagine what Heron is thinking about to countenance your leaving Town at this time!"

"The Duke does not have the ordering of my life," Pandora maintained stoutly.

In fact, she was not clear quite how the Duke felt about her imminent departure, but could not suppose that he felt anything special. He behaved very well as he had always done, taking her driving in the park occasionally, though since she had once happened to mention that she would rather like to ride in the mornings, when it was quieter, he had provided a nicely behaved mare for her use and they were now more frequently to be seen, by anyone who chanced to be abroad at such an hour, cantering along the deserted walks before the dew was off the grass.

Putting on her blue riding habit for the first time in months gave Pandora a sense of freedom greater than she had known since she had come to London. It was cut on military lines and became her trim figure surprisingly well. It also filled her with nostalgia.

"I was used to wear a riding habit more often than conventional dresses," she said when Heron was pleased to compliment her upon the rather dashing black shako adorned with a red plume, which she wore set straight on her head, but tipped a little rakishly over her eyes. "It was by far the most practical mode of dress, in the circumstances."

"Well, you will be able to ride as often as you please at

Chedwell. My head groom will be delighted to have someone to help exercise the horses."

It seemed as though her new life was destined to fulfil all her most cherished dreams. And with only a few days to go, she began to pack up her belongings yet again, but this time in a spirit of happy expectation.

As a final treat she was to be taken to Covent Garden theatre, where a special gala entertainment was being performed in honour of the city's most illustrious visitors. It was to be an evening she would never forget. A glittering assembly was already filling the auditorium to overflowing by the time they arrived, and the Duke of Heron's box was no less crowded. His guests included friends known to Pandora—and some with whom she was only slightly familiar.

Lady Margerson, who had been prey to severe misgivings that it would be a sad crush, had in the end overcome her scruples; partly because Pandora had begged her to and partly out of a natural curiosity to know who was to be there, she had armed herself with an enormous fan, donned her finery, and set forth, determined to enjoy herself. The fan proved invaluable, not only to herself but also to those about her, the heat being all but overwhelming. People would be fainting all over the place, she predicted, complacently wafting the air.

The programme in its entirety was prodigious, including no less than four separate spectacles; an Allegorical Festival was to be followed by the highly acclaimed Historical Romance (revived for the sixth time, with new scenes, music, dresses, *and* decorations) of Richard Coeur de Lion, during the third act of which there was to be included a *grand pas de deux* by Monsieur Soissons and Mrs. Parker, and a *pas de trois*. Who could want more? But more there was.

Before ever the entertainment got under way, however, the audience were to be treated to a spectacle of a different kind, no less magnificent but infinitely more provocative. The curtain had been drawn up, "God Save the King" had been sung with great enthusiasm by the

Regent, the Czar, and a large proportion of the audience, and the sovereigns had just seated themselves after a chorus of acclamations, when fresh applause broke out.

"What is happening?" demanded Lady Margerson, who was so firmly wedged in her seat that any movement was rendered well nigh impossible.

"Can't see a deuced thing, ma'am," said Mr. Chessington at her side, with a lack of interest which she found astonishing. He had come, as had her ladyship, at Pandora's behest, though in general he found the theatre a dead bore and theatre audiences frequently indiscriminate in their applause.

The Duke felt much the same, but as host he felt it incumbent upon himself to satisfy her ladyship's curiosity. He therefore rose and leaned forward. They heard him say "Good God!" and chuckle softly to himself as he turned back to his guests, who were by now agog, including Pandora, who had seen what was happening, but did not understand its significance.

"Caroline, our beloved Princess of Wales, has just walked into her box," Heron announced whimsically. "She is wearing a black wig, a positive shower of diamonds, and is at this moment graciously accepting the plaudits of the audience, the deepest obeisances of the Czar, and a less-than-loving acknowledgement from her husband!"

Sir Henry guffawed. "The deuce! Well, you have to give her full marks for sheer effrontery!"

Pandora craned her head over the side to get a better view of Princess Caroline, but the excitement was over, everyone was sitting down again, and there was only a shimmer of diamonds. She didn't mind. For her, it was all part of the magical quality of the evening. From the moment the entertainment began, she was totally engrossed.

Heron, who had arranged the visit solely for Pandora's pleasure, paid little attention to what was happening on stage. He sat aside in the corner, with one arm resting carelessly along the padded rail, watching the rapt face, the slim, still figure unaffected by all the restless posturing that went on around her, her simple dress uncluttered by the feathers and spangles, the frills and furbelows, or the glitter of jewels so necessary to her supposedly more fortunate brethren.

He had never seriously questioned why he so continually put himself out for Pandora and her brother, for to question would bring him perilously close to forcing an admission that he had no wish to make. Even now, as his blood quickened, he shied away from the trap of too-coherent thought. He liked his life exactly the way it was—without encumbrances.

During the first interlude he was at his most urbane, employing his quizzing glass to survey the scene. In the next box, Lord and Lady Sefton's party were enjoying themselves. A statuesque beauty with the face of an angel caught his eye.

"Miss Arabella Fairlie," supplied a humorous voice at his side.

"Thank you, Harry."

Sir Henry grinned. "Think nothing of it, dear old fellow. Happy to oblige. Miss Fairlie is a connection of Lady Sefton's, only lately come to town. Ten thousand a year and on the catch for a husband, or so I am reliably informed."

At that moment, the young lady in question laughed— an unexpectedly grating sound. Heron sighed.

"I think not," he said, with just a hint of regret.

"Poor Miss Fairlie—to be so summarily dismissed," said Mr. Chessington, strolling toward the door in search of friends.

"Still, it does leave the field clear for the rest of us, eh, Miss Carlyon?" Sir Henry sounded vaguely envious. "Y'know, you're a dashed lucky fellow, Robert, you have but to crook your little finger and women flock to surrender themselves!"

Pandora turned away from the laughter, spreading her arms along the velvet rail, hands joined, her chin resting pensively on her fingertips. She didn't like it when they talked like that! Especially she didn't like the Duke being so . . . What was the word she wanted? Flippant? Superficial. That was it. As though he didn't really care for anything or anyone.

Below her heaved a sea of splintered light. She blinked, and the scene resolved itself into people once more. Her eye was suddenly caught by an elaborately coiffured head, its gilded perfection vaguely familiar.

"Oh, Gemini!" she exclaimed.

At once the Duke came to stand beside her, his hand on the back of her chair—and it was at that precise moment that Octavia looked up and saw the two heads close together. Her eyes widened in disbelief, grew first thunderous, then speculative—and finally, the visible struggle with her emotions completed, she managed an ingratiating smile, fingers tightening on Frederick's arm, a whispered word . . .

Pandora succumbed to a most unworthy urge—and inclined her head graciously. She saw Octavia's lips tighten angrily, and immediately felt much better.

"Most impressive," murmured the Duke in her ear. "I had no idea you harboured such vengeful notions!"

"I don't!" she cried, knowing that she lied. But she had lost his attention, for when she turned to look up at him, his gaze had already wandered to the box opposite, where Lady Sarah Bingly was laughingly surrounded by a bevy of young men. Pandora had never seen her look more lovely, though her shimmering gold dress was so revealing as to make one blush for her.

As though aware of Heron's interest, Lady Sarah lifted her jewel-bright eyes in provocative challenge. It was hard to tell whether it had the desired effect. There had been a coolness between them of late—since the musical evening, in fact—and the Duke's face never gave anything away. His bow now was no more than polite, but it would surely be difficult to resist such an open invitation! A little of the magic went out of Pandora's evening.

Her spirits were somewhat restored, however, by the Historical Romance, which was everything it had promised, and the *pas de deux* and *pas de trois* most tastefully performed. It was such a pity Mr. Chessington had missed it, she declared, rousing Lady Margerson from the comfortable doze into which she had fallen. Her lady-ship hastily agreed, and wafted her fan with renewed vigour.

During the second interlude an exceedingly jovial elder-ly gentleman came to their box and was greeted by Lady Margerson with cries of delighted surprise, and introduced all round. He wore an unfashionable velvet coat, and beneath it a handsome brocade waistcoat spattered with snuff stains.

"Such a fortunate coincidence, my love!" she exclaimed to Pandora, whose attention had been momentarily di-verted by the vanishing figure of the Duke, who had just been handed a note. "Lord Russet was your Grandfather Wyndham's most particular friend! Lud, Alastair, what times we had!" She sighed. "And what a long time ago it all was!" This reflection seemed to send her off into wistful contemplation.

With a smile, Lord Russet handed Pandora to her chair and indicated the Duke's vacant one. "May I?"

"Oh, yes—please do, my lord." Involuntarily Pandora glanced up, and was just in time to see Heron entering Lady Sarah's box, bowing over the hand she extended to him with such an air of certainty.

"Well, well, this is very pleasant, by George," his lord-ship was saying affably. "Small world, what? Not that I'd ever have guessed you were out of Vernon's stable—a regular out-and-out goer he was! We ran some pretty rum rigs in our salad days, I can tell you!" He seemed to recollect to whom he was speaking, *harrumped* a little, and begged her pardon.

But Pandora dragged her attention from the box op-posite and begged to know more about this somewhat disreputable ancestor of hers, and the old gentleman was soon carried away again.

"Abandoned most of his rackety ways when he met your grandmama, God rest her—now, you *do* have a look of her, bless me if you don't! A positive angel, little Lucy was . . . never a word of censure passed her lips, though she must have known about his little weakness . . ."

"His . . . weakness?"

"Faro, m'dear," murmured his lordship. "Couldn't keep away from the tables . . . played all night, many a time. I mind once . . ." At this point he took out a little enamelled snuffbox and went through the ritual of inhaling, spilling some in the process, and flapping ineffectually at it with his handkerchief while Pandora waited impatiently. "Vernon had a disastrous run of luck at White's . . . dropped fifteen thousand pounds in one night . . . a sensible man would have cried quits . . . contemplated suicide, even! But Vernon"—a deep throaty chuckle shook the brocade waistcoat—"took back to Rundell and Bridge's a diamond trinket he'd had made for Lucy on their wedding, got them to make him a replica, then pledged the original . . . won back most of what he'd lost . . ."

Pandora felt the faintest of cold shivers run down her back. "What . . . kind of a trinket was it, do you know, sir?"

"Deuced pretty thing . . . a necklace with some sort of flower petals strung out . . . very delicate workmanship."

"And what happened to the original, do you know?"

"Ah, now, there you have me, m'dear. All I do know is that, to my knowledge, Vernon never redeemed it. Made no bones about it. Well, as he said, it was a splendid copy—fool anyone but an expert, and Lucy was none the wiser, so why waste good gambling money!" Lord Russet seemed to feel that this comment might do less than justice to his old friend in this child's eyes. "Make no mistake," he assured her, leaning forward to pat her hand. "He was a fine man, your grandpapa—best in the world. Nerves of steel in a tight corner—passed some of that on to you, I'm told. Thought the world of your grandmama! And now . . ." He glanced with some relief toward the door. "His grace will be wanting his chair back . . ."

He came to his feet with the aid of a gold crutch cane, and bowed over her hand. "Been a great pleasure, m'dear. Perhaps we'll meet again, eh, what?" He glanced toward Lady Margerson's recumbent figure. "Tell you what, won't disturb Tilly . . . give her my regards."

He harrumped in his throat again and tottered away, stopping at the door to exchange a word with the Duke and never noticing the peculiarly blank look in the eyes of the girl he had just left behind.

It took Pandora several moments to collect her thoughts, but soon she was firmly reproaching herself for leaping to wild conclusions over what could most kindly be described as the wandering and probably inaccurate reminiscences of a very elderly gentleman. After all, she reasoned, if Grandmama Wyndham's necklace had been a fake, Mr. Bridge would have recognised it as such immediately, even if the Duke, upon what had been no more than a cursory glance, had not.

She determined to put the matter from her mind, and with the help of the entertainment and the excellent supper party at Grillon's which followed, she succeeded admirably. Also she was very much moved by the many quite genuine expressions of regret that she was leaving town.

"Only to be expected, m'dear, when you think about it," Fitz Chessington reasoned in his gentle fashion when she confessed her surprise to him. "Only got to take a look at us—under all the posturing, our lives are sadly jaded. Along comes a delightfully unspoiled creature with her clear-eyed view of life . . . laughs at our follies . . . don't simper or dissemble . . . deuced refreshing, don't you see?"

"You are very kind, sir . . ."

"Not kind at all, m'dear . . . simple truth. Never could turn a pretty compliment." Clearly embarrassed, Mr. Chessington changed the subject. "Robert taking you to Chedwell, is he?"

"Yes," Pandora said with a troubled smile. "I did suggest to his grace that I could perfectly well take the stage, but he looked down his nose at me—the way he does, you know, when he is on his high ropes."

"Devilish top-lofty?" he ventured at his most droll.

"Devilish!" she agreed with a grin.

It was not until the evening was over and she sat alone

in her bedchamber surrounded by half-filled bandboxes—chairs piled with items carefully selected for the cottage—that Pandora was forced to pay heed to her troublesome conscience.

Suppose that Lord Russet's story had been the simple truth? He had described the necklace with disturbing accuracy . . . why should he be any less clear about its ultimate fate?

"A splendid copy." She could hear his voice now. *"Fool anyone but an expert."*

Well, Mr. Bridge was an expert—but an expert perhaps who, when he discovered the truth, was loath to risk losing the patronage of a valued client by suggesting that the client's friends were something less than honest.

Forget it, she told herself recklessly, with one eye still on the bandboxes. You sold the necklace in good faith . . .

And were paid far more for it than you expected, said the unrelenting voice of her conscience. Infinitely more than you now know it was worth.

She undressed like a child, by rote; washed herself, brushed out her hair and, hunched against the counterpane on her knees, hurried through her prayers with an irrepressible sensation of guilt. Finally she blew out the candle and climbed into bed.

For a long time she lay on her back staring at the vague shadows formed on the ceiling by the gracefully dipping larch fronds outside her window, fighting the truth. Torturing herself by reliving her plans, she walked in her thoughts through each room in the cottage, seeing the boys there, while the tears rolled unheeded from the corners of her eyes and soaked into her hair.

Long before the ceiling lightened and the shadows faded, she knew what she must do.

12

The Duke of Heron was in the Yellow Saloon, toying with his third glass of Madeira and contemplating a stroll to White's with something less than enthusiasm, when Ambrose Varley came to inform him that he had a visitor.

"Not now," he said abruptly. "I am in no humour for making polite conversation."

"As your grace pleases." Mr. Varley hesitated, then added casually, "The young lady did say that it was a matter of extreme urgency and that she would very much appreciate it if you could see your way clear—"

"Miss Carlyon," said Heron, recognising the turn of phrase. "Why did you not say so in the first place? Where is she?"

To the casual onlooker the Duke's reaction must have appeared unremarkable, but Mr. Varley was observing him closely and noted with interest how his fingers holding the glass tensed, a sharpening in his voice. Having just met the young lady for the first time, he was even more intrigued. Not his grace's usual style at all.

"I believe Pinkerton has shown Miss Carlyon into the library, sir."

Heron was out of the room almost before his secretary had finished speaking, his step impatient.

The footman opened the library doors and closed them again silently behind him. Pandora was standing looking out of the window, though from the rigidity of her stance he doubted whether she saw anything. She had removed her bonnet and was twisting the ribbons between her fingers. She started nervously as he came in, swinging round to face him with something between relief and desperation.

"Pandora? Is something wrong?"

She stood, deprived of speech, not knowing quite how to begin.

Heron crossed the room swiftly, removed the mangled bonnet from her unresisting fingers, and took both her hands in his, noting how they trembled very slightly.

"What is it?" he demanded. "William? Has something happened to William . . . or Courtney?"

"Oh, no!" she said quickly. "Forgive me. I am behaving very stupidly."

"Not at all."

He led her to a chair and sat her down. The door opened again to admit Pinkerton, a young footman at his heels bearing a tray.

"I took the liberty, your grace," he said quietly. "There is some ratafia for the young lady, or some cordial if she would prefer it."

"Thank you, Pinkerton."

Heron's hand hovered over the decanters, and then, with the faintest of shrugs, he poured a glass of cordial.

"Oh, thank you," Pandora said, and drank gratefully.

Having provided himself with a drink, he drew a chair forward and sat, not too close, apparently at ease while observing her thoughtfully over the rim of his glass. Her eyes were shadowed and faintly red-rimmed, as though she had not slept. And the freckles were very prominent against her pallor.

At last she looked up.

"I am very much afraid," she said, "that I cannot after all t-take the cottage." The words were out, and she gave a little sigh, as though relieved of a too-heavy burden.

If she had expected him to show surprise, she was disappointed. He said merely, "Would you care to tell me why?"

"It's . . . a little complicated, but I will try."

She set her glass down on a nearby table and proceeded to treat her gloves very much as she had her bonnet ribbons. Her voice, halting at first, grew in confidence as she related the gist of her conversation with Lord Russet on the previous evening.

"I fear that the story is true, sir. His lordship described the necklace rather too well to allow of much room for doubt. And so, you see"—she spoke in a low voice, without quite meeting his eyes—"I have come by a great deal of money to which I am not entitled."

"Are you not rather underrating Mr. Bridge?" drawled the Duke. "I can assure you that his knowledge of stones is quite prodigious."

Pandora could remain still no longer. It was like being pinned down to a board—a specimen for close examination. And she had long since learned that the Duke's drawl was at its most pronounced when he was becoming annoyed. But as she stood up, he rose also—and that was even worse, for now he stared down his nose at her in a very unnerving inquisitorial way. She linked her fingers, stiff-armed, and blinked down at their backs.

"Well, I have thought about that, too," she continued doggedly. "And . . . and I suspect that he knew it for a sham when he bought it, or at any rate very soon afterward . . ."

"And took no action?"

Without looking up, she knew that his lip curled.

"No. Because I can quite see that it would be very difficult for him to . . . expose the fraud. He could not know how slight your connection with us was . . . and he risked incurring your displeasure . . . might perhaps lose your patronage."

He uttered a sharp bark of laughter. "Egad! You've a devilish queer notion of business!"

Pandora flushed. "I believe I am right, nonetheless."

He made an impatient gesture and took to prowling about the room, straightening the already immaculately regimented rows of books, and when he spoke at last, it was as though he held his temper on a tight leash.

"Why have you come to me?"

Pandora opened her mouth to reply—and closed it again.

Because turning to you has become as natural to me as

breathing! She wanted to shout the words aloud. Because you are the pivot of my life, my friend and confidant, my strength—and if you were not there, I should be a rootless plant doomed to wither away!

Would he smile or simply look uncomfortable if he could read her teeming thoughts? For she had only to remember last night, and the ease with which Lady Sarah had drawn him to her side in spite of the coolness between them of late, to know that she could never hope to figure in his affections in *that* way.

She said in a stifled voice, "I hoped that you would tell me what to do."

"Do?"

"About setting matters right with Rundell and Bridge as soon as possible. The difficulty is, I have spent rather more than I had intended . . . almost half of the principal, in fact. There was Courtney, you see, and the cottage, and then, I did give a little to Sergeant Blakewell . . . oh, only a little," she added hastily as his head came up, "f-for the soldiers coming home. Mr. Lewis was to invest the remainder for me, but"—she was rushing to finish before her courage ran out—"I wondered . . . do you think it would be in order for me to send what there is to Mr. Bridge with my deepest apologies and a promise to—"

"No, I do not!" Heron cut ruthlessly across her fine reasoning. "It's past and done with. Forget it!"

"But . . . that would be dishonest!" Shock made Pandora appear unwittingly censorious. "I feel quite badly enough as it is, but at least until now I have acted in ignorance. If I keep what is left, knowing it to have been acquired by fraudulent means, I should be plagued by the most dreadful feelings of guilt!"

"Oh, good God in heaven defend me from a pious conscience!"

Flicked on the raw by her implication that he was lacking in scruples, Heron flung the words at her with a suppressed savagery that made her blink. The intricate pattern on the circular carpet swirled before her eyes.

"If that is how you feel, then I am s-sorry. It was

wrong of me to trouble you." She choked on the words, turned away, stumbling toward the door.

"Pandora!"

She shut her ears to the peremptory note in his voice and had almost reached the door when he strode across the room and seized her arm, swinging her round, holding her against all her struggles.

"Let me go!"

"Not until we have talked," he said inexorably. Then, with less force: "Oh, be still, you absurd girl!" He felt a slackening in her resistance to him and concluded with something of his old mockery, "Perhaps . . . if I apologise?"

Pandora looked up at him suspiciously, but his face was a blur.

"I am *not* pious!" she gulped indignantly through her tears.

"Of course you are not," he agreed gravely. "It was *odiously ungracious* in me to imply that you were. But I have apologised, you know—and I really don't know what more I can add. Perhaps we should blame this room. We came to cuffs here once before, if you remember."

She gave a short hiccuping laugh. "Now *you* are being absurd, sir!"

He produced a fine cambric handkerchief and proceeded to dry her tear-streaked face with great care. A small sniff escaped her, and he obligingly offered her the handkerchief and bade her make use of it, which she did to such good effect that she was presently staring at the crumpled remains in some embarrassment. He told her to keep it, though he hoped she would have no further cause to use it on his account.

"It seems we have both come down from the boughs, at any rate, and before we become embroiled once more in matters of high finance, there is something I must set right."

He turned away from her abruptly and walked to his desk.

"I daresay that I, too, should apologise," she acknowledged a little shyly. "You know how my tongue runs away with me, and I had not fully considered that . . . being born into first circles, you will never have suffered the mortification of being without funds, and therefore cannot . . . Oh, Gemini!"

The Duke had just opened a drawer and was lifting onto the desktop a slightly shabby but indisputably familiar jewel case. As she drew nearer, staring first at it and then at Heron in disbelief, he indicated that she should open it. The necklace lay on its velvet bed, winking up at her as though defying her to denounce it as a sham.

"You have had it all this time? But how . . . why?"

"My own knowledge of stones is also fairly prodigious," he said dryly.

"So you knew . . . immediately?" Pandora was sufficiently impressed to forget, momentarily, the wider implications. "Well, I do think that was very clever of you, for it seemed to me that you only glanced at it for a moment. I suppose Mr. Bridge knew that you knew—and assumed from what you said that you wished him to proceed as though the necklace was what it purported to be?"

"Something like that," the Duke agreed.

Pandora's brow puckered. "But . . ."

"Why the quixotic gesture?" he finished for her.

She nodded.

"Can one explain such things rationally? Suffice it to say that I came upon you both at a propitious moment— your brother afire with the eager expectation of acquiring a handsome set of regimentals, and you, my dear Miss Carlyon, like a mother hen with your feathers all set on end by that bumptious young assistant, determined that he should not be disappointed." His mouth quirked at the memory. "How could I possibly stand aside and see you vanquished?"

Her grey eyes widened to their fullest extent. "Then your astonishing generosity really was prompted by the whim of the moment?"

"Does it seem astonishing to you?" He shrugged.

"Well, perhaps you are right. But, then, I had not expected that you would ever need to know."

His revelation rendered Pandora almost speechless; that anyone could be so well-breeched as to make such a gesture possible was quite outside her comprehension; that the Duke *was*, and had exercised his beneficence on her behalf, completely overwhelmed her. It also meant, and the thought struck her with a jolt, that it was to him she was now indebted. She said as much, haltingly, and was swiftly disabused.

"You owe me nothing, since I purchased the necklace knowing it to be worthless."

"But I can't take so much from you! It wouldn't be right!"

"Humbug!" he said.

She stood before him wearing her most stubborn face and looking about sixteen in her muslin dress with its tiny sprigs of roses scattered across a pale grey background. She had obviously braided her hair in haste, for in places it was already escaping its pins.

The solution was simple, of course—if she did not laugh in his face! It was, he freely admitted, a laughable proposition. He had never been quite clear how she saw him—as something between an older brother and a confirmed roué mayhap!

She would certainly never look at him as she had looked at her golden-haired young artilleryman, but then, she had nothing to hope for from that quarter. Whether she knew it or not, the gallant Captain was not for her, and it would be a pity were she to dwindle into spinsterhood waiting to minister to her brothers, who would, he suspected, be dedicated first and foremost to their own respective passions. Worse, she might marry some insignificant little Cit who would stifle her impulsive, independent spirit and have little idea of how to cope with William.

"I think," he said almost casually, "that you had better marry me. I can then look after you and William properly."

Yet again Pandora was deprived of speech. The singing

in her blood made her feel slightly dizzy, and robbed her of breath. Wild colour flooded her cheeks and faded again.

"The idea does not appeal to you?" His voice sounded harsh. "There is someone else, perhaps?"

She struggled to take herself in hand. "No . . . that would be absurd. Who could there possibly be?"

"I have no idea," he said casually. "Your Captain Greville, perhaps?"

"Oh, no!" She could feel herself turning scarlet, for had she not once had just such a dream? In consequence her laugh was self-conscious. "Gracious! Hugo could never be persuaded to see me in *that* way! His taste runs to ladies of more voluptuous charms, as . . ." She had almost said "as I thought yours did," but stopped herself in time. "I am just Hugo's little sister," she finished lamely, and did not notice the curious look he gave her.

"Well then?" he pressed her to answer.

"I . . . you cannot be serious!"

"Why not?" His eyes were very close, intense, awaiting an answer.

"Oh . . . for any number of reasons."

"Name some," he demanded.

Pandora sought frantically. "You have frequently insisted that you had no wish to marry."

"I've changed my mind."

"Well, then, there are others more fitted for . . . I'm not . . . You can't seriously want me for your Duchess!"

"You think not?" A faint smile lit his eyes. "I could do a lot worse, believe me."

Pandora wanted to say: You don't love me. But her courage failed her.

"Try thinking of some advantages," he suggested dryly. "I can offer you a choice of several houses—all excellently appointed—in which to live, as many dresses and the like as the most extravagant young lady could wish for, the very best of educations for William . . . you would even be able to help your beloved soldiers more positively—"

"Stop, oh, please stop, my lord Duke!" She pulled

away, angry that just for a moment she had allowed herself to be seduced by beguiling vistas. "How could you think I might be tempted by mercenary considerations!"

He pulled her back, laughing. "Silly! I was merely bamming, as you and William are wont to say."

"That's another reason, don't you see? Duchesses don't say things like 'bamming.' "

"Mine will." After a moment's deliberation he removed the pins from her hair and watched it spill around her face, straight and shining. He threaded his fingers into its silkiness, cupping the narrow sensitive face in his hands. "She will be impetuous, entirely lacking in pretension, and delightfully unconventional—and everyone will envy me!"

Pandora held her breath, unsure how to respond to this unexpected tenderness, which set every fibre in her trembling with new and inexplicable sensations.

"You really *are* serious!"

"Of course."

His lips touched hers briefly—too briefly; then he released her. She felt deprived, cheated—and that in turn made her angry.

"You haven't said why you wish to marry me, my lord Duke," she accused him. "And I haven't yet agreed."

Her truculence lent the situation a diverting piquancy, made the more amusing in Heron's eyes by her complete unconcern that mere contentiousness might lose her the most vainly sought prize on the Marriage Mart.

"No more you have," he said agreeably. "Do you mean to reject me, then?"

"I . . . fear that I should, because the advantages all seem to be on my side, and I don't really see what you will gain from such a marriage." She sighed in a troubled way. "But I don't think I have the strength of mind to say no."

She was so preoccupied that she didn't notice the slight tightening of his mouth. He continued to regard her for a moment in silence, then turned away to ring the bell.

"So we are agreed," he said. "My secretary can begin making the arrangements."

From that moment, Pandora's life began to assume an air of unreality. She wasn't sure what she had expected, but in the event, very little changed. The Duke continued to treat her very much as he had always done, though in those first days she had the feeling that she had somehow annoyed him. But when she asked, he told her not to be a goose.

It came as a relief to learn that their betrothal was not to be announced. The prospect of being obliged to face the *grandes dames* of society, of becoming the cynosure of all eyes, had filled her with apprehension.

"If you are agreeable," said the Duke, "I feel you should remove to Chedwell as planned. I would, however, prefer that you go straight to Clearwater, not to the cottage . . ." He saw the disappointment in her face. "Yes, I know, but it would be pointless to move in, only to be obliged to move out again in a matter of days. We will let Mrs. Briggs have the cottage."

"Are we . . . is it then to be so soon?" Pandora wished her heart would not leap at the prospect. She had schooled herself, or so she had thought, to accept the limitations of their relationship. If she had harboured any lingering hopes, his absorption with practicalities must have served to quell them. So many decisions, and all of them taken for her.

There was no virtue, he said, in delay. "We can be married quietly at Chedwell, thus avoiding the considerable ordeal of a London wedding at the height of the Season." When she did not at once agree, he looked at her with a frown. "You don't hanker after a grand society wedding?"

She was quick to reassure him, and thought that she detected a glimmer of relief. Well, she was hardly the stuff that society brides were made of, after all. Small wonder if he did not wish to show her off. It was a pity about the cottage, but she could see the sense in his argument. She had been less happy, however, about keeping the news from Lady Margerson.

"It does seem the shabbiest of tricks after all her plans

for me," she sighed, while acknowledging her ladyship's chronic inability to keep a secret.

"It won't be for long." The Duke was firm. "I promise she'll be at your wedding. I propose to invite her to Clearwater some days before, on the pretext of seeing you settled." As an afterthought he said, "Is there anyone else you wish to invite?"

She assured him that there was not. "Certainly not Octavia!"

He smiled at her vehemence. "No young ladies to attend you? I confess I have never seen you with anyone special."

"The only ones I know are the daughters of Lady Margerson's friends, but their conversation is all of balls, and what they are to wear, and the latest young man upon whom their fancy has lighted." She threw him a guilty grin. "I find them dreadfully tedious sometimes. Perhaps I am more used to men. I like you and Mr. Chessington and Sir Harry very much better."

The Duke looked quizzical. "Poor little Pandora! When you are a married lady, I shall seek to introduce you to some rather more stimulating female company."

Pandora wasn't at all sure she wanted stimulating female company, but she kept the thought to herself.

13

The wedding of the Duke of Heron to Miss Pandora Carlyon was celebrated on a perfect day in late June in the parish church of Chedwell, with no fanfares, the only crowd being an enthusiastic group of well-wishers from the Duke's estate, for although Pandora had been there for less than three weeks, she had already made a favourable impression upon the local people, especially the estate workers and their families, who were fast growing used to seeing her riding among them and whose names she unfailingly remembered, so that they soon came to overlook the fact that she was not quite what they had expected.

The bride's half-dress of cream silk edged with lace and fastened with pearl rosettes (bought dagger-cheap at a little shop in the Pantheon Bazaar before she left town) was worn over an underdress of peach-bloom satin. To complement it she had spent rather more than she had intended upon a stylish bonnet of cream chip-straw, shallow-brimmed and very high in the crown, trimmed with peach-bloom ribbons, which moved a jubilant William to remark in considerable awe: "I say, Dora, you look as fine as fivepence! I'd no idea you could look so pretty!"

The dress had inadvertently caused Pandora's only outright clash with her betrothed, who, upon learning that his bride was contemplating making her own wedding gown, had been more than a little incensed. It was, he said forcefully, absurd and quite unnecessary, when she might go to Madame Fanchon, or whoever she wished, and order as many clothes as she pleased. "It is very well to be unconventional, but duchesses, my dear child, most assuredly do not make their own dresses!"

But Pandora, who had acquiesced so willingly to all the plans made on her behalf, had proved immovable on this point. When she was a duchess, she told him stubbornly, she would strive to please him in all things, "but I do so want to make this particular dress! And I promise that I will not disgrace you."

Short of ordering her to obey him (a course which he wisely eschewed), there was little more he could do, though for all of an hour afterward he wore his most inflexible look, which made her wonder if the victory had been worthwhile.

But when the day dawned and Heron arrived at the church, at his most elegant in a morning coat of dove-grey superfine, so that even Mr. Chessington could not outshine him, he could find no fault with Pandora's appearance—quite otherwise, in fact. He had never seen her look so well, if a little pale.

Lady Margerson, who considered pallor in a bride to be an essential requisite, thought that her protégée looked almost beautiful, though she could have wished for more flounces and much more lace—and bridesmaids. She sighed heavily over Heron's wishing to celebrate his nuptials in this hole-and-corner fashion.

"Such a highly respectable marriage, my love!" she had murmured through her tears, having recovered from the initial shock of arriving at Clearwater to find Pandora on the verge of matrimony. "Far away and above anything I could have hoped for, though I am sure I shall never forgive you for being such a sly-puss as to keep it from me!"

But though she could have wished for more people in the church to honour so solemn an occasion—in her opinion, a mere eight people including the bride and groom *and* the priest could be considered little short of niggardly!—she had to own the ceremony itself to be most moving. Supported by Mr. Varley, she wept silently and copiously throughout, no more so than when Heron took Pandora's hand in his.

Fitz performed his part with careless grace and kept his thoughts to himself, as he had done when Heron first confided the news to him with the wry observation that he was like to be accused of cradle-snatching. Fitz wondered a little, but only said in his droll way: "Never knew you to give a toss for what anyone said of you, dear old fellow. If the little lady is content, I don't see you beginning now."

But watching Pandora when they returned to Clearwater for the wedding breakfast, Fitz thought her composure to be a little more on the fragile side than was usual; on at least one occasion when she believed herself to be unobserved, her hands crept up to her cheeks in a gesture which he might well have attributed to an excess of maidenly nerves, had he not also seen the expression in her eyes when they rested for a moment on Robert. It was the despairing look of someone yearning for that which is beyond her reach. Just for a moment he surprised in himself a strong surge of anger against Robert.

Pandora was in fact finding the occasion something of an ordeal, yet she could not wish for the day to end, knowing that she would then be alone with the Duke.

If only dear Lady Margerson would not keep throwing out arch hints about love nests. Her ladyship had partaken rather too liberally of the champagne and was by now inclined to be sportive. The final embarrassment came when she began to quiz her about the honeymoon.

"I'll wager Robert is to take you somewhere very special?"

"Oh! I . . . that is . . ." Pandora's glance flew to Heron, as a palpable silence ensued.

"We have not settled anything as yet," he said smoothly. "We thought to stay at Clearwater for a while and decide where to go at our leisure."

William, who had been debating with himself his chances of attempting what remained of the syllabub, looked up with sudden interest.

"Are you going away?" he asked. "Oh, good. If it's somewhere interesting, can I come too?"

"Incorrigible boy!" Lady Margerson's ample form

shook. "As if Robert would want you along to spoil sport!"

The syllabub momentarily forgotten, the boy looked from one to the other. "Sport? Is it to be a sporting holiday, then? I don't think my sister will enjoy *that* very much, will you, Dora?"

His sister could feel the tide of colour flooding her face. She hardly knew where to look, until, inadvertently catching the Duke's eyes, she found amusement lurking in their depths, and the tension was dissolved in laughter.

More mystified than ever, William turned to Mr. Chessington, who smiled gently at him.

" 'Tis nothing to fret over, dear boy. Just grown-ups behaving foolishly. We frequently do, you know."

William gave up in disgust and returned to the far more interesting pastime of investigating the contents of the dishes on the side table.

"I'm sorry that you should have been embarrassed," said Heron when he later walked with her to the suite in the West Wing, whence her belongings had been taken that morning from the guest bedchamber she had occupied since her arrival.

"It d-doesn't matter," she said, striving for a light air. The housekeeper had already made her familiar with the wing: "This is his grace's room, ma'am," she had said, leaving Pandora with an impression of rich velvet hangings and much dark woodwork. "And next to it a dressing room, and this will be your bedchamber, ma'am . . ."

They stopped now at the door, and Heron opened it, standing aside to let her enter. It was a beautiful, gracious room and looked the more so in the soft lamplight. The young maidservant who had been appointed to look after her turned from her tasks to bob a curtsy, saw that her mistress was not alone, and in a shy soft voice murmured something about forgotten towels and slipped from the room.

Pandora smiled nervously, averted her eyes from the bed, and crossed to the dressing table, aware that he followed her. She rearranged several of the little porcelain

167

ornaments and dabbled her fingers in an open dish filled with potpourri.

"I wondered why the house smelled so fresh and sweet when I first came, but I see these are everywhere."

"Grandmère brought the recipe with her from France. You had better ask her for it, since you get on so well together."

They were making conversation, thought Pandora in a panic. He would think her terribly gauche. The mirror against the wall showed their faces very close, his a little above hers, shadowed like strangers.

"There is so much to learn," she said jerkily. "I hope I may not disgrace you, sir."

Heron turned her to face him. "You could never do that, my dear." He cupped her chin in his hand, smiling down into her eyes. "But you will have to stop *sirring* me, you know—and there must be no more *my lord Duke*, either. My name is Robert."

"Yes. I will try to remember." Her answering smile was fleeting, her voice reduced to a whisper by the beating of her heart right up in her throat. There was a wholly unstudied, pliant look about her as she swayed toward him that took him off guard.

He kissed her softly parted lips, and they clung to his with a sweet innocence such as he had not known in a very long time. Desire stirred in him and he caught her close, his mouth growing more demanding. Taken by surprise, Pandora started and began to tremble and Heron cursed himself for a fool. In the face of her innocence, all his years of careless philandering rose up to accuse him and he released her almost abruptly.

"You must be tired," he said huskily. "Get to bed now. I'll send your maid into you."

It sounded very final. Pandora watched him stride to the door and with a sense of urgency knew that she must find the courage to speak before he left the room.

"My lord . . . Robert . . . please wait!"

He turned in that half-impatient way by now so familiar to her.

She clasped her hands nervously in front of her. "You

168

must be aware that I have never . . . that is, oh, I do so want to be a proper wife to you, b-but you will have to help me . . ." Dear God, what a mull she was making of it! Perhaps if she cared less, she would do it better.

Did she, Heron wondered bleakly, have any idea how much like a sacrificial offering she appeared standing there in her demure dress, a tell-tale trace of desperation in her eyes. With a muttered exclamation he returned to her side and took the pale face between his hands, feeling an instant quiver run through her.

"Don't!" he said tersely. "Don't look like that! There is all the time in the world. I have no intention of rushing you into anything before you are ready . . ."

"I *am* ready," she said tremulously. "Quite ready, I promise you."

His eyes searched her face and she met them unwaveringly.

"Well, then," he said softly.

But their wedding night was not an unqualified success. Heron was full of tenderness, but his concern lest he hurt or frighten Pandora put an unnatural constraint upon him. This in turn confused his bride, who from lack of experience was unsure of what was expected of her—and in spite of his assurances that next time it would be different, she was left with a feeling of dissatisfaction and the lingering impression that she had somehow failed him.

Lady Margerson and Fitz returned to town the following day, and in all the bustle of departure it was easy enough to display sufficient animation to fend off curiosity.

Her ladyship took her leave amid tears of happiness and expressed the hope that she might see them in town before too long.

"Shall you present her, Robert?" she asked, catching Heron on his own for a moment.

"I think not," he said, frowning. "The autumn will be soon enough."

"The child will find her life vastly different, certainly."

169

Lady Margerson glanced at his impassive face and, recalling his rackety past, said with sudden urgency, "You will be good to her?" Almost at once she wished the words unsaid, for he pokered up and said in his most distant manner that such was his avowed intention.

William, too, left them to return to the Brearlys'. It had been decided that for the present he should continue there during the week for the sake of his studies, returning to Clearwater at the weekends.

It seemed very quiet when they had all gone. Heron was in his most restless abrupt mood, and Pandora was suddenly filled with the enormity of the step she had taken. With the memory of the previous night like an invisible barrier between them, she wondered if he were already regretting his quixotic gesture in marrying her.

She longed for a return to the old relationship. They had always been able to talk—had never been awkward in one another's company as they were now. But one could not go back. Perhaps being married was always like this where there was not mutual love. If so, she must strive to adjust to it.

At dinner she made a determined effort to be cheerful despite the formality of their surroundings, and in part at least she succeeded, for as though suddenly realising how carelessly he had been treating her, he began to respond in kind; although she was aware that he was drinking rather more than was usual, the remainder of the evening passed off reasonably well and her own stretched nerves began to ease.

That night she lay for a long time staring up at the ornately gilded tester of her vast bed, its ceiling depicting "The Judgement of Paris," with the beautiful godlike young man leaning forward to bestow the golden apple upon Aphrodite. Occasionally, as the pretty French clock on the mantelshelf chimed with exquisite tuneful precision, she glanced toward the door that divided her room from Heron's.

As time passed she shrank a little further into her pillows. She shed no tears, but when she could no longer delude herself that he might still come, she extinguished the lamp and turned on her side, curling up in a ball for comfort.

In the room beyond Heron sat slumped in a chair. So clear that she was almost a physical presence he saw Pandora, her face pale with its look of strain as she valiantly tried to show a brave front. He heard again Lady Margerson's exhortation to him as she left. Finally, he cursed and reached once more for the brandy bottle.

The days passed with surprising swiftness as Pandora subjugated her disappointment in a firm resolve to become the kind of duchess of whom Heron could be proud. And as if to show his approval of her good sense, she found her husband unexpectedly helpful. There was a subtle difference in their relationship which she could not define, but found quite pleasing.

In fact, the Duke had also made a number of decisions, the most important being a determination to set Pandora's mind at ease and to woo her with patience—a virtue he had not until late possessed to any marked degree. For almost the first time in his life—certainly since the early days of his infatuation for Mariette—he was discovering in himself a love that transcended mere selfishness on his part. He had little doubt of his ability to teach Pandora to return that love, but this time he would not rush his fences.

So it was that the Duke and his young Duchess were regularly to be seen driving or riding round the estate and the home farm. It had surprised Heron to notice how very much at home Pandora was already with people in general.

"Well, I expect I find them easy to know, because they are the kind of people I understand," she explained. "I called on Mrs. Briggs yesterday. She has made my little cottage very pleasant."

"Your cottage?" He glanced at her quizzically. "Do you then still hanker after it?"

"Oh no!" she said, blushing a little. "I am beginning to find being a duchess most agreeable."

He laughed, and she blushed the more.

In the house it was different. It was so grand and she

was diffident, afraid that any ideas she might propose in the way of change would offend some unknown shibboleth. Yet she very much wished to introduce a few more homely touches.

"The house is so very beautiful," she confessed anxiously. "But it is a little like . . . like . . ."

"Living in a museum," he suggested with a whimsical drawl.

"Well . . . I did wonder whether perhaps, in just one or two of the rooms . . . the little drawing room, for instance? It could be so much more welcoming with only a very little change. It gets nearly all of the morning sun . . ."

"My dear child, do as you please. It is your house now, and heaven knows, it needs a woman's touch!"

Later, he lounged in a chair with one leg thrown carelessly over the arm, watching with amusement the growing confidence with which his wife directed a pair of footmen in the rearranging of furniture in the little drawing room. And bowls of flowers had begun to appear everywhere.

"Much better," he approved. "We shall make a hostess of you yet. This place already feels more alive than it's done for years. Grandmère tended to favour formality in her younger days and since she took to her own rooms, no one has bothered. Mama, of course, never liked Clearwater and hasn't been here in years!"

"Your Mama?" Pandora, flushed with her exertions, looked up in surprise, brushing back a strand of hair. "Is she not . . . that is, I had always assumed that she was dead."

"Good Lord, no! Or at least, not to my knowledge." His grin had a boyish air. "She married again, soon after my father died when I was nineteen—a diplomat of sorts. The last I heard, they were in some benighted South American state, but it could as easily be China by now. Mama don't trouble herself with tedious correspondence!"

"And the Comtesse is her mother?"

"They never hit it off. Mama was ever a butterfly," he added, as if that explained all.

172

And when one remembered the rigid conformity of the Comtesse, it did.

"Oh, that reminds me, sir." Pandora saw him lift an eyebrow. "I'm sorry. I do try to remember, but it isn't very easy . . ." The eyebrow quirked. "Robert," she said obediently, her mouth curving into a quick, crooked smile. "Do you think, Robert, that your carpenter could adapt a chair with wheels? It would then be possible to get the Comtesse out into the garden. It can't be good for her to be forever indoors. The sun is so warm, and at the very least she could sit on the terrace, though I hope in time she might consent to let me push her down as far as the lake."

Heron stood up, his tawny eyes mocking. "I shouldn't think you've a chance," he drawled, "but I doubt that will deter you."

"It is certainly worth a try, if you've no objections. We could take the children, too," she added enthusiastically. "Have a picnic!"

He strolled to the door. "I hope when you say 'we,' you do so in the purely regal sense, and do not think to include me."

"Coward!"

He put his head back round the door. "And Madame Daubenay won't love you, either."

Pandora sighed. It was true that Madame had not taken to her. Clearly she resented Pandora's frequent visits to the old lady and the growing closeness between them, the more so as she saw how much good these visits were for her charge. Jealousy was evident in the cold eyes that followed Pandora's every move, but she didn't mean to be put off.

As soon as the chair was ready, she set about convincing the Comtesse that she would come to no harm if she was suitably wrapped up and that she need go no further than the terrace if she did not care to. In the end, it was Madame Daubenay's opposition to the scheme that decided the matter. The Comtesse resented being ordered about and commanded the chair to be brought.

Before long a small procession was regularly to be seen

making its way down to the lakeside on fine days—the Comtesse being pushed by a footman, with Pandora at her side, the nursemaid following behind with the children, and two more footmen bringing up the rear carrying the picnic. The old lady blossomed as though she had been released from prison; the gardens rang with laughter as Pandora encouraged Eduard to run about like any other child instead of behaving like a tiny adult.

Sometimes, at weekends, William would consent to accompany them. He treated the little ones with a kind of lofty tolerance, but struck up a curious friendship with the Comtesse.

And even Heron, for all his declared abhorrence of these family airings, was occasionally to be found in their midst.

But these new pleasures suffered a slight setback when they were obliged to go briefly to London, the Duke and Duchess being commanded by the Regent to attend a glorious fete at Carlton House in honour of Wellington, the all-conquering hero. Pandora was in a quake at being flung so drastically into society.

"Must I go?" she pleaded, to be told with unusual brusqueness by her husband that it would be the height of ill manners to refuse the royal summons.

Her anxiety was only partially alleviated by the decision to take William with them. There were to be great celebrations in London's parks for the entertainment of the populace. Mr. Oliver had written to tell William so, one of the many highlights being regular balloon ascents.

"It would be a great pity if William could not be there," she explained to Heron, plumping up the sofa cushions and settling back with her feet tucked under her. "He is very grateful to you for the handsome way you have sponsored Mr. Oliver."

He watched her, remembering their second meeting and her preoccupation then with cushions. It brought an enigmatic gleam to his eyes as he retorted, "So he should be. It was deuced difficult, I can tell you. Oliver is almost as stubborn as you."

174

"I'm not!" But she laughed. "How *did* you persuade him?"

"Appealed to his better nature . . . said I was counting on him to further William's knowledge of aeronautics and to help guide the boy's fertile imagination along practical channels. I then pointed out," he concluded blandly, "that he would be in a much better position to do this if his own work were not held back for want of funds."

They arrived in London to find the city undergoing a transformation, its parks hardly recognisable, with Oriental temples, pagodas, and bridges sprouting forth even as one looked. All vied with one another for splendour and each had its own speciality. In Hyde Park, the Serpentine was to be the setting for a mock naval battle, and already the booths and drinking parlours were proliferating in order to accommodate the unexpected crowds, while St. James's Park had acquired an illuminated Chinese bridge.

But it was undoubtedly Green Park which could lay claim to the *pièce de résistance*, for here a towering Castle of Discord was nearing completion. On the first night in August, preceded by a realistic representation of the siege of Bajados, and with the aid of fireworks, rockets, and a small army of workmen, this hideous edifice was to be dramatically transformed into a Temple of Concord.

It was this magnificent concept (an inspiration of the Prince Regent) which captured William's almost undivided attention. He would spend hours watching the workmen and then come home to explain the intricacies of the structure to anyone prepared to listen, prompting the Duke to murmur with weary resignation that the occupants of Heron House must be better informed upon the subject of transmogrification than anyone else in town.

"Sir William Congreve has contrived it for the Prince Regent," William told Pinkerton, who, it was known, was prone to indulge him shockingly. "It's jolly clever really. The Castle and the Temple are so constructed that they are able to be turned under cover of the smoke."

Pinkerton showed himself to be suitably impressed.

"We used some of Sir William's new rockets in the

Ardour, you know. They were a great success, too, because although Lord Wellington had little expectation of their aim being anything but erratic, the Frenchies didn't trust them either, so they kept their distance!" William's eagerness faded. "That's when Pa was killed," he concluded with a sigh.

Pandora was given little time to think, let alone stand and stare. Hardly were they settled when Heron bore her off quite ruthlessly to the showrooms of Madame Fanchon. She protested that it could hardly be the thing for him to accompany her and that Lady Margerson would probably be happy to perform this office, but "That's all you know, my girl!" he retorted, and before he had finished reminding her of his views concerning her ladyship's taste, they were in Conduit Street and Madame was coming forward to greet them.

Though discreet, her effusiveness toward the Duke in particular left Pandora in little doubt that this was by no means his first visit to Madame's luxurious establishment. How many of his light o' loves, she wondered with unholy glee, had been dressed at his expense by Madame? His face, inscrutable as ever, gave little away, but the thought continued to divert her throughout an experience that would in other circumstances have sunk her!

Madame expressed delight that she was to be accorded the inestimable privilege of dressing her grace, whose romantic whirlwind marriage had . . . (A penetrating glance from the Duke at this point warned her to have a care.) Madame took the hint and gave herself over swiftly to particulars. Youth and dignity—such an intriguing combination, and what a happy coincidence that her grace was quite out of the usual style—it would make of her an enchanting original! Pandora could not but admire the shrewdness of one who could pass off plainness as "out of the usual style." She felt obliged to confess at once that all she wanted was a gown to wear to the Regent's fete, and since she had lost her father not six months since, it must be reasonably discreet.

Heron derived a certain malicious pleasure from noting the quite visible degree of havoc his wife's innocent comment had evoked in the renowned modiste's breast; to design a spectacular gown for such an occasion must advance her reputation immeasurably; to contrive such an effect within the limits her grace had set (and with such unpromising material to work on) would require every ounce of her undoubted genius. And upon the outcome rested her hopes of capturing the Duchess's patronage for the future.

Madame rose magnificently to the occasion. Silver gauze, she announced with authority, very light, very ethereal, with an underdress of soft rose-pink satin—simply but beautifully cut. She glanced speculatively at the Duke, but addressed herself to his wife. "It is true that the train is usually *de rigueur* for court functions, your grace, but from France only recently I have received fashion plates of the latest Parisian designs. You see"—she rustled to produce them—"the hem is to the ankle only, the skirt, of simple bell shape, just the style, if I may be permitted the observation, to compliment your grace's most charming quality of youth. Soon it will become the rage of London, but only think how delightful it would be to become a setter of fashion . . ."

The Duke silently applauded La Fanchon's quick wit. As Pandora looked toward him in a troubled way, he said blandly, "Why not, my dear? Madame is right. The style might have been contrived with you in mind. So much so, in fact, that I believe we will pursue it further."

Thus for the next hour Pandora found herself being draped in swatches of the most beautiful materials, pinned and tucked and turned about; she grew dizzy from looking at pattern cards, exclaiming over this, discarding that, her initial shyness about expressing her opinion fading as her interest grew.

Only as they returned at last to St. James's Square, the carriage piled high with bandboxes containing hats, shoes, gloves, and accessories of all kinds, did the extent of her extravagance hit her. Oh, why had Heron not curbed her headlong spree?

"My dear foolish girl," he drawled as she voiced her

dismay in stammering tones, "it is nothing! You might have as many dresses again tomorrow an' you wished!"

But this Pandora utterly repudiated. She had more than enough, she vowed, to last her for the rest of her life! Nevertheless, the churning excitement of that afternoon stayed with her until the night of her society debut.

14

Nothing in her experience until now could have prepared Pandora for the spectacle of Carlton House *en fête*. So diverted was she by the sheer opulence of the occasion that she quite forgot to be nervous.

The evening had begun promisingly. The hairdresser summoned by the Duke to dress her hair achieved the impossible, drawing it back into a smooth shining knot high on her head that bore little relation to her own botched efforts. Around the knot he secured a diminutive frill of silver gauze which rested like gossamer against the pale gold of her hair, and as a final triumphant touch, one fresh pale pink rosebud.

Heron came into the room as Betty was putting the final touches to her gown. He stood for so long without speaking that she grew nervous.

"You don't think . . . ?" she began, one hand fluttering up to the brief bodice, cut lower than she would ever have attempted for herself, making her feel a little self-conscious. "It isn't too . . . ?"

"Certainly not," he said, almost brusquely. His glance travelled down to the slightly stiffened hem of the skirt, which swayed as she moved, showing a tantalising glimpse of ankle, and silver slippers with diamonds glinting in their heels. "It is very well!"

"Truly?" She gave a nervous half-giggle. "I feel like Joan of Arc about to go to the stake."

He laughed. "Perhaps these will make you feel more the thing."

He put a soft leather box into her hands. She looked quickly at him and then opened it with fingers that shook slightly. A single pear-shaped diamond drop on a necklet winked up at her, together with two smaller identical drops for her ears. Her mouth formed a soundless "Oh," and Betty gasped, "Oh, your grace!" as Heron fastened the clasp around his wife's neck and stood back, waiting patiently for her to fit the earrings.

"Yes," he said with a little nod of satisfaction.

His obvious approbation gave Pandora an unconscious grace and dignity which carried her successfully through the ordeal of entering Carlton House amid a throng of eminent people passing in slow procession through the house and into the great hall beyond, which the Prince Regent had commissioned John Nash to build for the evening's festivities. The immense edifice quite took her breath away.

"You don't seriously expect me to believe that the Prince went to all this trouble just for a party?" she whispered, staring in awe at the vast umbrellalike ceiling painted to resemble the soft white muslin draping the walls. "I have cut my eyeteeth, you know!"

"Hand on heart!" murmured her husband, amused by the note of censure in her voice. "You should know, little doubter, that his royal highness eschews anything of a paltry nature. Am I not right, Fitz?"

They had come upon Mr. Chessington soon after the formalities had been completed, standing just inside the door, quizzing glass raised, pensively surveying the ornamental temple in the centre of the room. From its depths, massed with banks of flowers, floated the disembodied flowing cadence of a waltz.

"I fear that Prinny has overreached himself this time." He sighed. "Have you *seen* the walls of the avenues leading to the supper tents, my dears? Lined, every one, with transparencies depicting riveting themes such as Military Power and the Overthrow of Tyrants! One can only conclude that they are aimed to appeal to his esteemed guest of the evening." He turned his sleepy eyes upon Pandora as she remarked humorously that Wellington was unlikely to notice them unless they were pointed out to him.

"Robert, be so kind as to introduce me to your exceedingly stylish companion. She is turning all heads!"

"I do hope that you are quizzing me," Pandora said, pleading.

"Looks well, doesn't she?" said Heron.

"Enchanting," agreed Fitz. "More than one lady this evening is like to be sick with envy." His glance came to rest meditatively upon Sarah Bingly, who was staring at Pandora with hard, assessing eyes. Magnificent as ever in one of her clinging gowns—this one in a dull gold satin, and with diamonds sparkling in her rich dark hair—it would be fair to say that few women in the room could hold a candle to her. Yet Fitz was prepared to hazard that she would willingly change places with the slim young girl at his side.

As he still watched, she touched the arm of her companion and moved purposefully forward, her features arranged in a teasing smile.

"Robert!" Her husky voice was faintly chiding. "So you have decided to brave the wrath of your friends at last? How unkind of you to marry so secretively and then hide your little duchess away, depriving us of the chance to wish you both well!"

"You must permit us a little selfishness," he said smoothly. "We have been enjoying ourselves so much in the country that we were loath to leave, even for so short a time."

"Really?" Her laugh trilled out. "I had no idea you were so enamoured of country life!"

"Perhaps Robert has had little incentive until now," said Pandora in her clear light voice.

"Bravo, little one!" murmured Fitz softly.

Heron looked at his wife with new eyes. He had not appreciated until now how much grown in confidence she was after only a few weeks as mistress of Clearwater.

Lady Sarah turned to the florid young man at her side. "You know Arthur, of course. Except for her grace," she added sweetly. "Duchess, may I present my brother, Lord Shilton."

"My lord."

"Ma'am." The young man's glance was frankly admiring. "May I be permitted to say how delightfully you look?"

"Thank you." Pandora smiled.

"And how daring of you, my dear Duchess, to make your debut in such a dramatic fashion!" said his sister with apparent admiration.

Before Pandora could reply, there was a stirring in the crowd nearby—a clear voice, jovial, decisive. The words didn't carry, but the whooping laugh that followed was unmistakable, sending a deep pleasurable shiver of nostalgia through her.

Soon the Duke of Wellington was approaching their group, greeting Lady Sarah, with whom he was clearly already acquainted, his deep-set eyes appreciative of her incomparable beauty, and Pandora had time to look with affection on the well-remembered features, the hair slightly grizzled, blue eyes that could be so chilling, and the prominent nose.

His glance moved on politely, and was arrested by the slim figure in silver gauze.

"Well, bless my soul! Surely it can't be . . . Miss Pandora!" He took her eagerly outstretched hands, his eyes twinkling. "My dear young lady, how you have grown!"

"Oh, sir, how glad I am to see you!" Both her hands remained clasped in his as she related her changed circumstances and presented her husband and Fitz.

"So, my dear Duchess—we are both gone up in the world, eh!" His laugh rang out once more.

"Yes, sir, so we are."

"You are a fortunate man, Heron. Deuced fortunate!" He stayed some time talking in an animated way about the conclusion of his Peninsular campaign and reminiscing with Pandora. He asked after her brothers and was delighted to hear about Courtney. "I was deeply distressed about your father, my dear. I can ill afford to lose such gallant, dedicated men." He pressed her hand. "Well, now, I must get along—no doubt we shall meet again."

And he passed on, bowing to one person, shaking hands with another.

"So that's the great man," mused Fitz. "He don't cut that great a figure at first sight, but it becomes apparent as soon as he speaks!"

"Oh, yes! He has the most tremendous influence on the men," Pandora exclaimed as the group broke up. "They don't always love him, but they trust him implicitly!"

"Really?" murmured Lady Sarah, sounding bored.

Left alone with her brother, she continued to smile, but there was soft fury in her voice. "Something will have to be done about that little upstart!"

"The little Duchess? But why? Charming creature, I thought!"

"Did you?" She spat the words out, and he looked at her curiously.

"Drop you for her, did he?" His laugh held a touch of brotherly malice. "A novel experience for you, Sal. Still, plenty more fish, what? Forget her."

"I want her discredited—ruined!" she said through her teeth. "And you, little brother, are going to help me!"

He frowned. "Don't involve me! Besides, it won't get you Heron back."

"That is the last thing I want! And you *will* help me, Arthur, unless you wish to lose the very handsome allowance I pay you." She laughed at his discomfiture. "I knew you would change your mind. Don't worry, all I want is a man—young, attractive, preferably with army connections—who would be willing to seduce a young lady for a consideration." She moved away, saying over her shoulder, "He should not prove too difficult to find— among *your* friends."

Pandora, unaware of the enmity she had generated, was enjoying a marvellous evening. She came in for a great deal of teasing, but much of it was kindly, and she received a surprising number of invitations. The Season was almost over, but the Duke of Wellington's arrival in London had precipitated a number of last-minute balls and soirées in his honour.

Heron introduced his wife to the Prince Regent, who was most affable in his congratulations. She in turn was fascinated by his immense girth and the richness of his dress, but although she had heard many spiteful things said about him, she found his manner most kindly.

She drank a great deal too much champagne, which made her feel light-headed, full of goodwill toward all the world, and exceedingly talkative. And when her amused husband finally carried her off home amid protests, the dawn was already breaking, but she was reluctant to be handed over to Betty. The maid had been dozing in a chair and had to be roused in order to put her happily intoxicated mistress to bed, not an easy task, for it was almost impossible to keep her still while she unravelled the complexities of the hairdresser's art. Finally it was accomplished, her mistress was safely in bed, the lamp extinguished—and she could snatch a little sleep for herself.

But when Betty had gone, Pandora found it impossible to settle. Her head tended to spin when she laid it on the pillow, but on her feet she felt fine. Light was filtering under the curtains as she draped a wrap about her shoulders and pattered across the room to her husband's door.

He looked a little nonplussed to find her there when he answered her knock.

He stood aside to let her pass, and closed the door. He was wearing a black brocade dressing gown, exotically frogged, which she eyed approvingly, and he carried a wineglass in his hand, which she also eyed approvingly. "Is that champagne?" she asked.

It was not, he said, his brow arched quizzically. "My dear, why are you here? Do you feel unwell?"

"No." She shook her head with considerable care. "I feel wonderful."

"Then shouldn't you go back to bed?" he suggested.

"I don't care for it in there on my own," she said, enunciating very precisely. "I want to be with you, Robert. I am your wife, after all." Her voice grew a little plaintive. "Sometimes I think you don't like me . . ."

He felt a great wave of love surge up in him for the endearing comic figure swaying slightly in her demure nightgown with her wrap slipping off her shoulders.

He moved away to put down his glass. "I like you very much," he said gently. "But we'll talk about it tomorrow."

She giggled enchantingly. "That's all right, then, because tomorrow's already today!"

He turned back to find the wrap on the floor and the buttons of her nightgown already undone. "Pandora! For heaven's sake!" he besought her, and moved forward swiftly to stop her, but not swiftly enough.

She was already shrugging it off her shoulders, and a moment later it slithered into a heap at her feet. He gazed helplessly at her, knowing full well that he ought to bundle her up and carry her back to her room, knowing that she was not responsible for her present actions. But there was something touchingly comic and vulnerable and desirable all at the same time in the sight of her standing with her silky hair tumbling round her shoulders, fanned out above modest breasts, her slim waist swelling into the curve of hip and thigh. She was quite blatantly offering herself to him, and he was lost.

He moved closer, very close. "My dearest girl, are you sure this is what you want?"

"Oh, yes!" she said tremulously.

He swept her off her feet and laid her gently on the bed.

Pandora woke slowly, unwilling to relinquish the cocooning clouds of sleep. She felt vaguely different, and wondered why. Then a memory—was it dream or reality?—came into her mind and a hot blush spread from her toes slowly upward. She opened one eye warily, and then the other, surprised to see her own room as sunlight sliced narrowly through the closed curtains.

As her mind cleared, she knew that it had not been a dream—Robert's passion, his infinite tenderness, were vividly real, as was her own eager response. Her whole body melted now, remembering. Much later and less clear was memory of being carried back to her own room, demurely nightgowned once more, with Robert whispering in her ear that Glyn would be deeply shocked should he find her in his master's bed—and she giggling into his chest and telling him that he was being very silly. . . .

She raised her head off the pillow and groaned as her head swam. It must have been the champagne, she decided —glasses and glasses of delicious bubbly champagne. . . . She was sitting hunched up with her head in her hands when the door presently opened.

"Please, Betty, be quiet!" she implored.

"Oh, dear," said Heron with a hint of rueful laughter in his voice. "I rather thought you might be feeling a trifle out of sorts, so I have brought you a little of Glyn's unfailing remedy."

Pandora peered at him through her fingers, reluctant to look him in the eye. He was fully dressed and looked quite unbearably fresh, which had the effect of making her feel worse.

"I rather think . . ." she began miserably. "That is, I fear I must have behaved very shockingly last night."

"Disgracefully," he agreed, sounding severe. " 'Abandoned' would, I believe, best describe your behaviour."

"Oh, no!" Her head dropped a little lower.

He sat on the bed beside her, removed her hands gently but inexorably from her face, and tilted her chin up. She saw that his eyes were alight with laughter.

"My darling goose, you were entirely delightful! I am only sorry that I didn't think to ply you with champagne from the first."

"It is indelicate of you to say so!" she protested. "And most unfair, besides, for I have been very willing from the first to . . . to be a p-proper wife to you." This last became somewhat incoherent, as his tender mirth filled her with confusion. But soon his merriment became infectious and she too succumbed, laughing and holding her head by turns. He persuaded her to drink the excellent physic prepared by his valet.

"He doesn't guess it is for me?" she enquired anxiously, sniffing before sipping warily. It smelled terrible and tasted worse.

"My dear sweet wife! Glyn is the soul of tact. He might

hazard a guess, but the rack wouldn't drag an admission from him!" He watched her face wrinkle up in disgust. "Yes, I know, but it works. Toss it off. It's by far the best way."

She did so, and shuddered. But the effect was almost magical, which was just as well, as they were promised somewhere for almost every moment of that week.

She had no need now for champagne; the happiness bubbling constantly inside her was quite as intoxicating, without any distressing aftermath. To be sure, Robert had not actually said he loved her, but there could surely be little doubt of it. There was a new intimacy between them, an indulgence in his attitude toward her that was marked by others as well as herself. Sometimes, the way she felt frightened her a little, for surely such unconfined joy could not last!

Lady Margerson was quick to note the change when Pandora visited her to regale her with an account of the fete, which she had felt unable to attend. The child's grey eyes sparkled and her improved looks were not solely due to her new elegant image. Her ladyship was content.

"You seem to be mightily in demand for someone who vowed she had no use for society!" she quizzed her.

Pandora bit her lip ruefully. "Oh, well, I daresay I shouldn't care for it indefinitely, you know. We stay only until William has had his fill of fireworks and balloon ascents and the like—and then we shall all go home." Her eyes twinkled. "But it is surprisingly agreeable to have lots of new clothes and be made much of by important people. I only hope it may not go to my head!"

"That I would very much doubt," said Lady Margerson.

In all her excitement, however, Pandora did not forget those less fortunate. For a wedding gift, Heron had given her, besides her grandmama's necklet, now reset once more with diamonds, the lease of a pair of houses close to Sergeant Blakewell's, which he had suggested the sergeant might oversee on her behalf, for a small remuneration, to act as a temporary refuge for those men of her old regiment who found themselves destitute. Nothing could have pleased her more.

The sergeant, once he had recovered from the shock, agreed and had set about organising the running of the houses in a very businesslike way so that they should not become a mere doss-ken for idle scroungers. Those who could, paid, however small a sum. A strict reckoning was kept and regular accounts rendered to Mr. Varley of what was spent.

As soon as Pandora found a spare moment, she persuaded Heron to let her take William along to see what had been achieved.

"But quietly, please—just the two of us, and not in your grand carriage? The last thing I want any of them to feel is that I have gone up in the world and am there to make a kind of grand tour of inspection!"

"No. That would never do," he agreed gravely. "But I really cannot permit my wife to take a hired hack, you know." She saw that he was laughing at her. "I believe we do have a relatively unremarkable chaise somewhere in the stables. Grimble shall have it cleaned up a little." Now there was a definite glint in his eyes. "He can drive you there himself!"

It was made very clear from the set of Grimble's shoulders as he later complied with the Duke's instructions that he felt the whole equipage, not to say the whole expedition, to be very much beneath his touch. But Pandora's understanding and William's easy chatter went a long way toward mollifying Grimble, and by the time they arrived in Peg Street, he had learned a considerable amount about the flying artillery as the RHA was wont to be called.

It was William too who made the whole visit such a success, seeking out the odd face he knew, asking eager questions, and arguing amiably about shared experiences.

Pandora, for her part, was happy to see how much good the venture had done Sergeant Blakewell. He was, in a sense, in command once more. And Alice, too. She had quickly involved herself, her sharp tongue giving short shrift to many a troublemaker.

Pandora left, feeling more than ever grateful to Robert for enabling them to win back their pride and give them a sense of purpose. She hoped that her father would have been pleased.

15

Captain Denby Austin was handsome, reckless, and bored. His was a nature that craved action, excitement, risk—and the Peace had deprived him of these. Small wonder that he turned to the tables, throwing himself into gambling in the same neck-or-nothing fashion that had characterised his exploits in the Peninsular, but with less success.

Being badly dipped, he had borrowed, and borrowed again, until he found himself hopelessly in debt and with nothing before him but the Fleet. So when Lord Shilton had offered to clear his debts and put something in his pocket besides, he listened. It seemed a deuced lot to pay someone for simply flirting with a young lady (a habit that came naturally to him anyway). That the lady in question was a duchess added piquancy; that she was also married, a hint of danger.

It was easy enough to infiltrate society; the braided dolman of an officer of hussars was sufficient passport, for uniforms were everywhere lionised and, worn with an air, could ensure one a welcome almost anywhere.

Pandora met him first at a soirée, where he was all politeness and charm, though his eyes betrayed an interest. He was in Hyde Park on the following morning when she rode with Robert. Once again, beyond the usual pleasantries, he conversed mostly with the Duke, though occasionally she caught him looking at her, and much as she rebuked herself for it, found the experience not unpleasing.

She found herself dressing for Lady Chorley's ball with extra care, attributing her excitement to having received only a little earlier two letters sent round from Brook Street by the faithful Binns. They were written in Bermuda, the usual hurried note from Courtney, but Hugo's full of anecdotes about their journey designed to make her laugh.

Its contents had just been devoured for the third time when Heron came in as ever to admire and approve. Pandora stood up to shake out the deep cream folds of her mousseline de soie skirts. The colour warmed her skin, and Betty had dusted her cheeks with rouge and applied a very small amount of carmine to her lips. The effect was, in her husband's teasing words, "vastly fetching!"

She turned back impetuously to pick up her reticule, and the letter fluttered to the floor. Heron bent to retrieve it and in so doing the opening greeting jumped out at him: "Dearest Princess." He handed it back without comment, and she did not notice his sudden quietness.

"It's from Hugo. He writes most entertainingly about their exploits thus far! I will tell you all later." She smiled happily. "As well I don't have to rely on Courtney for news!"

Lady Chorley's rooms were crowded and, the night being warm, the windows stood open to the balmy air. The Duke of Wellington made a promised appearance and stayed for some time talking amiably to people and watching the swirling couples, before retiring with Lord Chorley to the library.

Pandora found it very hard being at a ball in half-mourning and not being able to dance. She could not think that Papa would have minded in the least—he liked nothing better than to see her enjoying herself—but, as Heron's wife, she would not dream of showing disrespect by flouting the conventions.

She was not short of company, meanwhile. According to Fitz, she had definitely "taken," and if she cared to come up to town next Season, he had no doubt of her being much in demand. Heron, when appealed to, agreed, but she thought he seemed a little preoccupied.

Rather surprisingly, Lady Margerson had decided to attend the ball, it being, as she told Pandora, one of the few opportunities she might have of seeing the Great Man at close quarters without fear of there being too much of a crush, for many people had by now left town.

But she very soon found the atmosphere too warm for comfort, and Pandora took her to a small retiring room some way from the ballroom and stayed there talking to her for a while until her carriage arrived and she was seen safely on her way.

So it was that Pandora found herself retracing her steps down the wide empty corridor just as the opening strains of a waltz drifted out from the ballroom. Without conscious volition her feet moved to the music, and with a conspiratorial grin at a wooden-faced footman, she began to dip and sway and turn.

"Bravo!"

She gasped and stood still, and found Captain Austin leaning against the wall silently applauding her, his eyes laughing to behold the guilt writ large on her face.

"You waltz beautifully, Duchess! Perhaps, if you would do me the honour?" He held out a hand.

"Oh, no!" she said quickly. "You know I cannot. It wouldn't be proper!"

"And do you never do anything improper?"

He was flirting with her quite incorrigibly and she knew that she ought to repulse him. But no one had ever flirted with her before (except Hugo, and he only did it in fun, which couldn't be held to count), and she found it a peculiarly exhilarating experience.

"It does seem a pity to waste the music," he continued persuasively. "And if we were to dance out here just for a little while, no one need ever know." He watched her bite her lip pensively and pressed his advantage. "It could surely do no harm, and you would make a poor soldier very happy, dear ma'am!" he concluded with a mock humility that didn't reach his eyes.

She tried to look severe—to think of Robert, who would be angry if he knew—but her mouth curved irrepressibly, and perhaps because the captain reminded her a little of Hugo, she succumbed. Soon she was wishing that she had not, for he swirled her round with increasing intimacy and murmured compliments of a decidedly intimate nature in her ear.

"You are being very silly," she said firmly, "and I think we should stop now."

He smiled down at her in a way that would have disturbed any woman who was not a block of wood. "How can you ask me to stop when you dance like an angel, sweet divinity?"

"Do angels waltz? I confess I hadn't thought about it." She was babbling now. "I learned in the army, as I expect you did."

He suppressed a vague feeling of exasperation and continued valiantly, "Of course, I was forgetting that you were also in the Peninsula. Why did I never meet you there?"

Diverted for a moment, Pandora giggled. "I doubt, Captain, that you would have given me a second glance an' you had!"

His gallant denial came out smoothly, but there was no denying that he found the giggle unsettling. In fact, the young lady herself was unsettling. She was proving rather less easy to seduce than he was used to, and rather to his surprise, he found he liked her the better for it. A pity that his debts were so pressing.

He accepted the challenge of her resistance and set himself to pursue his conquest of her once more with a subtle blend of outrageousness and gentle cajolery. But Pandora, with a growing sense of panic, was oblivious of his charms. At any moment someone might see them, and she begged him to let her go.

"I can't do that, sweetheart," he said, and there was something in his voice suddenly that frightened her. He began to whirl her ever faster, and she saw with horror that they were fast approaching the entrance to the ballroom.

"Oh, please!" she gasped, feeling sick and dizzy with apprehension. "You can't . . . you mustn't! Captain, this is beyond a joke . . . you must let me go!"

But they were already crossing the threshold, fully circling the floor until they reached one of the window embrasures. He whisked her through the partly drawn curtains and out onto the shallow balcony.

"And now, to recompense me a little, just one kiss!" There was a strange wildness in his laugh as he drew her close, containing her struggles with ease, his mouth finding hers though she sought to prevent it.

She wrenched herself free, distressed beyond measure. "How could you?" she whispered, the back of her hand pressed to her trembling lips. "Oh, how could you?"

His smile was bitter. "How, indeed?" He caught her arm as she would have fled, and felt her flinch from him. "Easy, my dove," he said wearily. "I will hurt you no more. But if you don't want a scandal crashing about your ears, we had best be circumspect."

He drew her unresisting hand through his arm and they emerged just as the dance ended. He led her to a chair and was heard to be most solicitous about her momentary faintness before leaving her.

Naturally the escapade had not gone unnoticed. Pandora's flustered appearance was marked by those who thrived on such incidents. She however was aware only of her husband who stood a little way off, his face quite expressionless.

"Oh, Robert!" So deep was her need for his understanding that she was sure she must have called his name aloud. But no sound came, and after a moment he turned away.

She was dimly aware that Captain Austin had returned and was presenting her with a glass of cordial. Then he bowed, thanked her with his inevitable charm, and departed. She felt that all eyes were on her and unconsciously sat a little straighter, listening to the buzz of conversation coming in waves, the occasional trill of laughter.

Fitz strolled up and, having reassured himself about her health, began talking in his gentle way about generalities. She was deeply grateful to him and tried to tell him so. But he would have none of it.

"I have made a scandal, haven't I?" she said flatly.

"Nothing of the kind, m'dear. A trifling indiscretion, no

more. The gabble-grinders will chew on't for a day or two, but most of 'em will be off to Brighton or the country or wherever very soon and all will be forgotten. My word on it."

"I don't think Robert will see things quite that way."

Mr. Chessington regarded her wan face with sympathy. "No, well—stands to reason he'll be a bit miffed. Blow to his pride and all that! Deuced fond of you, though," he added, almost as an afterthought.

And that about summed up the situation, thought Pandora, stifling a wild urge to laugh as her husband made his way toward her. She had done the unforgivable—and his pride was bruised. No matter that *she* might have been ill-used!

To all outward appearance his manner was all concern as he bent over her, his fingers lovingly circling her wrist, caressing it, but his meticulous politeness frightened her, and the caressing fingers were like bands of steel.

"Wasn't feeling quite the thing," said Mr. Chessington helpfully.

"Go away, Fitz, there's a good fellow." Heron's voice was expressionless. The dandy looked ruefully at them both and took his leave.

"So. You felt a trifle faint, I believe? Too much exertion, perhaps," he continued in the same manner. "I am happy to see you recovered. Clearly the fresh air revived you! How quick-witted of the Captain. I must make it my business to thank him."

That dangerous silkiness had crept into his voice now. It made her say hurriedly, "You must not . . . the fault was mine . . . that is, it may have looked a little misleading, but . . ."

"Only to those who do not know you." The music was beginning again, and his fingers tightened on her wrist. "We must reassure everyone that you are quite well again."

"Oh, no! I don't want to dance. I didn't mean to before! I just want to go home," she pleaded.

His smile was a travesty. "Unfortunately, we cannot always do as we want, madam wife. Since you have chosen

195

to break with custom, we will dance, if you please, and you will appear at least to enjoy it."

The remainder of the evening was unrelieved misery, though she did her best not to show it. But the journey home was much worse. Heron could not be brought to talk about what had happened, and when she persisted, said tersely, "Not now."

At Heron House, he tossed his hat and cane to a waiting footman, and without pausing in his stride, carried straight on to the library, with Pandora half-running to keep up with him, her sense of guilt fast turning into grievous injustice. He waited for the door to close.

"Now," he said, turning. "I will hear your explanation."

"And if I don't choose to give you one?" she returned pugnaciously.

He looked momentarily surprised, but his expression hardened again almost at once. "Impertinence won't help matters."

"I don't mean to be impertinent, Robert," she cried. "But I deeply resent being treated like a half-wit child. I am, after all, your wife."

"Precisely. And when *my wife* behaves with little more decorum than a back-street trollop, I believe I am entitled to an explanation."

Pandora recoiled as though he had struck her. "Is that how you saw me?"

"It is how many people saw you, my dear," he said harshly. "I was obliged to fend off several oh-so-innocent enquiries as to whether you were now out of black gloves, together with much speculation about Captain Austin—was he a friend from your army days, or even a relation, perhaps, since you were clearly on such familiar terms with him."

"Oh, no!"

His lip curled. "I suppose the uniform proved an irresistible lure, your partiality for all things military—and handsome young officers in particular—being what it is."

"That is unfair, and untrue!" She remembered the letter. "If you are referring to Hugo . . . well, I have known him forever, and he is just : . . Hugo!"

"Do you say so?" There was mild disbelief in the words. "Then I am forced to conclude that your recent popularity has gone to your head and has led you to believe that you may do as you choose. Certainly the girl I knew, the girl I married, would never have disported herself in such a fashion."

He had hurt her deeply; it showed in the pallor of her face, where the rouge stood out starkly, vying with her freckles for prominence. He wanted to sweep her into his arms, to tell her he didn't mean any of it, that he was a jealous fool—but there was a frightening, untouchable dignity about her which warned him not to try.

"I never wanted fine clothes," she said over the constriction in her throat, "or to mix with your society friends. But, as you remarked earlier, we cannot always choose what we want, and it would be dishonest to say that I have not enjoyed these past weeks. But it is becoming clearer to me with every minute that I should never have married you."

"Now you are being absurd beyond measure," he said stiffly.

"No! I'm facing facts," she cried. "I told you I shouldn't know how to go on as a duchess, and tonight has proved it. Perhaps it *was* the uniform that drew me to Captain Austin. He reminded me of . . . of someone . . ."

Greville, thought Heron savagely. That damned letter!

"But that isn't really important," she continued doggedly. "You see, you weren't angry because what I did was so terrible. Oh, it was silly, but from what little I've seen, ladies frequently behave foolishly without being unduly censured. What infuriated you, my lord Duke, was that my conduct made you an object of ridicule before your friends! Oh, I don't blame you for it, but I can't guarantee not to let you down again, for I cannot change what I am." She forced herself to look him in the eye—and rather wished that she had not. "And so the sooner I go back to Clearwater, the better."

"I see. You mean to turn tail and run?" he drawled derisively. "Very heroic! And what, pray, do you hope to achieve? Sneak away now, and you'll play right into the tattle-mongers' hands. It will delight them to be able to say that I have turned you off." He saw the look on her face and added with quiet fury, "Stubborn little fool! Can't you see that it's you I am thinking of, not myself?"

Pandora sighed. "I'm tired. I can't think anymore tonight."

He shrugged angrily, and made no attempt to stop her as she walked to the door, saying only as she left, "If you won't consider yourself, think of William. He has been looking forward for weeks to the celebrations. Will you now spoil things for him?"

Lady Sarah was less than pleased when the world failed to fall about Pandora's ears. When she saw the couple at the theatre on the following evening, and later at an exclusive supper party, as though nothing had happened, she was furious. She accused Arthur and his friend of bungling, and refused to pay one penny of Captain Austin's debts until they redeemed themselves.

But the Captain vowed that he would not lift one finger more to contribute to Pandora's discomfiture. He was not usually troubled by conscience, but her grey eyes wide with distress had risen to reproach him more often than he cared to admit. So Lady Bingly could keep her money, and he would find some other way to replenish his funds.

"Well, that's that," said Arthur, secretly relieved that his sister's plans had been thwarted.

"Fool!" she said, her mind already busy. "You don't think I mean to let it go at that, do you?" And as he stared: "For a start, I want Captain Austin followed. If I am not mistaken, he is riddled with the kind of stupid quixotic gallantry that will drive him to see that girl again to tell her all! If he does, they must both disappear."

Her brother looked at her as though she had gone mad. "What *are* you driving at, Sal? Disappear?"

Her sapphire eyes were jewel-hard. "It's very simple, brother dear, I want them got rid of—permanently. There are ways of arranging such things. And the world"—she smiled—"including Robert, will suppose that they have run off together."

Pandora was amazed to discover that one could actually go through the motions of living—could converse with reasonable liveliness and lucidity, laugh when required to do so, eat sufficient to avoid comment, even sleep if one were tired enough—and yet feel utterly dead inside.

She had no way of knowing how Robert felt. Since the night of their quarrel, he had made little attempt to communicate, though in public he played the indulgent husband with conviction enough to deceive the most prurient eye. At home, too, he was careful to keep up appearances, especially in front of William, but somehow he contrived never to be alone with her.

Perhaps he thought her too light-minded to care deeply about what had happened. If he did, there was no way she could convince him otherwise, and to sink into a despair would be despicably poor-spirited, though there were moments when his increasingly long absences during the day brought her close to it.

Fitz was unfailingly kind and supportive, providing his willing escort when needed and never once embarrassing her with awkward questions, though he was clearly puzzled by the situation. Whether he said anything to Heron, she wasn't sure, but their manner toward one another seemed a little cooler than was usual. Several times it was on the tip of her tongue to ask, for it grieved her to think she might have caused a rift between them, but it wasn't easy to ask Fitz anything if he didn't wish to be asked.

William helped by just being William. His mind was so often preoccupied with higher things that he was seldom sensitive to the moods and whims of others. So he was very much taken aback when, having enquired of Pandora for the third time in as many minutes whether she was not taking him to watch Mr. Oliver try out the latest improvements he had made to his new balloon as she had promised, she snapped his head off.

"Well, I wish you'd have said if you didn't want to be bothered," he declared with an air of justifiable grievance. "I could have gone with Mr. Oliver, if I'd known, but he'll have left ages ago! And Heron isn't here either. I must say, he seems to be out a great deal just lately. Still, I 'spect dukes have a great many calls on their time."

To his consternation, he saw the sudden tears standing out in his sister's eyes. "Oh, Lord, Dora—it's not like you to be a watering pot."

"No. Idiotish of me!" Pandora forced a laugh. "Too many late nights, I expect. Of course I'll take you. Go and ask Grimble to put the horses to . . . oh, the landaulet, I think, as it's such a nice day, and I'll fetch my hat and a parasol."

"Look, you don't have to come if you don't feel up to it." William, much chastened and thus disposed to be generous, couldn't forbear to add hopefully: "Except that it might be just the thing if you're feeling glumpish!"

He couldn't for the life of him think why she gave him such a bear hug. Girls were very odd sometimes.

As they drove through Green Park, the sounds of hammering echoed above the many other clamorous noises as workmen put the final touches to a pavilion being erected outside Buckingham House from where the Prince Regent and his guests would be guaranteed an uninterrupted view of the Jubilee celebrations two days hence.

The press had made alarming predictions of the drunkenness and rioting which would accompany the affair, and like many other people, Fitz thought the whole thing excessively vulgar, just what one would expect of Prinny, but William had no such qualms. He was full of happy expectation, and chattered nonstop about the latest tit-bits he had gleaned, so that Pandora had only to listen as they made their way to the field a little way out of town where Mr. Oliver was conducting his tests. As William clambered down, he pointed eagerly to the casks standing close to the balloon, a hosepipe extending to the gently wafting silk bag.

"I say! We're only just in time. It looks as though he intends an ascent very soon!"

William found Mr. Oliver deep in an argument with his assistant over the latest refinement he had made to the valve, which he was certain would do away with any danger of it sticking at the crucial moment. He greeted William with a smile, and seeing the landaulet standing a little way off, said, "I do hope your sister will pardon me if I don't come to greet her just now."

"Yes, of course she will. She can see how occupied you are. Do you mean to take it up?" William asked, hopping at his side. "Can I come too?"

Mr. Oliver looked doubtful, but was soon won over and sent William to ask Pandora if it would be all right, and if so, to assure her that he would deliver her brother safe home afterward.

"But you will wait and see me go up, won't you, Dora?"

She smiled and agreed, adjured him not to be a nuisance, and told him to hurry back, for the bag was already filling up fast, swelling into an enormous sphere of vivid-banded colours shimmering in the sunlight. She and Grimble watched as William climbed into the brightly painted boat beneath, the securing ropes were released, and the balloon soared majestically upward. She saw his hand waving and waved back.

"Oh, it does look quite splendid, does it not?"

"Very impressive, I'm sure, your grace," admitted Grimble, his head craning upward to follow the balloon's progress. Already it seemed frighteningly high.

"William says they can reach as much as two thousand feet."

"Is that a fact?" Grimble sniffed. "Well, no offence, ma'am, but give me good solid earth any day. If the good Lord had meant us to fly, I reckon as he'd have given us the wherewithal to do it proper."

Pandora watched the fast-diminishing sphere and shuddered faintly. "Yes, I feel rather that way myself," she confessed. "But I wouldn't dream of admitting as much to my brother."

There seemed little point in remaining where they were any longer, but before she could voice the thought, her ear picked up the heavy thud of hooves coming fast toward the bend in the path which skirted the small copse at their backs.

"Someone in a hurry," she said.

A moment later the rider came into view, and with a stab of irritation she saw that it was Captain Austin. "Drive on, Grimble," she said clearly.

"Ma'am." Grimble acknowledged the command and moved to pick up the reins.

"Ah, thank goodness!" the Captain exclaimed, drawing alongside. "I saw you leaving town and feared that by the time I was saddled up you'd be gone. Look here, I must speak to you—there is something you should know—"

"I'm sorry, but there can be nothing I wish to hear, sir. You will oblige me by going away at once."

"No, wait!" he said urgently. "Please, I beg of you, ma'am—hear me out!" Swiftly he dismounted, looped his horse's rein over the back of the carriage, and was at the door before she could deny him further. "No trickery, I promise you!"

Pandora was flustered. He looked so contrite, so full of entreaty, that she hesitated, glanced at Grimble, who held the ribbons at the ready, decided that his very solid presence was protection enough, and said, "Oh, very well. You had better come up, though I cannot see what you hope to gain from this intrusion."

He had hauled himself into the carriage almost before she was finished speaking, and was saying earnestly, "Nothing, I swear—except perhaps your better opinion of me. Yes, I know," he said as her head lifted, "I behaved despicably, but I had no idea . . . it was only later I learned that I had been an unwitting pawn in a jealous woman's vile scheme to bring ruin upon you!"

This sounded so like high melodrama to Pandora that she was inclined to smile, except that as he cast a soldier's eye over the surrounding terrain there was something in his listening stillness that stirred the hairs on the back of her neck, as of old.

"Do you think we could get moving?" he said uneasily. "We're a mite too exposed here for my liking."

The words were hardly out when violence erupted without warning. A small band of hard-faced men burst from the copse and were upon them before Pandora could do more than cry out. Grimble had no time to raise the horse pistol he always kept in readiness; the burliest of the men made short work of him with a sickening blow across the head which felled him instantly.

Pandora was too angry to heed her fright; she beat the man furiously about the head and shoulders with her parasol, gouging his cheek with the ferrule until with an oath he wrenched it from her grasp, broke it in two with insolent ease, and tossed it away, pushing her back at the same time into a heap on the seat.

Captain Austin was faring little better. He was very much hampered by the lurching carriage as the horses shied and reared in panic, while his own horse, pulling the opposite way, was also rearing in an effort to free itself. In struggling to keep his feet, he was no match for the assailants and very soon suffered the same fate as Grimble.

Pandora, very much alone now, was prey to a terrible feeling of helplessness. The man who had struck Captain Austin pushed past his slumped figure to sit beside her; another climbed in at the other side and clamped an arm about her, containing her resistance with good-natured proficiency.

"Easy does it, Duchess! Meself, I don't hold with striking ladies, but Harry, now—'e ain't arf so perticler!"

The big man had settled himself on the box, pushing Grimble's inert body over the side with one heavily booted foot; the thud as the groom hit the ground made Pandora gasp with a shared agony.

Suddenly all was quiet again. The Captain's mount had struggled free and run off, the man on the box had the reins in his hand, and the one holding the horses let them go and leaped up to join him.

"What do you want with us?" Pandora, drawing on the experience of years of surviving tight corners, fought down hysteria to speak calmly.

The least hostile of their captors shrugged. "Not for us

to know or to say, Duchess. Just doin' what we're paid for."

"Stow magging and manging back there, Joss!" growled the burly man, whipping up the horses. "You too, lady, if you don't want a touch of the home-brewed!"

Pandora grimaced, and glanced across at the Captain, who lay against the side squabs, alarmingly pale and still, blood gently oozing from a gash across his temple. She took a handkerchief from the pocket of her dress and looked steadily at the man named Joss. "May I stanch his wound? I won't try anything stupid." Her glance lifted for a moment to the balloon floating high and free against the blue sky, and her mouth crooked in a faint wry smile. "After all, there really isn't anywhere I can go, is there?"

16

Heron was in the Yellow Saloon with Mr. Chessington, the latter ensconced in a comfortable wing chair watching his friend prowl the room. They were perilously close to quarrelling when William burst in upon them, all mud, freckles, and eagerness.

"Oh, hello. Is Dora back yet, do you know? Only she'll be wanting to know how I went on. I've had a famous time, I can tell you! I made an ascent with Mr. Oliver at last—from Plover's Field. We went *miles* up . . . well, about twelve hundred feet, actually. Only then the wind died and we weren't able to cover any great distance . . ."

William's voice trailed off as he detected a lack of interest in his audience. He looked from one to the other—and grinned sheepishly.

"Sorry. I'm intruding. I didn't think . . ."

The Duke surveyed the dishevelled figure with damping austerity.

"Obviously. But then, why should you think?" he drawled. "Pray do not be imagining that you need feel the least compunction about erupting into my rooms unannounced"—he raised his quizzing glass—"and looking more of a complete shag-rag than usual."

William, unexpectedly finding himself on the receiving end of one of Heron's set-downs, flushed and bit his lip. "I'm sorry," he said again. "I'll go and change."

Heron watched the drooping figure almost to the door before saying impatiently, "Oh, for heaven's sake, come back, child!"

William turned politely, but the enthusiasm had died from his eyes. "If you please, sir, I'd as lief go and change. I *am* rather dirty, as you say, and besides, I do want to see Dora."

"As you will," came the curt reply. "But I doubt you'll find her home."

The door closed. Mr. Chessington crossed one yellow-pantalooned leg elegantly over the other and studied the gleaming toe of his hessian boot thoughtfully as the silence stretched. Heron flung away to stare down into the hearth. At last he turned.

"All right, Fitz—say it. I made a complete mull of that!"

Mr. Chessington transferred his studious gaze to his friend's face. "It was not one of your more elevating performances." He paused. "You are not usually so clumsy in your dealings, Robert."

"No. No, dammit, I'm not."

The exquisite's eyes remained steady. "Do you want to talk about it?"

"Oh, God, Fitz, I don't know what to do for the best!" He sank into a chair opposite. "That cursed affair the other night! We had words, Pandora and I . . . and now we hardly speak." He sighed. "She said she ought never to have married me . . . and I begin to think that she is right."

"So do I. She is clearly tied to a blockhead who don't see what's under his nose!"

"Oh, I see well enough." The lip curled. "I am in almost six and thirty, Fitz, and most of those years have been squandered on women not fit to breathe the same air as Pandora." His friend's snort of derision in no way mollified him. "Oh, I know she likes to call herself a realist, but she's only nineteen, and for all her open manner, still full of shining innocence and dreams of romance."

His companion's voice was dry. "But presumably you considered all this before you married her?"

Heron got up and restlessly prowled the room once more. "Well, of course I did. But you can have no idea how refreshing I found her frankness. There was a rapport between us from the first. She never once bored me, you see—and so, God help me, I convinced myself that she needed taking care of—that they both needed taking care of. But what I never admitted, even to myself . . ."

"Yes?" Fitz prompted, his glance suddenly keen.

"I'm in love with her, Fitz." The admission came with a curious humility. "Dammit, the other night I was so wild with jealousy, I wanted to knock that young coxcomb's teeth down his throat!" Heron's laugh was mirthless. "For behaving exactly as I would have done myself at his age. Diverting, is it not?"

"Excessively. So now you have convinced yourself that you have deprived Pandora of some young buck's undying love?" Mr. Chessington stood up. "I suppose it has never occurred to you to tell *her* all this? I thought not." He strolled to the door. "Be advised by me, dear old fellow, and do so with all speed." Looking back, he smiled. "Your experience with the opposite sex may be legion, Robert, but you plainly cannot see what is under your nose!"

It was considerably later when William put his head round the door and asked diffidently if he might come in.

Heron, roused from thought, was filled with compunction (a novel experience) as he saw how the boy hovered uncertainly. "I beg you will disregard my earlier ill manners, William. I was confoundedly blue-devilled!"

"Oh, I don't mind that, sir." William grinned with relief. "P'raps there's something in the air today—Dora was decidedly miffy this morning, too." His grin faded. "About Dora, sir. She isn't back yet. You don't think anything's happened to her, do you?"

The Duke had been growing a little uneasy himself. He had asked Pinkerton to put back dinner and to let him know the moment his wife came home. But to William he was reassuring.

"With Grimble in charge? Never. Any number of things might have delayed them, you know."

"Yes, of course." The boy sighed. "It did cross my mind that she might have gone somewhere with that cavalry officer."

Heron's hands tightened on the arms of his chair. "Cavalry officer?"

William frowned. "Well, I can't be sure, because we were quite high up by then. But I did see someone ride up and get in the landaulet . . . and he looked to be wearing a hussar uniform."

"I see. And did you happen to notice what happened next?"

"Well, I was a bit occupied." William frowned over his recollection. "But Mr. Oliver pointed the carriage out to me shortly after, and . . . well, you get a terrifically wide view of things up there, sir, and I remember thinking it was funny because it was going toward the river instead of coming this way, so p'raps they were going to visit someone?"

"Yes, that will be it."

William wondered why Heron should look so peculiar all of a sudden, and why he started when the door opened. It was Mr. Varley asking for a word with his grace. The Duke heard the note of gravity in his secretary's voice and said in his calm way as he left the room, "Go and tell Pinkerton to serve you your dinner, William. I expect you are hungry, and there seems no point in waiting further. I will join you shortly."

"I did not wish to alarm the boy, sir," said Mr. Varley as they hurried to the parlour belowstairs where Grimble lay on a couch, blood congealing on his head, his face grey.

"It's a miracle that he got back here at all, your grace," muttered the undergroom who hovered close. "On a strange horse, 'e was, all slumped over, like!" His voice sank still lower. "Looks mortal bad, don't 'e?"

The Duke bent over the couch, his voice calm, unhurried. "Grimble . . . can you hear me?"

After a moment, the groom's eyelids fluttered open, the eyes dull, uncomprehending. "Head . . . hurts like the devil . . ."

"Yes, I know, old chap. The doctor will be here directly." He spoke slowly and clearly. "Can you remember what happened? The Duchess . . . ?"

He waited. Then:

"Four of 'em . . . hard villains . . ."

Heron felt as though his heart was being squeezed. "And Captain Austin—do you remember about him?"

But the groom's eyes had closed again.

"I think he's lost consciousness again, your grace."

The Duke swore silently and straightened up. He was already turning away when there came the merest thread of sound. He bent close.

". . . pawn of . . . jealous woman . . . he said . . . ruin . . . Duchess . . ."

He could make little sense of it. The doctor came bustling in, and after a word, they left him to it and went up to the library.

"Not much to go on, Ambrose."

"No, sir." Mr. Varley had never thought to see so much anguish in his employer's eyes.

"I mean to find her, you know. Even if she and Austin have . . ." He recollected himself and stopped short.

Mr. Varley took a deep breath. "If you'll pardon the liberty sir, that's pure gammon! Her grace has eyes for no one but you."

He was surprised to hear a short burst of laughter.

"So everyone keeps telling me!" The Duke buried his head in his hands. "Oh, God . . . where do we begin?"

"Well, sir, as I recall your telling me, young William saw the carriage going toward the river, and if that is so, it occurs to me that we do have a formidable source of help in that quarter."

Heron lifted his head slowly. "Sergeant Blakewell and his friends—of course! They'd do anything for Pandora! Ambrose, you're a genius!"

"No, sir."

"That carriage wouldn't exactly escape notice in an area like that." He stood up with an air of purpose. "Look, would you get down there and organise things? I have been thinking over what Grimble said—and there is something I must do."

Lady Sarah Bingly was about to leave for a dinner engagement when the Duke of Heron was announced. A feeling of unease gripped her.

"Tell his grace I am not at home," she snapped.

"How very ungracious of you, my dear," Heron said, striding past the gaping servant and making her an exaggerated bow. He looked her over with an air of studied familiarity which brought a faint flush of anger to her cheeks. "Exquisite as ever. Going out? Well, I won't detain you. The fact is, I am a little concerned about my wife and felt convinced that you could help me."

Alarm flickered in her eyes, and she was betrayed into a wild tinkling laugh. "My dear Robert, if you will marry a naive little nobody, I am not surprised that you are concerned!"

Sarcasm had been a mistake. She realised it at once, but the damage was done. He closed upon her with frightening speed.

"Where is she, you unscrupulous little bitch?" he said softly.

She raised a hand to strike him, but he seized her wrist in a punishing grip, his tawny eyes paled to a chilling yellow like the eyes of a wildcat. He forced her back until she was brought up against a Louis Quinze commode and could go no further.

"You are mad!" she hissed. "Let me go or I shall scream!"

"Try it," he invited cordially. "It would give me a great deal of pleasure to throttle you! Now, then"—he gave her wrist a persuasive twist—"where is my wife?"

"I don't know!" she cried, and as his grip tightened even more painfully, "I tell you, I *don't* know!" The look in his eyes frightened her, yet she could not keep a hint of triumph from her voice. "More than likely she is by now well out to sea!"

The chair creaked as Pandora shifted her position in order to look round the small bare room into which they had been unceremoniously thrust, their hands and feet firmly bound. Captain Austin lay on a pile of sacks in the corner near the filthy casement through which the fast-fading daylight filtered. He moaned from time to time, but had not answered when she tried to call him. There was no way of telling the time, but she supposed it must be early evening.

Would Robert be wondering where she was? Perhaps he hadn't even noticed her absence. Thinking of him filled her with a great aching need. Suppose she never saw him again? She rebuked herself for the sin of despair. Papa had taught her always to think positively.

From somewhere close by came the steady slap of water against a stone wall or jetty. So they must be near the river, and rivers were a mighty convenient outlet for disposing of unwanted people—or bodies. Her mouth, already dry, grew drier. The sooner they could get away, the better.

"Captain Austin?" She tried again. "Oh, Captain, do please wake up!"

He muttered something unintelligible. Pandora feared he was concussed, so if they were to escape being fed to the fishes, it would be up to her. Her hopes of creating a scene when they arrived had been thwarted by her captors, who had stuffed a noxious rag into her mouth, removed her pretty hat, dragged the pins from her hair, and had thrown a piece of sacking over her head and shoulders.

"Can't have all the neighbours gawping, now, can we?"

They had removed the Captain's distinctive jacket, too, and now he shivered occasionally in his shirt sleeves, though the room enveloped them in malodorous stuffiness, and she was sure she had heard mice, maybe rats, scuttling about. As darkness came, they would probably grow bolder, and though she was no stranger to vermin, there was something repellent about being tied up and subject to their whims. It would be too much to hope that one might gnaw its way through her bonds.

At least she no longer had to suffer the choking rag. She had Joss to thank for that. "No one'd hear you if'n you did shout your head off." He had given her a few sips of porter, too, when they were alone for a few minutes. It was not really to her taste, but it removed that other, fouler taste. He was clearly unhappy about the situation, but Pandora had sized him up very quickly as a born follower of orders, unlikely to go against his mates.

"What regiment were you, Joss?" she asked suddenly.

"Fifty-seventh, ma'am," came the prompt reply.

"Then you have a proud record. Isn't this a bit of a come-down?"

He shuffled uncomfortably. "A man has to eat, ma'am."

"Perhaps so, but surely . . . ?" She looked at his tough scrawny little body and sighed. "Oh, well."

"I'll have to be going." He picked up the piece of cloth, his eyes pleading for understanding. "I'm sorry about this, straight I am."

"Yes, I know."

"You really a Duchess, ma'am?"

"Yes." She viewed her surroundings ruefully. Not exactly Carlton House! "But before that, I was with the army too . . . artillery. I'm Colonel Carlyon's daughter."

"Gawd Almighty. You never are! There's some of your lot got a ken not far from 'ere . . ." He stopped, conscious of being indiscreet. And then, as a thought struck him: "Someone said as it was bought by some swell cove like a . . ." His eyes widened. "Like a Duke?"

"My husband," she said. "It was his wedding present to me." The thought of Sergeant Blakewell not far away was absurdly comforting.

"Oh, Gawd!" he said again.

"You won't tell the others?" she pleaded.

"Stop jawing in there," came a growl from beyond the door.

"I'll have to go, ma'am . . ."

An idea stirred. "Joss, don't leave me here in the dark without a light. There are rats, I think."

He treated her now with an awkward deference that would have been comical in other circumstances.

"Can't promise anyfink, ma'am," he'd mumbled.

But now, as the casement window showed its little patch of sky turning to an indistinguishable darkening grey, he sidled in furtively with a scrubby bit of candle in

212

a holder. It flickered feebly as he set it on the table. "Best I could manage," he muttered by way of apology.

She thanked him, but watched in dismay as the closing door almost extinguished it, and with it her only hope.

It seemed to take her an unconscionable time to shuffle to the table, the cord chafing her ankles with every tiny movement, the noise sounding alarmingly loud in the silence so that every moment she expected someone to come rushing in.

But that was the least of her difficulties; positioning her wrists over the candle flame, near enough to have some effect without dropping them so low that they put it out, and without being able to see what she was doing, was well nigh impossible; the effort of holding the position steady once she had achieved it made her perspire, and the strain on her arm and shoulder muscles caused them to tremble so much that a fear of failure superseded all else. She tried to empty her mind of thought, concentrated fiercely, and could hardly believe it when at last she felt a slight give in the cord's tension. A few moments more and it fell apart, but one end, in falling, guttered the candle.

"Oh, devil take it!" she exclaimed, furious with her own clumsiness.

"Who's there?" came a blurred voice from the corner.

To Pandora it was the most wonderful sound in the world at that moment. Crawling to Captain Austin's side, she struggled to free her ankles with fingers numbed of all feeling, while the words spilled over themselves in her relief.

"So you see, we must be quiet," she whispered, untying his hands and feet. "How do you feel?"

"Devilish queer," he muttered thickly. He tried to sit up. "Oh, God . . . my head! And I can't see a damn thing!"

"No, I'm afraid that's my fault." Pandora explained about the candle. "Please, you must lie quiet. I mean to try to get help."

"Must let me . . ." he began, then sank back with a groan.

Now that her eyes had adjusted to the darkness, she

found that just sufficient light filtered through the window to enable her to see what she was doing. The window had a latch, though she doubted it had been opened in years. Her hands and feet were suffering the excruciating discomfort of returning sensation, but she forced herself to think of other things.

"Perhaps," she mused, "'if I can drag the table against the door without them hearing, it will hold for as long as it takes me to release the window catch and climb out."

"Make too much noise . . . two of us together . . . lift the table."

Captain Austin had hauled himself upright and was sitting propped against the wall.

Pandora eyed him doubtfully. "I really don't think—"

"Dammit, Duchess!" he exploded softly. "I refuse to sit here doing nothing while you—"

"Oh, pride!" she scoffed. "Very well, but do take care."

With her arm for support he slid up the wall to stand for a moment, eyes shut. "Ah!" he gasped, and then, taking a deep breath, "Now, your grace, lead on, if you please."

Laughing shakily, she put a shoulder under his oxter, and they staggered drunkenly across the room. The table was heavy, but between them they jammed it hard up against the door. The noise seemed to echo through the dark room, but no sound came from beyond. The effort had exhausted the Captain, however, so Pandora moved the chair close to the table and made him sit.

"You can hold them off," she said placatingly, and turned her attention to the window. Kneeling on the wide sill, she tried it. It was solidly stuck. "I'll have to bang it," she said, attacking the surround with clenched fist. Just as the top was beginning to give, there was a shout from the other room and pandemonium seemed to be breaking loose. Pandora renewed her efforts, the door reverberated with rattles and thumps, the table rocked and there was much shouting. A few minutes more of that and all her effort would have been for nothing.

Then the window gave, and fresh air rushed in. She

turned swiftly to the captain, holding out a hand. "Come on. I'm sure you can make it!"

"No. I'll slow you down."

"But I can't leave you here! They'll kill you!"

"They can try." A touch of the old audacity showed briefly; then he put his weight against the table and said tersely, "It's you they really want, so stop agonising, girl . . . and go!"

A bellow of rage galvanized her into action. "I'll bring help!" she vowed, gathering her skirts. Turning round and clinging to the edge of the sill, she began to lower herself backward out of the window.

There was a crash that made her jump and almost lose her grip. One of the door panels splintered. A hand pushed through and groped around for the obstruction. Captain Austin seized it and hung on grimly.

"Pandora? For God's sake, answer me! Are you all right?"

"It's Robert!" she cried, her face transfixed. "Oh, do please let him in quickly!"

The Captain staggered back, attempting to drag the table, but already the pressure against the door was shifting it. Light flared suddenly. The Duke squeezed through, to behold his wife doggedly grasping the sill.

"I can't get back!" she gasped.

"Don't try." Heron was across the room in a stride, lifting her back into the room bodily, crushing her to him so tightly that she could hardly breathe.

"You're hurt!" he exclaimed as he felt her wince.

"It's nothing . . . my hands . . ."

The candle had singed them and the rough sill had rubbed the sore places red raw. "It doesn't matter!" she insisted as he exclaimed in horror. "Just hold me! And tell me . . . how are you here? Have you killed those awful men? Oh, poor Joss!" She was laughing and crying and talking all at the same time.

"Hush. Later," he murmured. "I will explain all later, when we are out of this place. Oh, my darling intrepid, *impetuous* love! Another moment and I would have been too late!"

215

His endearments entranced her so much that the rest hardly registered. "Oh, what did you call me?" she sighed dreamily. "Am I really your love? You have never actually said so until now."

"That is because, according to Fitz, I am a blockhead," he said against her hair.

"Oh, no!"

"Not anymore," he agreed, and proceeded to demonstrate his feelings in a way that left no room for doubt.

"Oh, yes! You really do love me!"

"Of course I love you! I adore you!" he said fiercely. "If anything had happened to you . . ."

"Well, it didn't." Pandora emerged rosily from his embrace to find that they were being watched with varying degrees of interest and satisfaction.

"Josiah!" she exclaimed, picking out the sergeant's laconic grin amid a sea of faces. "I was on my way to try to find you."

"Then it's as well we got here when we did, Miss Pandora," he said with a chuckle, "for you'd never have made it."

"Oh, I don't know," she protested. "I am very resourceful, you know."

"We are all well aware of that, my love," drawled her husband softly, "but you see, that window opens straight onto the river."

———————

It was September, and Clearwater was dressed in its most glorious autumn colours. The visits to the lake had become much less frequent and were now confined to the children. The Comtesse had improved greatly through the summer, but now tied to her own rooms more and more in spite of Pandora's efforts to interest her, she was slipping away from them. Pandora's sadness was tempered by the knowledge that at least they had made her happy for a short while.

They had come back to Clearwater very soon after her ordeal, staying in London only until William had witnessed the grand opening of the Jubilee celebrations, with all its attendant excitements. He had been much put out to have missed Pandora's "great adventure," and Heron was in his black books for several days after the event for not including him in the rescue. But the prospect of another ascent with Mr. Oliver, coupled with the news that he was to go to Charterhouse in the autumn, soon drove all else from his thoughts.

Lady Sarah left town in a great hurry. Rumour had it that she was bound for Vienna, where the Peace Congress was shortly to be held, no doubt amid much gaiety and pomp.

The story of her vengeful attack on the Duchess of Heron had leaked out in the way such stories do, though every attempt was made to suppress it.

"Is it really true, my love?" Lady Margerson had summoned her carriage to take her to St. James's Square the instant she heard the news, a very natural concern for Pandora mingling in her ample bosom with a desire to know *all*. "Sarah Bingly actually hired a band of thugs to make away with you, and you and Captain Austin were to be taken out to sea and . . ."—the word almost choked her—"*drowned*?"

"So we believe."

"Well, I never liked the woman, but . . . it don't bear thinking of!" Her ladyship had recourse to her vinaigrette. "Only consider . . . if Robert had not found you when he did!"

Pandora preferred not to dwell on the dread alternative, but knew that Lady Margerson would be content with nothing less than the full account of how Robert had left Lady Sarah's house in near despair; of how he had then gone to seek out Mr. Varley and Sergeant Blakewell, who already had a small army of men out asking questions.

"Of course, the carriage had been hidden, but someone remembered having seen it drive up to the house standing alone at the end of a row backing onto the river. So they came and broke in."

"Fancy! And what of that poor man Austin? Not but what he brought the misfortune upon himself."

217

"He paid dear," said Pandora quickly. "But he will recover."

In the event, Robert had been quite charitable about Captain Austin. But she had been relieved to receive a note from him, apologising for bringing so much trouble to her, and saying that he was going away to recuperate.

Grimble, too, though his injuries were rather more severe, was improving daily, and they had hopes of his eventual recovery.

Now, at a comfortable distance from the events, and in her own little drawing room at Clearwater, with Robert's arm about her and her head resting on his shoulder, she could almost feel sorry for Lady Sarah.

"After all, she could be sitting here instead of me," she reasoned, nestling closer, "and to that extent I can perfectly understand her disappointment. Though I never could understand why she hated me to the extent of wanting to kill me."

Heron's arm tightened. "And you never will, my dearest love, because you don't give a fig for worldly vanities. But to Sarah you were a growing threat. Not only had you, an insignificant nobody, snatched me from under her nose—her assessment, not mine," he drawled, dropping a kiss on the top of her head, "but she was obliged to watch you bidding to become the rage of London . . . and, a final blow to her vanity, you possess the priceless gift of youth."

"Then I am certainly sorry for her."

Heron kissed her long and deep. "I do love you!" he murmured.

The door opened to admit William brandishing letters. "From America!" he cried, and stopped, eyeing them with disapprobation. "Oh, you're cuddling again!"

"Um," sighed Pandora. "You may open the letters if you wish."

"Thanks, I will," he said, making a silent resolve never to get married. "Anyway, you'll have to stop in a minute," he added with relish. "I saw Nurse on her way down with the children."

"Abominable little thatchgallows!" said the Duke amiably. And then to his wife with a sigh: "If this nursery half-hour is to become a regular practice, I believe I must seek refuge elsewhere."

Pandora sat up, looking flushed, her grey eyes wide and considering, with a hint of laughter trembling in their depths. "Oh, dear, and I had hoped to get you nicely into the habit over the next month or two."

He sat back, regarding her with dawning realisation. "You mean . . . ?"

William, in the act of opening Courtney's letter, came to lean over the back of the sofa. He looked from his sister to Heron and back again. "Another baby!" he exclaimed. And then, with an awkward smile: "Oh, well, if it's yours, I 'spect it won't be so bad." A thought struck him. "I say! I shall be an uncle!"

"William," said the Duke, "go away, there's a good fellow."

About the Author

Sheila Walsh lives with her husband in Southport, Lancashire, England, and is the mother of two daughters. She began to think seriously about writing when a local writers' club was formed. After experimenting with short stories and plays, she completed her first Regency novel, *The Golden Songbird*, which subsequently won her an award presented by the Romantic Novelists' Association in 1974. This title, as well as her other Regencies— *Madalena, The Sergeant Major's Daughter, Lord Gilmore's Bride, The Incomparable Miss Brady,* and *The Rose Domino*—are available in Signet editions.